Faithfully Yours
Lois Richer

Recycling programs
for this product may
not exist in your area.

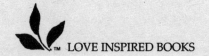 LOVE INSPIRED BOOKS

ISBN-13: 978-0-373-78697-8

FAITHFULLY YOURS

Copyright © 1998 by Lois Richer

www.LoveInspiredBooks.com

Printed in U.S.A.

But the Lord said unto Samuel, Look not on his
countenance, or on the height of his stature;
because I have refused him: for the Lord seeth
not as man seeth; for man looketh on the
outward appearance, but the Lord
looketh on the heart.
—1 *Samuel* 16:7

To my husband, Barry,
on our fifteenth wedding anniversary, with much
love and appreciation for your unwavering support.

Chapter One

"That man will turn my hair gray," Gillian Langford sputtered, twisting the emerald engagement band around the ring finger on her right hand in frustration.

"Not yet, I hope," Mary Teale teased, her eyes flashing. "This is only your third year teaching—your first at JFK Elementary."

"And it may be my last in the fair town of Mossbank, North Dakota," Gillian retorted. "I'm not kidding! Mr. Nivens is so strict, I've forgotten half of the six thousand rules he's made in the past five weeks." There was a sudden silence in the staff room, and Gillian turned around in her chair to see why, her heart sinking as she did.

"That fact is very evident, Miss Langford." Her nemesis stood behind her, his face hardened into the usual stern lines. "I would like to speak to you privately, please. In my office."

"Now?" Gillian heard the squeak of surprise in her voice and wished she had been able to control it. He didn't need to know how badly her feet were aching.

"If you please?"

She forced herself to follow his tall form and noted the short, precise cut of his hair above his stiff white shirt collar. Jeremy Nivens was at all times perfectly groomed with never a hair out of place or a spot on his tie. Gillian hated that. She felt like a grubby child when she stood next to all that neatness.

"Be seated, Miss Langford." He sat stiffly behind his massive desk, his back ramrod straight, arms resting on the desktop. "I wanted to discuss this afternoon's unfortunate incident with you."

Gillian frowned. What in the world was old Jerry talking about now, she fumed, and then corrected herself for using the term bestowed on him by the other teachers. Actually, Jeremy Nivens wasn't all that old, her aunt Hope had assured her. But you couldn't tell it from his unyielding demeanor.

Gillian had noticed other aspects about him, too. He was certainly good-looking with that tall, lean, wide-shouldered body under a perfectly tailored suit. He had the long, straight, haughty nose of an aristocrat with the same high cheekbones and patrician features.

As she stared across at him, Gillian almost grinned. This situation reminded her of her own school days and the times she had been reprimanded by the principal. Only this time it was more serious; her job was at stake. Mr. Nivens's chilly blue-gray gaze was focused directly on her. Again.

"I'm sorry, I don't quite follow," she said softly, rubbing her shoeless foot against the carpet on his office floor. "Did something unusual happen today?"

"I'm speaking about that disgraceful display on the playground this afternoon." His icy stare wiped the smile off her face. "My science students were totally unable to concentrate on their work, with you and your students racing about, shrieking like wild animals."

"It was phys ed," she told him shortly. "They're supposed to run around. Goodness knows, they needed a breath of fresh air after the stuffiness of this school." She had referred to the current heat wave, but it was obvious from the grim tightening of his face that the principal had taken her reference personally.

"Rules and regulations do not make a school stuffy, Miss Langford. They make it an orderly place where children can learn more easily." As he spoke, Mr. Nivens flicked a speck of dust off his gleaming oak desk and straightened the already-neat sheaf of papers on top into a military-precise line. "Which is why the children can't run in the hall, use profanity or chew gum on the school premises. If everyone follows the rules and conforms to what's expected of them, the school year will progress smoothly. For all of us."

His eyes narrowed. "Which is why I suggest you get rid of the blue and yellow chalk and use the *regulation* white in your classroom. Colors are only to be used for special occasions. Now, about your, er, outfit."

Gillian glanced down at herself worriedly. So far in one month's teaching at JFK a button on her blouse had come undone in his presence, he'd reprimanded her for wearing sandals and not wearing hose in the classroom, and he'd given her a lecture on the advisability of keeping her hair tied back, after one of her students had inadvertently caught his watch in it. What now?

"My suit?" Gillian stared down at herself.

She'd chosen her current outfit partially because of the dull brown color that couldn't be easily marked, and partly because it had a lack of buttons, zippers or other fasteners. And she definitely had panty hose on, Gillian grimaced. She'd been sweltering in them all afternoon. His glare was frigid and she bristled under the indignity of it all.

"What's the matter with my clothes this time, Mr. Nivens?" she demanded, a blaze of indignation lighting up her clear green eyes. All her life her parents had told her to make allowances for people who had beliefs different from her own, but Gillian figured she'd given Jeremy Nivens about as much room as he was going to get.

"Well," he began solemnly, folding his fingers tepee style on top of the desk. Gillian caught a faint tinge of pink on his cheekbones. "I'm sure it's a wonderful suit for some things but it does not, er, lend itself to gymnastics." His eyes followed the smooth, fitted lines of the knit cotton as it hugged her well-shaped form and emphasized her obvious assets. "Your skirt, for instance. It's far too short."

"It's below my knees," she sputtered angrily.

"Perhaps. But when you bend over to get the ball, it has certain, er, disadvantages. Both front and back." Jeremy averted his eyes from her angry, red face. "And I can hardly imagine those shoes are meant for football."

It was the last straw in a long, tiring day and Gillian felt her usual calm demeanor explode. She bent over and retrieved her shoes, barely noticing the way her neckline gaped slightly in the front. She stood, thrusting her long curls behind her ears, and glared at the man behind the desk.

"Why you rude, obnoxious man! I wore these stupid heels because you said we had to be dressed in a businesslike fashion at all times. And I bought this suit because thus far in my employment there has not been one item of my clothing in my wardrobe that you deem suitable for the business of teaching. Well, tough!" Gillian practically bellowed the word.

"From now on I wear what I want, when I want, the way I want. If you have some complaint, I'll be pleased to take it up with the Human Rights people. Your only business is with my job, and I do that very well."

"Miss Langford, if you would kindly be seated…"

"No, I won't. I've tried to go along with your silly little regulations and your unceasing demands for weeks now. I've taught in other schools and never had anyone question my taste in clothes. And I'm not taking it from you anymore.

You're making my life miserable, and you're doing it on purpose. You think I'll quit, don't you?" She stared at him as the thought dawned. "You think that if you keep at me, I'll give up and leave. Well, I'm not going," she told him firmly.

"Miss Langford, I am not trying to force your resignation. I merely wanted to advise you that the entire grade-six class was ogling your, er, posterior this afternoon!"

Jeremy Nivens's generally unmoving face was full of fury. His dark eyebrows drew together as he glared down at her, mouth pursed in a straight, disapproving line. He had surged to his feet and now stood towering over her, even though Gillian stood five feet eight inches in her stocking feet.

"I was trying to spare you some embarrassment," he offered a moment later, in his normal hard tones.

"You know what? Don't bother! From now on I'm going to wear exactly what I've always worn to teach my classes. I'm sorry you don't approve of slacks but I like them. And shorts. And jeans. And when the occasion demands, I will wear them."

"Business attire is the only appropriate apparel in this school," he began his lecture again. Gillian walked to the door in her stocking feet and pulled it open, ignoring the icy coolness of his words.

"I work with twenty-eight first-graders. I have to be comfortable, to be able to get down on their level when I need to. I certainly don't need to dress up for some high-powered, executive-type office. If you want to institute a school uniform, fine. But until then, don't try to force me to conform to your strictures." Her green eyes glittered with frustration as she thrust the last stab home.

"You know, Mr. Nivens, you could have closed the blinds if the view was so disturbing," Gillian told him savagely. She tossed him one more angry glance over her shoulder and then strode from the office, high heels dangling from one finger as she left the school, muttering dire epithets all the way home. As she walked, she reviewed her stormy relationship with Jeremy Nivens.

"Of all the nerve," she grumbled. "For two cents I'd go back to Boston and St. Anne's without a qualm."

But she knew it was all talk. She couldn't go back; not now. Since Michael's death she hadn't been able to face living alone in the city, remembering their special haunts, driving past the places they'd gone together, attending the same church they'd attended together and where they had planned to say their vows. The pain of his death was too new, too fresh there. She'd had to get away, and Aunt Hope had been the answer to her prayers. In a lot of ways.

"Hello, dear. Did you have a nice day at school?"

Gillian had been so preoccupied with herself she hadn't noticed the slim woman busily raking leaves on the front lawn. She studied her tall, blonde aunt curiously, noting her ageless, blue eyes that still sparkled and the lean, athletic build Hope worked so hard to retain.

"Nice," she griped angrily. "No, it was rotten. That Carruthers child is a klutz. She spilled the glue all over me. Again. And the Stephens's youngest son is deaf—I'm sure of it." Gillian flopped down on the top step with disgust. "If that weren't enough, that contemptible man nattered at me about my clothes again—said I shouldn't wear these shoes for phys ed. Imbecile! As if I didn't know that."

"Well then, dear, why *did* you wear them?" Hope's voice was quietly curious.

"Because he's ordered us to wear business dress at all times," Gillian bellowed and then grinned wryly. "Sorry, Auntie. I'm taking it out on you, and it's not your fault. But don't worry. I told him that from now on I'll wear what I blasted well please." She spread her arms wide and stared up at the bright sun. "You'd think I looked like a bag lady or something, the way he talks to me."

Her aunt smiled thoughtfully as she stared at the tattered shreds of her niece's panty hose. "Well, those stockings would certainly qualify, my dear." She chuckled.

"Don't you start now," Gillian ordered. "I've had enough for one day. Petty little man." She glared at the cement walkway as if it was to blame for her problems.

"My dear, there are bound to be adjustments with a new principal. You may just have to bite your tongue and accept the changes. Not all change is bad, you know. The possibilities that are ahead of you are endless. Open your eyes."

"I don't want to. They're too tired." Gillian faked a snore. "Thank heavens it's Friday. I intend to relax tonight." She sprang to her feet and leaped up the three stairs. Gillian was almost through the door before she remembered her manners and turned back. "Is that okay with you, Hope, or have you something special planned?"

Her aunt swept the rest of the crackling red and gold leaves into the huge black bag and neatly tied the top. Gillian noticed that her aunt's pale aquamarine pantsuit was as pristine as it had been this morning; her shiny blond hair swaying gently in its neat bob as she lifted the bag and deposited it at the curb.

"Gillian," her aunt chided her softly. "You don't have to keep asking me that. I want this to be your home, too. Please don't feel pressured to involve yourself in my activities. Feel free to go out with people your own age, dear."

"Then you are going out," Gillian muttered, dropping her shoes in the hall and curling comfortably on her aunt's pale floral sofa. "What has bustling Mossbank scheduled for the inmates tonight?"

Hope favored her with a look that spoke volumes about her niece's attitude, but she answered, anyway.

"The church has a fowl supper on tonight. I offered to help in the kitchen." As she spoke, she lifted a huge roaster from the oven. Immediately the house was filled with the succulent aroma of roasting bird and tangy sage dressing.

"I always thought it was a 'fall' supper. Doesn't matter, I'm starved," Gillian breathed, closing her eyes. "Maybe I should go with you. I could help wash up afterward. Who all goes?"

"Almost everyone," her aunt chuckled. "It's an annual event. If I were you I'd get there early." Her astute eyes watched as Gillian twisted the glowing band around her finger. "Please don't think I'm trying to boss you or anything, dear."

Gillian felt her body tighten at the sad but serious look in her aunt's eyes.

"You know you can say anything to me, Hope. I won't mind." Gillian examined her aunt's serious countenance. "What is it?"

"Don't you think it's time to put Michael's ring away, Gilly? He's gone and he's not coming back," she said in a soft but firm tone. "You have to move on."

"I'm not sure I can." Gillian stared at the floor, her mind flooded with memories. "We would have been married by now," she whispered, tears welling in her eyes.

"Oh, darling." Her aunt rushed over and hugged her. "I'm so sorry. I know it hurts. But, dear—" she brushed Gillian's burnished curls off her forehead and pressed a kiss there "—Michael loved life. He wanted to experience everything. Now that he's with God, I don't think he would want you to stop living. There are marvelous things in store for you. You have to accept the changes and move on…go out and find what God has planned specially for you."

"I already know my future," Gillian whispered at last, pressing herself away and straightening the hated brown suit.

"I'm going to teach, Auntie. I'm going to focus my energies on my students and their needs." She smiled sadly at her aunt's worried look. "You and I have a lot in common, you know. We've both lost the men we loved—you in the Vietnam war and me because of some stupid drunk driver.

"I'm sure I couldn't do better than follow your example. Teaching will be enough for me. It has to be." Gillian choked back a sob and smiled brightly.

"Sweetheart," her aunt began slowly. "Don't use me as a role model for your life." Her eyes were shadowed, and Gillian saw her aunt's face grow sad. "I have had opportunities to marry that I sometimes wish I had taken." She shook her blond head and focused on her niece. "Be very sure of what you ask out of life. You may just get it."

"Right now," Gillian said, grimacing. "I'd settle for Mr. Jeremy Nivens moving to another country. At the very least, another school." She made a face. When Hope chuckled, Gillian plucked at the repulsive brown fabric disparagingly. "I'll just go change and we can go to the fall or *'fowl'* supper."

Which was probably how she ended up pouring tea for Jeremy Nivens that evening, she decided later.

"Miss Langford," he murmured, his gray-blue eyes measuring her in the red-checked shirt she wore tucked into her denim skirt. "You look very, er, country tonight."

Gillian knew he was staring at the spot of gravy on her shirt, and she would have liked to tell him how it got there, but instead, she swallowed her acid reply with difficulty. After all, this was the church.

"It's comfortable," she told him shortly. "Do you take cream or sugar?" She held out the tray, knowing perfectly well that he took neither. When he waved it away she turned to leave.

"The meal was excellent." His voice was a low murmur

that she barely caught. "Is there anything I can do to help out? As a member here, I'd like to do my bit."

"I didn't know you went to this church," Gillian blurted out, staring at him aghast. School was bad enough. A person should have the sanctity of their church respected, she fumed.

"It is somewhat less formal than the English one I've attended for years, but I find it compatible with my beliefs. Besides, my great-aunt goes here." He nodded his head at a woman Gillian identified as Faith Rempel.

Although Gillian certainly knew of Faith from her aunt's vivid description of one of the two ladies she called her dearest friends, she herself had never actually met the woman formally.

"Oh, yes," she murmured. "Mrs. Rempel. She's *your* aunt?" It was strange to think of such a happy-looking woman as the old grouch's relation. Gillian watched in interest as a grin creased the principal's stern countenance.

"Apparently my aunt, your aunt and another lady have been great pals for years. I believe the other lady is Mrs. Flowerday. They seem to get along quite well. It must be nice having friends you've known for a long time." His voice was full of something—yearning?

Gillian stared at him. He'd sounded wistful, just for a moment. "It must? Why?"

"Oh, I suppose because they make allowances for you, afford you a few shortcomings." He smiled softly, glancing across at his aunt once more.

"Why, Mr. Nivens," Gillian sputtered, staring at him in shock. "I didn't know you had any."

He looked startled at that; sort of stunned that she would dare to tease him. A faint red crept up his neck, past the stiff collar, to suffuse his cheeks.

"There are those," he muttered snidely, glaring at her, "who say that I have more than my fair share."

It was Gillian's turn to blush, and she did, but thankfully the effect was lost in Pastor Dave's loud cheerful voice. "Just the two folks I was most hoping to corral at this shindig."

Gillian winced at the stomp of the cowboy boots that missed her bare toes by a scant inch and the thick beefy arm that swung around her shoulder. Pastor Dave was a cowboy wannabe and he strove constantly to perfect his image as a long, tall Texan, even when he remained a short, tubby Dakota preacher.

"What can we do to help you out, Pastor?" Gillian queried in a falsely bright voice. "Another piece of pumpkin pie or a fresh cup of coffee?"

"No sirree, Bob. I've eaten a hog's share tonight." The short man chuckled appreciatively, patting his basketball stomach happily. "No, I was hoping you and your friend here would consent to helpin' a busy preacher out with the youth group."

"I'm afraid I haven't had much opportunity to work with young people," she heard Jeremy Nivens begin nervously. "And with the Sunday school class you've given me, I'm not sure I'll have enough free time for anything else."

Gillian peered around Dave's barrel chest to stare at her boss's shaking head.

"I'm afraid I'm in the same boat, Pastor," she murmured, thankful that she wouldn't have to work with old, stuffed-shirt Nivens. Their contact at school was quite enough for her. She didn't need more proximity to know that the two of them would never work well together, especially not in the loose, unrestricted world of teenagers.

"Nonsense," Pastor Dave chortled. "Why, you folks just being here tonight is a good sign that you have Friday evenings free. And I know the young folk would appreciate having you whippersnappers direct their meetin's more than they would old Brother Dave." He whacked Jeremy on the back and patted Gillian's shoulder kindly before moving away. "I'll be calling y'all about an organizational meeting next week," he said, grinning happily. "See ya there."

Gillian stared aghast at the tall, lean man in front of her. It couldn't be. No way. She wasn't going to be conned into this. Not with General Jeremy Nivens.

"I don't think that man listens to what anyone says," Mr. Nivens muttered in frustration. "He bulldozed me into taking the Sunday school boys class, but I can't take on a bunch of hormone-crazy teens, too."

"Well, you don't have to act as if they're juvenile delinquents or something," Gillian said, bristling indignantly. "They're just kids who don't have a whole lot to amuse themselves with in a town this size."

"Hah!" He glared at her, his gray eyes sparkling. "They should be able to make their own fun. Why, these children have every advantage—a lovely countryside, acres of land and rivers and hills. They should be happy to be free of the inner-city ghettos that lots of children are enduring where they don't get enough to eat and—"

"Please," Gillian muttered, holding up one hand. "Spare me the sermon. It sounds just like something my grannie used to say." She shifted to one side as the family behind her moved away from the table, children gaily jumping from bench to bench.

"'When I was a child,'" she said in a scratchy voice meant to copy her grandmother's thready tones. "'We never had the advantages you young things have today. Why I walked three miles to and from school every single day, even when it was forty-below. In bare feet. Without a coat.'"

Mr. Nivens's eyebrows shot up almost to his hairline as he listened to her. When at last he moved, it was to brush off the crumbs from his pant leg and remove a blob of cream

Gillian had slopped on the toe of his shoe when Pastor Dave had grabbed her.

"You're being ridiculous," he murmured, stepping around her carefully. "No one could walk through forty-below without shoes or a coat and survive." He started up the basement stairs after tossing one frowning look at her bright curling tendrils of hair where they lay loose against her neck.

Gillian snapped the tray down on the table and motioned to the folk holding out their cups.

"Help yourself," she advised, with a frown on her face. "I've got something to say to Mr. Nivens."

"Go for it, missy," Ned Brown advised, grinning like a Cheshire cat. "That feller needs a bit of loosenin' up. Seems to me you're just the girl to do it."

As she raced up the stairs, Gillian decided Ned was right. She had a whole year of Mr. Jeremy Nivens to get through. She might as well start off as she meant to go on.

He was striding across the parking lot when she emerged—huge, measured strides that made her race to catch up. Fortunately, she wore her most comfortable sandals and could easily run to catch up.

"Just a minute, Mr. Nivens," she called breathlessly. "I have something I want to say."

He stopped and turned to stare at her, the wind ruffling his dark brown hair out of its usual orderly state. One lock of mussed hair tumbled down across his straight forehead, making him seem more human, more approachable, Gillian decided.

"I was making a joke," she said finally, aware that his searching gray-blue eyes had noted her flushed face and untucked shirt. "It was supposed to be funny."

"Oh." He continued to peer at her through the gloom, and Gillian moistened her lips. It was the kind of stare that made her nervous, and she shifted from one foot to the other uneasily. "Was that everything, Miss Langford?"

"My name is Gillian," she told him shortly, frustrated by the cool, distant frigidity his arrogant demeanor projected. "Or Gilly if you prefer."

"It sounds like a name for a little girl," he told her solemnly, his dour look suggesting that she take the information to heart. "At any rate, I barely know you. We are coworkers in a strictly professional capacity. I hardly think we should be on a first-name basis."

"Look, *Mr.* Nivens," she exhorted. "I'm trying to be friendly. That's the way people in Mossbank are, friendly and on a first-name basis. No one at school uses titles except in front of the children." She drew a breath of cool, evening air and counted to ten. "If you don't want to help with the youth group, fine. But don't pretend it's because they're too uncivilized for you to be around." Her eyes moved over his three-piece suit with derision.

"I doubt you and they would have anything in common, anyway," she muttered. "You're far too old for them."

His stern, rigid face cracked a mirthless smile.

"Not so old," he said sternly. "I was a teenager once, also, Miss Langford."

"Really?" Gillian stared at him disbelievingly.

"I'm sure of it." His eyes sparkled at some inner joke as he watched her.

"Well, anyway—" she shrugged "—if you don't want to work with them, just say so."

"I thought I had," he murmured so softly she barely caught the words. He studied her face. "Are you going to fall in with Pastor Dave's suggestions?" he demanded.

"I think I might," she mused, deliberately ignoring that inner voice that quietly but firmly whispered *NO*. "They really need some direction, and there doesn't seem to be anyone else." All around them the rustle of wind through the drying leaves and the giggles of children romping in the playground carried in the night air. The musky odor of cranberries decaying in the nearby woods wafted pungently toward them on a light breeze.

"But you're not that much younger than I am," he objected.

"In some ways," she said through gritted teeth. "You and I are light-years apart."

"I suppose that's true," he admitted at last. He turned to leave. "Good night, Miss Lang— Gillian."

As he walked away into the dusky night, Gillian stood with her mouth hanging open. For the first time in over a month, he'd called her by her first name. How strange! Perhaps the man really wasn't as stuffy as she'd thought. Maybe, just maybe, he'd unbend with time.

Then she frowned.

He hadn't outright refused to attend the organizational meeting, had he? Did that mean he intended to show up and offer his staid opinions?

"No way," she muttered angrily. "I don't care how much they need helpers. Mr. Jeremy Nivens is not going to work in the youth group, not if I have anything to say about it."

As she turned to go back inside, Gillian tried to ignore the sight of Jeremy almost lost in the shadows up ahead, children racing along beside him, chattering eagerly as he ignored them.

She had not misread the situation. He wasn't the youth leader type. Not at all.

Was he?

Chapter Two

"**W**hy are there two whole shelves of dog food and only one teensy section with tea?" Charity Flowerday muttered, as she hobbled up and down the aisles of Mossbank's largest grocery store, searching for the ingredients she needed for lunch with her friends. Although why she should have to search for anything was a mystery. She'd lived in this small farming community for almost seventy years. She should know where every single item was kept, she chuckled to herself.

"Ah, tea." She ran her finger along the shelf and plucked a package into her cart. "Now, dessert."

It was impossible to ignore the young towheaded boy in the junk-food aisle across from frozen foods. He looked much the way her own son had thirty years ago: freckle-faced, grubby, with a tear in both knees of his filthy jeans and his shirttail hanging out.

"School not started yet?" she asked in her usual friendly fashion. It wasn't that she didn't know. Why, her friend Hope's niece had been teaching at the local elementary school for almost a month now, and she was well acquainted with the schedule.

"Buyin' somethin' fer my mom," he muttered, turning

his face away and hunching over to peer at the varieties of potato chips currently available. It was obvious that he wasn't interested in carrying on a conversation. Charity shrugged before turning away to squint at the ice cream labels behind the frosted glass doors.

"Hmm, all pretty high in fat and cholesterol," she murmured to herself. Heaven knew women of her age couldn't afford either one, she thought grimly. "Arthur," she called loudly, hoping the proprietor would hear her above the roar of the semitruck unloading outside.

When Art Johnson didn't immediately appear, she shuffled over to the counter to wait for him. The grubby little boy was there ahead of her clutching a fistful of penny candy.

"Hello again, young man. I don't think I've seen you around before. Has your family just moved to Mossbank?" Any newcomer to their fair town was a source of interest for Charity, and she couldn't help the bristle of curiosity that ran through her. "What's your name?"

"Roddy. Roddy Green."

"Well, nice to meet you, Roddy. My name is Mrs. Flowerday. I live at the end of Maple Street in that redbrick house. Perhaps you've noticed it?"

"Nope."

Evidently young Mr. Green didn't care to know, either, thought Charity with a tiny smile. Kids nowadays were so different. They didn't bother with all the folderol of petty politeness and such. They just got down to the basics.

"Where's the old guy that runs this place?" the boy demanded sullenly, tapping his fingers on the counter. "I haven't got all day."

"Oh, Mr. Johnson often has to stay at the back while they unload the truck," she explained to him with a smile. "He counts the pieces as they take them off to be sure he receives everything he should. I'm certain he will be here in a moment."

"I'm here right now, Charity. Sorry to have kept you waiting. What can I do for you?"

Arthur Johnson smiled at her the same way he had for the past thirty-five years, and Charity smiled back. He had always been a friendly man who took pleasure in meeting the needs of his customers. When he looked at her like that, his face jovial, his balding head burnished in the autumn sun shining through the window, Charity felt her heart give a quick little patter. He was still such a handsome man.

"I was here first," Roddy piped up belligerently. He smacked the candy on the counter. "How much?"

Charity noticed Art's eyebrows rise at the obvious discourtesy, but she shook her head slightly.

"Yes, he was here first, Art," Charity murmured.

"All right, then. Twenty-nine cents, please, young man."

As Charity watched the child's hand slip into his pocket for the change, she noticed his other hand snitch a chocolate bar from the stand in front of him and slip it into his other pocket. She motioned her head downward as Art glanced at her, but this time it was he who shook his head.

"Thanks, son. Now you'd better get back to school."

"'Bye, Art the fart," the boy chanted, racing out the door and down the street. They could hear his bellows of laughter ricochet back and forth along the narrow avenue.

"Of all the nerve! Arthur Johnson, you know very well that child stole a chocolate bar from you," Charity accused, casting the grocer a black look. "Why did you let the little hoodlum get away with it? Didn't you see it clearly enough?"

"Oh, I saw it, Charity. My eyes are still pretty good, and that mirror really helps," Art chuckled. "But this isn't the first time I chose to do nothing about it. Not right now. Anyway, that chocolate bar will eat away at his conscience all afternoon. He's not getting away with anything." He pressed her shoulder gently as if to soothe away her indignation. "Now, dear lady, what can I do for my best customer?"

Charity preened a little at the complimentary tone, straightening her shoulders as she blinked up at him girlishly.

"Well, Arthur, I'm having guests for lunch today, and I want to serve ice cream. This may be one of the last really warm days we have this fall, you know."

"I see." Art led the way over to the freezers and tugged out a small round tub. "I have your favorite right back here, Charity. Double chocolate fudge pecan." He beamed down at her.

"Why, I can't believe you remembered. It's ages since I had this. It won't do for Hope, though," Charity said, grimacing. "She's always watching her fat content, and this is bound to send it over the moon." A tinge of frustration edged her words as she shoved the container back into the freezer. "Maybe we'd better have sherbet instead. A nice savory lemon."

"Charity, Hope Langford is so scrawny she could do with a little fattening up. Besides, you know you love chocolate. And this is the light variety with one-third less fat. It's really quite delicious." Art glanced at his hands self-consciously. "I tried it myself last week."

"You ate chocolate ice cream, with *your* cholesterol level?" Charity frowned severely. "You need a woman to look after you, Arthur."

They spent twenty minutes discussing their various health ailments before Charity strolled out the door carrying the container of chocolate ice cream and grinning from ear to ear.

Two and a half hours later Charity was welcoming her two friends to her cosy home and a scrumptious lunch.

"Isn't it lovely out today." That was her friend Faith

Rempel who simply never had a bad day. "I can't imagine more perfect weather for walking."

"I thought Jeremy didn't like you walking all over town," Hope Langford questioned. "Has he changed his mind?" Hope's voice was soft and shy, much like the woman herself. At fifty-six, she was the youngest in their group and much concerned over her friend's propensity to accidents. She had, at first, greeted the arrival of Faith's nephew, Jeremy Nivens, with relief.

"Oh, Jeremy's far too busy with school just now. He's trying so hard to make a good impression with this first principalship. The dear boy hasn't been hovering nearly as much this week." Faith brushed the permed lock of gray hair off her forehead absently as she stared at the other two. "I haven't seen him for three days," she told them cheerfully. "Or was it four? Let's see now…"

Charity laughed gaily.

"Oh, Faith," she murmured, leading them out to her small patio and the gaily set table. "Don't tell me you've forgotten what day it is again? I declare that memory of yours is—"

"Just fine," cut in Hope quietly. She frowned at Charity. "I think she does wonderfully well. And if we're talking about Jeremy, I don't think Gillian is particularly impressed with him. She says he's very old-fashioned."

They sat around the table, munching on the low-fat ham sandwiches and crunchy green salad as they discussed the newest educators at the local elementary school.

"Well," Charity murmured. "You must admit your niece is very advanced in some of her ideas. Why, just the other day I heard Gillian complaining about the textbooks. Said they were too passé to be any good!" Her white eyebrows rose with indignation. "We've had those textbooks for years, as you well know, Hope Langford."

Hope hid her smile behind her napkin. Her voice, when

she finally spoke, was the same soft tones they had come to expect from her. "Yes, I know the age of some of those books very well. I myself tried to have them replaced just before I retired from teaching. Unfortunately, some folk in the community felt they were adequate, so the money was not forthcoming." Her blue eyes sparkled with mirth at Charity as she smoothed a hand over her blond, chin-length bob. As usual, there wasn't a hair out of place.

"I can't imagine why anyone thinks the children of the nineties still need to focus so completely on President Kennedy's administration," Hope murmured. "Several things have happened since the early sixties, Charity."

"Oh, piffle." Faith stared at them vacantly for several moments, her brow furrowed. Her English accent became more pronounced as she spoke. "I've forgotten whatever it was we were going to discuss today."

"It's all right, dear," Hope whispered, squeezing the other woman's hand gently. "We were going to discuss our Christmas project. Isn't that right, Charity?" She glanced across the table warningly, her thin body rigid in her chair.

"Yes, indeed," Charity murmured gaily. "But not before we've had my special dessert." She rose to stand behind Faith's chair, her tiny frame hidden by the larger woman. "And of course, we'll have tea. You pour, dear." She squeezed the rounded shoulders affectionately.

It was difficult to scoop out the ice cream with her arthritic hands, so Charity took the carton and dishes to Hope for help. They both watched as Faith's faded green eyes lit up with excitement as she tasted her first spoonful.

"Nuts," she crowed. "This ice cream has nuts." She sighed with pleasure. "I do love nuts," she murmured happily.

As they basked in the warm, afternoon sun, sipping tea, chatting desultorily and ignoring the dirty dishes sitting nearby, Charity held her hands out for them to see.

"I'm afraid I won't be able to quilt this year, girls," she murmured, staring at her gnarled fingers and twisted knuckles. "I just can't manage the needle anymore."

They were aghast.

"But, Charity," Faith exploded. "You've always made a special Christmas quilt every year for as long as I've known you. It's a tradition in Mossbank." Her eyes were huge and filling rapidly with tears. "You can't just give up."

"Well, this year I am choosing something else for my Christmas project." Charity's brown eyes sparkled with a secret.

Hope cleared her voice, curiosity widening her china-blue eyes. "What?" she inquired softly.

"I've been praying about it, and this morning I got an answer. I'm going to take on a different kind of project—a person. A little boy named Roddy Green. I watched him steal a chocolate bar at the grocery store this morning when he should have been in school." Charity shifted her feet to rest on a nearby rock, exposing her puffy, swollen ankles. "And I decided he could use a friend," she murmured quietly. "Art told me a little about the boy, and I think we could both benefit from the relationship."

"I don't like that word," Faith told them both, absently pulling a weed from the huge pot of yellow begonias that sat nearby. "It's what Jeremy always talks about when I ask if he has a special girlfriend he's interested in."

"What word is that, dear?" Hope asked mildly confused.

"*Relationship.* My Donald and I never had a relationship, not once in thirty-five years. We had love and friendship and care and concern and sometimes arguments, but we never had anything as cold as a relationship." Faith spat the word out with disgust.

"Young people today do have a different way of looking at things," Hope agreed. Her blond brows drew together as she asked curiously, "And does Jeremy have a relationship with someone?"

Charity watched Hope twist her fingers together as she lounged in her chair. It was that unusual activity that gave the younger woman away, she decided. Hope never fidgeted. Charity wondered what her friend was up to.

"No," Faith answered the question sadly. "Jeremy says he's far too involved in his career to bother with females right now. He really wants to make a success of this school year." Her face drooped as she told them about her great-nephew's visit two or three nights before. "He was most uncomplimentary about my natural garden. Said it resembled a weed patch more than a flower garden. He even pulled up a few of my special species."

"He would." Hope's tones were dry. "He's got his nose buried so far into his policy-and-procedure manuals he can't see real people in front of him. Jeremy Nivens needs to realize that life is about more than school and books."

"He doesn't like me to have the fireplace going, either," Faith told them solemnly. "He said I'm liable to kill myself with it."

"It's gas," Hope cried. "It shuts itself off. What in the world is he so concerned about?"

Faith shrugged her shoulders tiredly, a wan smile curving her full lips.

"Jeremy worries about me, my dears. He's much like his father was, always fussing about things."

"Well," Hope drawled, staring thoughtfully up at the deep blue sky, "I think he needs something else to engage his mind. Something slightly more challenging."

"What are you up to?" Charity demanded finally. "Don't bother to deny it, I can see that glint sparkling in your eyes."

"Oh, tell me, too." Faith clapped her hands in glee. "I love it when you have a plan, Hope. It's always so wonderfully organized, just like you."

Hope smiled a peculiarly smug grin as her eyes moved from one to the other.

"You have to promise not to say a word," she said seriously. "Not a whisper to anyone. If this gets around, he'll never forgive me."

"Who?" Charity demanded irritably.

"Jeremy," Hope told them proudly. "I've decided to make Jeremy my Christmas project. I'm going to find him a wife so he'll be too busy to bother Faith anymore."

Her two friends sat in their lawn chairs, mouths gaping as they absorbed her news. The birds happily chirped around them as a neighbor's lawn mower hummed industriously.

"You mean," Charity asked, "you're going to throw him and Gillian together? I don't think—"

"Of course not," Hope said, cutting her off. "Gillian is a free spirit. She needs a man who can understand that, and not try to fence her in with a lot of silly restrictions. Besides, Jeremy's too old for her."

"Oh, piffle. Jeremy's not that much older than your Gillian," Faith chided, her eyes sparkling at the thought of her great-nephew married.

"In his approach to life in this century, Jeremy rivals Moses," Hope muttered dourly. "I was actually thinking of Letitia Chamberlain. She's a quiet little thing, and she'd do whatever he told her to."

"Well," Charity murmured, staring off into space, "I suppose if you've made up your mind, there's no point in me trying to change it. I do think it's too bad not to continue with your knitting though, Hope. Those mittens you donate are really needed in the cities. Why, I heard the mayor of Minot on the news the other day. He said they would need at least a hundred pairs in the schools this year!"

Hope smiled. "Oh, I'll still be knitting," she murmured. "And while I am, I can think of new plans for Jeremy." Charity watched the glint of mischievousness sparkle in her friend's eyes and wondered what she was up to.

"It isn't fair," Faith wailed sadly. "You have both chosen your projects, and I don't have one. What shall I choose? I'm not very good at matchmaking but maybe I could try for Gillian."

Charity met Hope's wary glance with her own.

"No!" They both said it together.

"What we mean, dear, is that you're such a good cook and you always do those wonderful dainty trays for the Christmas hampers. Maybe you should do that again." Charity nodded as Hope's soft voice soothed their friend.

"Of course I will continue with *that*," Faith told them firmly. "But I want a special project. Something really different." Her green eyes narrowed as she pondered the subject. Finally she stood to her feet.

"After all, I do have a bit of time yet. It is only the first week of October, isn't it? I shall think and pray about it. Perhaps the good Lord has some special work that I can do." Faith ambled out the front door, completely forgetting her purse and sweater as she strolled along, mumbling to herself.

"We should have thought of something for her to do, before we announced our ideas," Charity muttered, gathering up their teacups and setting them on the tray. "It's not fair to leave her like that."

Hope carried the dishes back into the house and set about washing them carefully in the old-fashioned sink. She had most of the work done before Charity hobbled in.

"Faith is a strong, competent woman," she stated firmly. "She's not senile, just a little confused sometimes. I think it will be good for her to think about a Christmas project rather than Jeremy's odious meddling, for a while." Hope shook her head with disgust. "That man would drive a saint up the wall."

"He's certainly been hovering around Faith since he came," Charity agreed. "I heard him telling her not to use the oven unless he was there. You know how she loves to bake. I can't imagine that she'll listen to him."

"It might be best if she did," Hope muttered finally. "I hate to say it, but her memory is getting worse. I've been checking up on her myself lately, just to make sure she gets home safely."

"Funny," Charity mused absently, rubbing liniment on the aching joints of her hands. "Arthur mentioned something about seeing her home the other night. Said he found her in the park, gathering leaves for her collection. In the dark."

"Well, I think we'll just have to be especially careful to keep track of her with Jeremy around," Hope said with a frown. "I don't like the way he keeps telling her not to do this or that, fussing if she goes for a long walk. She's not in prison, for heaven's sake."

"Yes, I'll watch her, too," Charity agreed, sinking into her easy chair. "Now about this project of yours? Do you really think you can find someone suitable for him? He's rather, er, old-fashioned, dear."

Hope grinned smugly.

"I know. That's why I've decided to hook him up with Flossie Gerbrandt. She's exactly the same."

"Flossie?" Charity shuddered. "I hate that name. Can't understand why Clara called her that. Always reminds me of a rabbit, for some reason." Her brow furrowed in thought. "I hope you know what you're doing, Hope. I just can't picture Flossie in her support hose and caftans going to church with the elegantly turned-out likes of him." She coughed discreetly behind her hand. "Anyway," she murmured repressively. "The Lord has his own plans for Jeremy Nivens. He doesn't need you to meddle."

"I'm just going to give the man a helping hand," Hope told her, stacking the plates in the cupboard. "Nothing wrong with that, is there?"

Hope sipped her tea pensively, staring at the embroidered Lord's Prayer on the wall. She was lost in thought until Charity's voice called her back to the present.

"Pardon?" she asked softly, enraptured by the picture her mind had drawn.

"I just wondered when you were going to get to work on your new project?"

"Soon, dear. Very soon." Hope returned her gaze to the figure of Jesus holding a sheep in his strong arms. "The sooner the better—for Faith, for Jeremy and for Gillian."

Chapter Three

Gillian stared at the cut on the boy's knee.

"Jed, I told you to stay with the rest of us. How did you do this, anyway?" She dabbed at the injury carefully, noting the dirt imbedded in the cut.

"I had to go pee" she was told in no uncertain terms. "When I was doing up my pants, I tripped on somethin'. It made me fall."

Gillian grinned. No responsibility for Jed. If something had cut him, it certainly wasn't his fault. She grimaced. There was no doubt in her mind that Mr. Nivens would believe that the cut was all her fault.

"Come, children," she called, ushering them ahead of her onto the path through the woods. "We have to get back to the school now. It's almost time for the bell. Quietly, Rowena."

Who are you kidding? she asked herself sourly. Quiet? First-graders? Not likely. As they stumbled and pushed and shoved their way back into the classroom, she glanced round surreptitiously. Her heart fell as she noticed the man in the blue pin-striped suit heading directly for her.

"Come along, children. Let's get your things together now. Don't forget to collect as many leaves as you can this weekend." She handed out knapsacks and lunch bags, just managing to grasp Jed's arm before he headed out the room as the bell rang. "Just a minute, Jed. We'll have to see to that knee."

"Miss Langford? What is the meaning of this bedlam?" Mr. Nivens's voice was raised to counter the excitement coming from the rest of the children now pouring into the hall.

She ignored him as she drew Jed over to the sink and began dabbing antiseptic from the first aid kit onto the child's knee. She held one bony little shoulder firmly as the boy wriggled.

"Ow!" His bellow was loud and angry.

"Has this child injured himself on school property, during school hours, Miss Langford?"

Old Jerry was in a cranky mood, she decided glumly. There was no way he would let her off easily for this one.

"We went on a nature hike, and Jed cut his knee," she told him, still gripping the child's wriggling shoulder. "If you could assist me with this, I'd appreciate it. I have to cleanse the area."

"He should be seen by a doctor," Jeremy Nivens began firmly, but he knelt beside the boy and peered at the affected area. "At least it won't require stitches," he muttered, taking the cotton from her hands and briskly wiping the grit and particles of soil away.

"That hurts, ya know," Jed shrieked. His face was red with anger.

"Nonsense. A great big boy like you wouldn't feel a little nick like this. You have to be strong when these things happen—stiff upper lip and all that." His finger slapped a Band-Aid across the knee with surety, and he pulled Jed's pant leg swiftly down.

"Huh?" Jed sat staring at the older man in perplexity.

Gillian bent down and stared into Jed's puzzled face. "He means that you were very brave for handling that so well, Jed. Here's your knapsack now. You'd better run and get that bus."

As the boy scurried from the room, he cast a suspicious look at Jeremy's suited figure. "My lip's not stiff," he told the older man seriously. "My leg is, though."

"Have a good weekend," Gillian called and waved briskly, watching the most daring member of her class dodge the other children in his rush to get to the bus.

"Miss Langford, you and I need to have a discussion."

She turned back wearily to face her towering boss's stern face. He had that glint in his eye, she noticed. The one that always spelled trouble. For her.

"Have a seat, Mr. Nivens. I'll just clean up a bit as we talk." She avoided his eyes as her hands busily picked up the shuffle of papers on her desk, brushing the bits of twigs and crushed leaves into the garbage.

"I would prefer to speak in my office. In a more formal setting." He was still standing, Gillian noted.

"Oh, why bother to walk all the way down there?" she murmured airily. "We're both here now. Why don't you just tell me what's on your mind?" Smoothly, without a pause in action, Gillian slipped the books into order on her shelves, removing a bubble gum paper from Jonah's reader. When he didn't speak, she finally glanced up and found his remote stare fixed firmly on her. "Well?"

"Miss Langford, do you ever read the notifications I leave in your mailbox?"

He brushed a hand gingerly over the edge of the table, checking for stickiness before reclining against it. It was the most relaxed she had ever seen him, and the sight was very appealing. As she watched, Jeremy brushed a hand through his hair, destroying the immaculately arranged strands. "Miss Langford?"

She jerked her gaze away from the silky softness of his hair and focused on his frowning face.

"Of course I read them," she muttered finally. Her thought winged back over the past few weeks, trying to recall which particular missive he could be referring to. If the truth were known, she barely glanced at his memos lately. She had been centering every bit of time and attention on her students.

Jeremy crossed his arms over his chest.

"Then I'm sure you noticed that I asked teachers to be particularly aware of permission notes and the necessity of having parents sign if their child was to be taken off the school property," he said smugly. "May I have the notes?"

"But we only walked through the land right next door," she told him wide-eyed. "Surely we don't need a permission slip for a little nature walk."

"I take it that you didn't bother to procure the signatures then," he bit out, shaking his head angrily. "Miss Langford, you cannot keep ignoring the rules that are part of the function of this school."

"Oh, but surely for a little nature walk…"

"Your *little walk* may have engendered a lawsuit," he rasped, standing straight and tall before her.

"What?" Gillian stared at him, half-amused. "Why would anyone sue the school?"

"What if Jed's cut becomes infected and requires further treatment? What if one of the children had been badly hurt? What if you were injured and they were without a leader?" His eyes were icy as they glared at her.

Gillian shook her head. "We didn't go to Siberia," she said softly, peering up at him in confusion. "We walked not fifty feet beyond the school property. Any one of them could have made it back safely, without trouble."

"Deidre Hall couldn't," he said angrily, standing directly in front of her. "What about her?"

Gillian thought about the young girl in the wheelchair whom she'd pushed through the undergrowth. She shrugged. "All right, Deidre needed my help. And I was there. Nothing happened. No big deal."

"Not this time, no." His jacket was unbuttoned, and Gillian could see the missing button on his vest as his hands planted themselves firmly on his hips. For some reason that lost button gave her encouragement; maybe Jeremy Nivens was human after all.

"Fine," she murmured softly, staring up into his stern face. "I admit I should have checked with you first. I'm sorry I didn't advise you of my plans or get the children's parents to sign permission slips. I'll ensure that it doesn't happen again." Gillian smiled placatingly. "Is that all right?"

"I don't think it is. You have perverse ideas on teaching that seem to dictate constantly removing the children from the classroom. I cannot condone that. The classroom is where they should be doing their learning, not in the woods."

Gillian tried to control the surge of rage that flooded through her at his words. How dare he criticize her efforts! She was a good teacher, darned good. And she focused her attention on teaching children to learn in whatever situation they found themselves.

"My students," she began angrily, "are learning to be aware of the things around them, whether or not they are in the classroom. Today they experienced all five of the sensory perceptions of fall. They saw things in a different way than they would have looking out the window at the woods."

"Five senses?" He jumped on her statement immediately, his voice full of dismay. "What did they eat?"

"We peeled the outer shell off acorns and tried to crunch the centers. They tasted the flavor of the woods," she told him proudly.

If it was possible, Jeremy Nivens's body grew even tauter

as he stood glaring down at her. His hands clenched at his sides, and his jaw tightened.

"They'll probably all get sick," he muttered angrily. His voice was cold and hard. "Why can't you learn to just follow the rules?" he demanded angrily.

"Why can't you learn to live with a few less rules and a lot more feeling in your life?" she flung at him. "This isn't a prison. It's a school—a place of learning and experimentation meant to prepare the children for the future. If you constantly deny them the right to find things out for themselves, how will they solve the problems of their world? You can't keep them under lock and key."

He stood there fuming, his anger palpable between them. Gillian could feel the tension crackling in the air and tried not to wince when his hard, bitter, exasperated tones stabbed at her.

"In the future you *will* okay all field trips with me, whether the students go fifty feet or fifty miles. Do you understand, Miss Langford?"

Gillian stifled the urged to bend over at the waist and salaam to him. He would find nothing funny in such an action, she knew.

"Yes, Mr. Nivens," she murmured softly. "I understand completely." Her voice held a nasty undertone that she did not attempt to disguise. "Would you also like to sit in on my classes and make sure I'm not teaching my students political activism or the making of pipe bombs?"

He turned to leave, stopping by the door for a moment. His eyes glittered with something strange as he smiled dryly at her. "Thank you, Miss Langford," he murmured slyly. "I may yet find it necessary to do that."

She could have kicked herself for offering, and spent the next hour mentally booting herself around the room for falling into his little trap. "Odious manipulator," she mumbled, checking her daybook for the plans she had made. "As if I'd let him in here to check up on me. No way." Of course there was really nothing she could do to stop him, Gillian knew. And if he decided she wasn't doing her job, he could call for a review on her work.

Why did Michael have to die? she asked God for the zillionth time. If he were alive, they would be married, and she would be in her happy, carefree position at St. Anne's, blissfully oblivious to the presence of Mr. Jeremy Nivens and his immense book of rules.

But there was nothing to be gained by going down that road. She would just have to learn to accept it and get on with living. The past was no place to dwell, and time *was* flying by.

Gillian laid out the work she had planned for the next school day and checked to see there were enough copies of the Thanksgiving turkey she planned to begin in art class next week. At least she had the children, she consoled herself. She would never have Michael's child, but she had twenty-eight needy ones in her classroom every day, and she intended to see to it that they got the best education she could offer.

Gillian was about two blocks from her aunt's house and dreaming of relaxing for the weekend when she saw the smoke. Thick, billowing, dark gray clouds of smoke rolling out the window of a house. Gillian raced across the street and dashed inside the open front door. This was Faith Rempel's home, she was pretty sure. And if she remembered her aunt's description correctly, Mrs. Rempel lived alone.

Gillian found the woman in her kitchen, slumped over a counter, the smoking remains of a pan with something resembling cherries bubbling blackly on the stove. She snatched a dish towel and grabbed the pan, dumping the entire contents into the sink and pouring water over it. Steam and smoke combined to cover her in a cloud of acrid odors.

"Mrs. Rempel? I'm Hope's niece. Are you all right?" Gillian checked the elderly woman's pulse and was relieved to find it seemed strong and healthy. When the green eyes opened, they stared at Gillian blankly. "Come on, Mrs. Rempel. We'll have to get you out of this smoke."

"Yes, thank you, dear. That would be lovely. I'm afraid my cherries jubilee didn't quite turn out. Such a pity." Faith Rempel's English accent was pronounced as she rose from the table with alacrity and waved her apron back and forth briskly, whooshing the air as she walked.

"Cherries jubilee?" Gillian couldn't believe her ears. Who made cherries jubilee at four-thirty on a Friday afternoon, for goodness sake? And wasn't the sauce supposed to be set on fire when the dish was served, not hours before?

She left Mrs. Rempel sitting on a patio chair outside and checked for further damage in the kitchen before opening all the windows and doors. Thankfully the light, afternoon breeze soon whisked the smelly fumes and billows of blue-black smoke away.

"I've brought you a glass of water, Mrs. Rempel. Are you sure you're all right?" The puffy lines in the woman's face had been there before, Gillian decided, checking her patient once more.

"Of course, dear. I'm perfectly fine." Faith's green eyes stared into hers. "Do I know you?" she asked curiously.

She grinned. "I'm Hope's niece, Gillian. I'm here teaching school."

"Oh, yes," Mrs. Rempel smiled brightly. "You're Jeremy's new girlfriend. You two make the sweetest couple." She stood suddenly and moved briskly to the back door. "I'll have to clean this mess up before he gets here. Jeremy hates a mess."

"I'll help you," Gillian offered, remembering that this woman, according to her aunt, had slight lapses in memory. That would account for her erroneous linking of their names.

How strange that such a lovely woman should be old sour-puss's aunt.

"Does he come every day?" she asked curiously. It seemed odd to think of her boss checking up on his aunt. More likely he came for a free meal so he wouldn't have to dirty his own kitchen, she decided, still fuming at his biting remarks.

"Almost every evening. We have dinner together. I was hoping to surprise him with a new dessert. Piffle," she grunted, glaring at the charred remains of the cherries. "Should have turned the heat down sooner."

Gillian grinned. So Jeremy Nivens came for a free dinner every night. Somehow she had known human kindness wasn't the reason for Jerry's visits. She wondered what he'd think of his aunt's messy kitchen right now.

"You know," she told Faith, smiling as she wiped down the counters and stove. "In our family we had a standing joke whenever Mom burned something. We always said she thought we must be little gods because she was serving us burnt offerings."

Faith giggled appreciatively.

"Underneath all this smoke, something sure smells good," Gillian told her seriously. She opened the oven door and sniffed appreciatively. "What is that?"

The older woman blushed, her salt-and-pepper head bending forward shyly.

"Oh, just a little rouladin. Jeremy loves beef, you know. I imagine you'll be cooking it often after you're married, dear." She scurried about, putting the last of the now-dry dishes away. "I just need to get a salad together and check the potatoes."

"Uh, Mrs. Rempel, Jeremy and I aren't getting…"

"Oh, silly me. Of course you aren't announcing it right away. I can understand that. You both being so new to the community and all," Faith twittered happily as she rinsed the lettuce and set it carefully in a colander to dry. She grasped Gillian's hand in her own and glanced at her finger. "Oh, you haven't found a ring yet?"

"No, we haven't," Gillian searched for the right words, but she needn't have bothered. Jeremy Nivens's aunt was lost in a world of her own, green eyes sparkling with happiness as she stared at her own rings.

"It seems just last week when Donald and I became engaged. He insisted that I choose my own ring, said it was going to have to last a good long time and he didn't want me wearing something I didn't like. It has lasted, too." She didn't say it, but Gillian could almost hear her thinking that the rings had outlasted the husband.

"He gave me that cabinet over there," Faith pointed to the corner china cabinet in the next room. "For our anniversary it was." Her green eyes grew cloudy. "I forget which one, but I remember Donald saying it was my special place for my little china dolls. He sent them to me from overseas during the war."

"Auntie Fay? Are you all right?"

The anxious tones of her authoritative boss jerked Gillian from her happy daydream of the past. It was strange to hear that note of concern in his voice, but moments later she decided she must have imagined it as he glared across the room at them.

"What are you doing here?" he demanded, staring at Gillian. "Oh, never mind right now. Auntie Fay, the neighbors phoned me to say that there was smoke coming from the house. Are you all right?"

"Oh, I'm just fine, thank you, dear. A wee bit early for dinner, aren't you?" Faith blinked up at him innocently as her hands tore the lettuce apart and placed it in a crystal bowl. "I'm afraid I haven't got the table set yet."

"There's no rush," he told her softly, his gray eyes gentle.

"As you say, I am early. I'll talk to *her* while I wait." His head nodded at Gillian, who felt an immediate prickling of anger.

"Yes, I suppose you two lovebirds do have some catching up to do. Go ahead out on the balcony and relax. I remember young love. Why, your fiancée and I were just talking about it." Her benign smile left Gillian smiling back, until Jeremy's rough voice roused her.

"Yes," he agreed, frowning severely as he grasped Gillian's arm in his firm fingers and tugged her from the room. "I think Miss Langford and I definitely need to have a discussion."

Obediently Gillian preceded him out the back door and sank onto one of the wicker chairs Faith had placed under the awning. She slipped off her new, black patent shoes and wiggled her feet in the fresh air as she summoned enough nerve up to glance at his forbidding face.

"Would you mind very much telling what in the dickens is going on in this nuthouse now? I mean since you are my fiancée and everything!"

His scathing tone rasped over her nerves, but there was no way he was intimidating her, Gillian decided. Once today was enough. She glared back at him, daring him to holler at her again.

"Well? Exactly when did we become engaged, Miss Langford?"

Gillian couldn't help it, the grin popped to her mouth, splitting it wide with mirth. "Since I'm your fiancée and everything," she murmured slyly, "don't you think it's about time you started calling me Gillian?" Laughter burst out of her at the stupefied stare on his face. "Well? Jeremy?" It was the first time she'd seen him dumbfounded, and it was very refreshing. "Honey?" She shook his arm teasingly.

A second later the grin was gone from her mouth as he tugged her into his arms and kissed her on the mouth. It wasn't a passionate kiss, or even a very practiced one. In fact, Gillian suspected it had more to do with anger than anything.

Still and all, it shook her. She liked the feel of his firm lips against hers, she decided dazedly. And his arms were strong, but gentle, around her.

"Wh-what are you doing?" she stammered at last, staring up into his glittery blue eyes. They had a wariness about them that added to the unreality of the situation.

"Kissing my fiancée. Surely that's allowed?"

Gillian stared at the transformation taking place in front of her. For once, the stern, haughty face had been replaced with a handsome, smiling countenance that drew her like a magnet. It was disconcerting to find that he affected her so. Clearly he wasn't nearly so bothered by that kiss. His entire demeanor was calm, cool and collected. Carefully she extricated herself from his embrace, stepped back and sat down.

"Not this early in the relationship," she murmured, peering up at him from between her lashes. When he said nothing, she pressed on. "Your aunt is a little confused," she told him quietly. "I don't know where she got the idea that we are a couple. Maybe it's due to the fire."

His face blanched.

"Then there really was a fire." He smacked his hand on his pant leg. "Darn. I was afraid of that." His eyes had dimmed to cool gray again. "What happened?"

"She was flambéing cherries jubilee, and I think they caught on fire, which in turn started the pot holder smoking. She had everything well under control when I arrived," Gillian lied. "I merely opened the doors and windows to let the smoke out. No damage done."

"No damage done?" Jeremy stared at her as if she'd grown two heads. "Miss Langford, really! My aunt almost burns her house down. While she's inside, incidentally. She decides to cook cherries jubilee in the middle of the afternoon, and then, out of the blue, decides you're my fiancée." His eyes narrowed as he stared at her calmly nodding head. "I don't think you are a very good influence on my aunt." He shook his dark head vehemently. "Not at all."

"Oh, I don't know," Gillian said, chuckling at his stern look. "I got her uppity nephew engaged to me without even trying. I must be doing something right."

The whole town was loony, Jeremy decided, staring at the vibrant young woman in front of him. Absently he noted the way her freckles drifted across her nose and cheeks.

It was her eyes that really got to him, though. They were like jade daggers, stabbing at him in angry little jabs as she bristled up in her chair.

"Oh, for goodness sake," she complained at last. "Can't you tell that your aunt's a little confused? Cut her some slack, would you?"

Jeremy stared. "I beg your pardon?" he murmured, trying to figure out what she was talking about. "Cut some slacks?"

Gillian Langford sighed, pleating her trousers between her fingers as she stared back at him.

"How old are you, Mr. Nivens?"

"Thirty." Jeremy was too shocked to stop his immediate response. "Why?"

"Don't take this personally," she told him with a teasing little grin that reinforced how beautiful Gillian Langford really was, "but you act like you're from another planet. Where have you been for the past thirty years?"

"England," he murmured at last. "At least for twenty-eight of them. I was raised in Oxford and attended school there. I was headmaster at a school nearby until this summer, when I returned to the States." His brow creased. "Why?"

Gillian's narrow shoulders shrugged. "Doesn't matter," she murmured, tugging her mane of reddish-gold off her face. "Anyway, the point is, your aunt is a little mixed-up. For some reason she's decided that you and I are engaged."

He laughed harshly.

"My aunt is a lot more than slightly confused. She is forgetful, absentminded, preoccupied and inattentive when she is cooking. That's why I'm trying to persuade her to sell this house and go into a nursing home."

"What?"

Jeremy winced at the shrill shriek of her voice. He would have pointed out that the whole affair was none of her business, but he didn't have time. Miss Langford advanced upon him like a Mack truck, letting nothing stop her surge of fury until she stood directly in front of his chair, green eyes glittering.

"You can't! No way. She loves this house and the memories that are hidden away in every nook and corner. You can't expect her to just give it all up. What about getting someone to live in?"

Jeremy snorted. She might be beautiful, this new teacher on his staff, but she wasn't in the least practical.

"In Mossbank? Population five thousand, and that's a high estimate?" He shook his head. "I don't think so."

"But a nursing home? She doesn't need it. She's perfectly self-reliant." Her lips had carried an angry tilt to them. "She just forgets things once in a while."

"I know," he nodded. "Like the fireplace going or the stove or the kettle. One day it will cause a fire. Like today?" He peered at her with one eyebrow raised inquiringly. "What aren't you telling me that she forgot today?"

"Nothing," Gillian answered stoically. "She just let the liqueur get a little too hot when she was flambéing the cherries jubilee. It was out before I got here. I told you that."

"Yes," he nodded slowly. "I heard exactly what you said. It's what you didn't say that has me worried." He studied the flaming sparks that reflected off her hair in the late-afternoon sun. "And it's knowing that my aunt is a loose cannon, waiting to go off, that is forcing me to consider a facility that can care for her."

"But you can't!" Gillian was aghast that he would consider such a drastic action. "She loves the freedom of cooking and cleaning in her own home. I can't believe that she's in danger. Not really." She glared at him through the fringe of bangs that fell across her forehead. "Anyway, Mrs. Flowerday and my aunt Hope will be watching out for her. And I certainly will. Among the three of us, she'll be well cared for."

Jeremy was shaking his head.

"But you can't be here all the time, and neither can I. There will be those occasions when she will decide to cook some elaborate dish at five in the morning and no one will be able to stop her. Next time she may well set herself on fire." His face glanced down at Gillian sadly. "I don't like it any more than you, but I simply will not take the risk of her hurting herself."

"I don't think you have the right to make such a decision," Gillian sputtered angrily. "You've only just arrived on the scene. Faith has been managing alone for years now. You can't just waltz in here and uproot her from everything that's familiar. It will only confuse her more."

"Oh, I won't do it right away. I'll talk to her, give her time to get used to the idea first." He stared out across Faith's ramshackle garden with its wild assortment of plants. "Look at her garden," he muttered, thrusting out one hand. "She's forgotten all about it."

"She hasn't forgotten it," Gillian denied, glaring at him. "She probably hasn't had time to get to it. Especially when she's fixing your meals all the time. That must be quite a burden for her." Her eyes sparkled angrily at him. "Can't you learn to cook, Mr. Nivens?"

Jeremy felt his eyes open wide, startled at the anger in her tones.

"Surely you don't think I come over for dinner just to get a free meal?" he said, furious at her categorization of his motives. "There are any number of restaurants in the town. I can certainly afford to eat regularly at most of them."

"Then why are you here?" Gillian Langford looked down her nose at him disdainfully, daring him to deny her conclusions.

"To make sure Aunt Faith eats at least one decent meal a day. If she thinks I'm coming, she makes a full meal. And eats it." He met her stare head-on. "Otherwise she would make do on tea and toast, and that's not very healthy."

Jeremy watched the dull flush of red suffuse her pronounced cheekbones, making the light sprinkling of freckles across her nose stand out. The reddish strands in her shining hair glittered. Lord, Gillian Langford was a beautiful woman.

He wondered why she wasn't married and how she'd come to live in Mossbank. His eyes swept down to the beautiful ring she always wore on her right hand. He'd noticed it before; many times. It looked like an engagement ring, but even he knew they were worn on the left hand. And no young man came by to claim her after school.

Which no doubt meant that the lady wasn't interested in men. Good! He didn't want to have to deal with overeager suitors hanging around the school, and he felt fairly certain than any suitor of Gillian Langford would be eager.

He glanced up and found her gaze fixed on him: dark, turbulent shadows clouding the green clarity of her eyes.

"My aunt must be about ready by now," he murmured. "Perhaps we had better go in." As he followed her into the house, Jeremy was forced to admit that today her choice of clothing was both suitable for school and extremely attractive.

She wore the long, slim slacks comfortably on her leggy frame, a matching teal silk shirt hanging loosely to her hips. The color was very flattering to her. A short, knitted black vest made the outfit complete and rendered it less casual looking. With her hair on the top of her head, Gillian looked coolly professional, and the picture irked him immeasurably. Why, he wasn't sure.

"Well, I'd better be getting home to Hope's," Gillian told the older woman cheerfully. "She's sure to have dinner ready."

"Yes, Hope is a good cook," Faith enthused. Her forehead pleated in a frown. "Although she does have a tight fist with the butter. Now, dear," she turned to Jeremy. "You are eating with Gillian tonight, aren't you? I would have made more if I'd known you were coming, but when I thought there would be just Art and me..." Her voice trailed away as she gestured to the smiling man seated on the other side of the kitchen table.

Jeremy stared at her in perplexity, wondering what was going on now. A sharp jab in the ribs brought him back to reality immediately, and he glared down at Gillian in frustration.

"Well, the truth is, Auntie Fay," he began, and then swallowed the rest of the sentence as Gillian cut him off.

"Of course he can eat with us. Hope is sure to have plenty. And if he doesn't like her cooking, I'm sure Jeremy can get something for himself."

Her eyes opened innocently to stare at him, and Jeremy smiled at the idea of cooking anything in his poorly stocked apartment. "You know me, Auntie Fay," he murmured, just under his breath. His eyes met Gillian's startled ones, and he grinned. "I'll do anything for a free meal."

He could see that she felt embarrassed at her previous assumptions about his motives for going to his aunt's, and he would have chortled with delight at the sight of it if the others hadn't been there.

"I just hope Hope isn't serving tofu," Gillian whispered in his ear, her shoulder pressing against his chest for just a moment. "My aunt is really into eating healthy, you know."

Jeremy felt his stomach lurch strangely. Tofu? As in that curdled white stuff?

"Well, I hope you and your girl have a real nice evening," Art said, smiling benignly. "Faith was telling me about your engagement. Congratulations to you both."

"But there is nothing to—" Jeremy gave up trying to explain as the willow wisp of a girl next to him tugged his arm none too gently.

"Thank you very much," he heard her say with a laugh. "I hope the two of you enjoy your dinner. Come on, *honey,*" Gillian said, wrapping her arm through his.

Before his wits returned, Jeremy found himself standing on the sidewalk in front of his aunt's house next to the beautiful woman who taught first grade in his school. She had removed her arm and he was thankful for that. It wouldn't do for the rest of the town to hear of their bogus engagement. Anyway, even that slight touch bothered him. A lot.

He felt the poke in his side and chanced a look down. She stood there, grinning from ear to ear.

"Well," she charged. "Aren't you going to offer me a ride to Hope's?"

Without conscious thought he opened the passenger side door and waited for her to slip inside his shiny black Mustang convertible. Her hand slid longingly over the leather-covered dashboard as he watched her snuggle into the fawn-colored bucket seat.

"Is that why you wanted to be engaged to me?" he asked solemnly, shifting gears before pulling away from the curb. "So you could ride in my new car?" He glanced at her and surprised a calculating look in her green eyes.

"Oh, that's just one of the many reasons," she murmured softly, sliding her shoes off and squishing her toes in the plush beige carpeting. "I'll tell you the rest of them over dinner."

As he negotiated the streets to her aunt's house, Jeremy frowned. Gillian Langford had arranged this, this misunderstanding, he felt sure. And it was because she had some ulterior motive.

Why then did he feel anticipation instead of fear at finding out just what the gorgeous redhead had in mind? he asked himself.

Chapter Four

❧

"Where did you get this car?" Gillian demanded, breaking the tense silence that hung between them. She brushed her hand over the cool, smooth leather. "It's fabulous. And it doesn't seem like the type of car you'd drive at all," she blurted out. "I mean…" Her voice trailed away in dismay.

Jeremy chuckled. "What did you think I'd drive? Some staid, old family sedan, I'd wager." He laughed out loud at the abashed look on her expressive face. "Don't ever lie," he advised. "You can't hide your true feelings worth a plugged nickel."

She bristled immediately, which was exactly what Jeremy had expected.

"I make it a habit never to lie about anything," she told him pertly. "I learned that in the Sunday school right there." Gillian pointed to the old church as they passed it.

"Did you grow up here?" he asked, suddenly curious about her childhood.

"No." She shook her head. "But I came to visit Hope quite a lot when my parents wanted their own holiday. It was great fun for me, coming from Boston to the freedom of this little town." Gillian pointed to the lovely park with its huge trees and carragana hedge. "We used to pretend there were little caves in that hedge," she told him. "We could hide or have tea parties or lunch and never worry anybody."

"It sounds like you had a happy childhood," he murmured softly.

"Oh, I did," she enthused, grinning as the memories surfaced from long ago. "Whenever I visited Hope's, I was the queen of the castle. She'd let me stay up as long as I wanted. Or at least as long as I could without nodding off." Her thoughts drifted to the times she and Hope had slept outside under the stars.

"I believe children need a regular bedtime." Jeremy's quiet voice interrupted her musings. "It's important for their health and their growth that a regular schedule is maintained."

"Oh, for goodness sake," Gillian snapped, glaring at him angrily. "There you go again with those silly rules. Why do you always do that?" She watched him blink in confusion.

"Do what?" he asked, frowning. "I never did anything. I merely said…"

"I know what you said. It's what you always say. For every situation in life you need a rule." She scowled at him with disgust. "Don't you ever just relax and enjoy the world around you without worrying if it's the right thing to do?"

"It's not a matter of relaxing," he muttered at last, gliding to a stop in front of Hope's compact two-story. "It's a matter of planning things out to get the optimal benefit out of life."

"But I did get the optimal benefit," she argued, sliding out of the seat as his hand went under her elbow. "If I'd been sleeping in my bed, Hope and I wouldn't have been able to discuss the constellations or where God lives, or how the angels come to earth. Those things were just as important to me as a few extra minutes of sleep."

She stared into his handsome face seriously. "My mom always told us that life is made up of little shining moments like stones in a necklace. They're what make the everyday routine things bearable, because we can take out those stones and remember them with pleasure during the bad times." She beckoned him up the stairs. "Come on in. Hope will have started something."

But unfortunately Hope hadn't. There was a note tacked to the phone informing Gillian that her aunt had gone shopping with Charity Flowerday.

"I'm sorry," she murmured, frowning up at Jeremy, who towered over her, now that she had removed her shoes. "I guess we'll have to find something for ourselves. Do you like tacos?"

His face was a study in contradictions. Gillian would have teased him about it except that he looked so unsure of himself.

"I—I don't know." His eyes met hers, and she was surprised to see uncertainty in their depths. "What is a taco?"

"Well," Gillian began, matter-of-factly arranging the ingredients she would need on the countertop and trying to ignore the spark of electricity she felt fluttering down her sensitive skin whenever Jeremy Nivens came near. "There are two kinds—soft and hard. I like the hard ones, although they're messy to eat."

He watched her defrost a package of meat in the microwave and then dump it into a frying pan. His forehead furrowed.

"Ground beef," he murmured.

"Hamburger, yes. With seasoning and spices. You put it into the shell and add vegetables and cheese to it." She watched his long patrician nose twitch as he caught a hint of the savory cooking odors.

"I'm not sure if I can eat such food," he told her seriously. "It smells as if it's spicy and my stomach is rather queasy about those things."

Gillian grinned at him, enjoying the look of uncertainty

on his handsome face. For once Mr. Jeremy Nivens was not in control. She was going to enjoy this.

As the meat cooked, she shredded lettuce and minced tomatoes. She put Jeremy to work grating cheese. As they toiled side by side, she chattered a mile a minute, hoping to put him at his ease.

"I love tacos. Especially with hot sauce. It just makes your mouth come alive. Michael used to…" Her voice trailed away as she realized what she'd said.

"Michael was your fiancé?" Jeremy's matter-of-fact voice inquired, eyes intent on the cheese as he carefully rubbed the slab of cheddar against her aunt's grater.

Gillian realized that she had been talking about Michael naturally for once, and although the pain was still there, it had diminished to the point where she could talk about him with fondness.

"Yes. He died in a car crash. Anyway, he used to tease me for being a wimp." Her mouth curved in remembrance. "He would load on the hot sauce until my eyes watered and I was coughing like crazy. Michael never even needed a drink of water. You know—" her eyes flashed to him and then looked away in embarrassment at the scrutiny she found there "—the Thai people clench their teeth together and then spread their mouth wide so they can suck air into their mouths, not blow it out. They claim it's the best way to cool your palate."

Jeremy was silent, steadily building the tower of cheese curls on the plate she'd given him. When he finally spoke, it was in a soft, careful voice that was totally unlike his usually brusque tone.

"It must have been very difficult for you," he offered. "Was that why you decided to move here?" His blue-gray eyes met hers steadily, his face set in its usual stern lines.

"Partially." She set the table quickly and scooped the browned meat into a bowl. "I just couldn't stay in Boston anymore. It reminded me too much of him and of what I'd lost." Carefully she removed the warmed tacos from the oven and placed them on the table beside the tomatoes and lettuce. A huge pitcher of lemonade and two large glasses completed the job.

"Okay, everything's ready," she grinned at him. As he gingerly set the cheese on the table, Gillian lifted a bottle from the fridge. "Now, for your first taste of tacos. Don't forget the sauce."

She murmured a short grace for both of them and then showed him how to assemble the items and bite off the end carefully so that the whole thing didn't crumble in his hand.

"It is rather good," he murmured, a surprised look on his face. "And not really hot at all."

"That's because you haven't used this yet." Carefully she spooned a small teaspoonful onto his taco. "Now try."

He gasped, and Gillian giggled as his eyes grew round with surprise. Seconds later he was glugging down a huge glass of lemonade.

"Good heavens," he whispered. "That was like fire." His eyes were huge as he watched her slather on the sauce and then chew the mouthful with alacrity. "How can you do that?"

"Practice." Gillian giggled. "Plus the fact that this is extra mild." He raised one eyebrow skeptically. "Don't worry. You'll get used to it."

Jeremy finished his first taco and started gingerly on a second, carefully avoiding her jar of sauce.

"You reminded me of a visit I once made to my aunt here," he told her as they sat companionably sipping the icy lemonade. "She invited me to stay while my parents attended some teaching sessions at the college. They were anthropologists, you see, and in order to maintain their grant status, they had to return to the States every so often for a report."

"Was that why you went to boarding school?" she inquired quietly. "Because they were so busy?"

He smiled, but his gaze was far away. Gillian wondered idly what kind of a childhood he'd had.

"Not exactly. They spent a lot of time on a dig in Egypt and then Israel. They wanted to make sure my schooling was uninterrupted." He smoothed the tablecloth idly, his voice low. "Anyway, every summer I came to spend several weeks with Auntie Fay. It was like a whole different world for me. The food, the clothes. Even the children were different."

Jeremy glanced up at her and grimaced.

"I'm afraid I didn't blend in very well, and I must have been an awful nuisance to have around. My aunt took me to the county fair and let me ride on the Ferris wheel until I was sick. I think I must have tasted every flavor and color of cotton candy and sugar cone there was, but it was the candy apple that finally did me in." His face had a wistful quality about it that tugged on her heart.

"I've never forgotten the pleasure she gave me in those days. Or the way she would tuck me in at night and kiss me." Jeremy glanced at her apologetically. "There aren't many people who will kiss anyone good-night in boarding school," he muttered quietly, his eyes downcast.

"But what about during the summers," Gillian demanded angrily. "Surely you lived with your parents then?"

She couldn't believe it when he shook his head, his sharp gray glance telling her that he thought she should know better than to ask such a silly question. Her tender heart ached at the words.

"Gillian, an archaeological dig is no place for a child. There are valuable artifacts lying about and open pits around which it would be dangerous for a child to play. Not that there was much to play with, anyway. Besides, it was far too hot, as I found out the one summer I insisted on visiting them.

I spent most of my time cataloging their finds. A layer of sand covered everything."

Gillian stacked the dishes into her aunt's dishwasher with a snap to her wrist that boded ill for the stoneware.

"I happen to feel that real, live children are more valuable than any old artifact from the past." She watched as he meticulously wrapped the leftovers and placed them neatly in the fridge. "It doesn't sound like much of a life for a child," she added finally.

He looked surprised.

"Actually it was a very good life. I was able to spend much of the summer studying for the next term. My grades were very good, and I finished my O levels a year ahead of schedule."

Gillian set the coffee to perk and waved him into the living room. She wanted to tell him that his rigid lifestyle had robbed him of the carefree play of a child, but who was she to judge. She could only sympathize with the little boy who had spent his time working on the Dewey decimal system for artifacts.

She had just poured them each a cup of the fragrant, steaming coffee when Hope's doorbell rang. It was Pastor Dave, in his usual jovial mood.

"I knew you two would be here," he said happily, his booted feet thumping heavily across the floor. "Heard about your good news, too. Congratulations." His round shiny face beamed down at them both.

Gillian could feel the tide of red suffusing her cheeks, as she realized from his sparkling glance that he'd heard about their supposed engagement from Faith.

"Well, thanks anyway, Pastor," she murmured, glancing at Jeremy's gaping mouth. "But we're not engaged. Mr. Nivens and I are merely colleagues."

"Oh, I remember. Faith did say you and your beau were

trying to keep things quiet. I'll respect your privacy, Gilly, girl. Don't you worry. At least for a while." He winked and patted her shoulder, then whooshed down onto the sofa.

Gillian gritted her teeth and willed him to listen.

"You don't understand, Pastor. Jeremy and I aren't engaged. Not at all." She glanced at her supposed intended for confirmation and saw a glimmer of mirth deep in his eyes. He couldn't be enjoying this, could he?

"Oh, you've had a little tiff, I suppose. Everybody has them, sweetie. You just have to work through your problems. And at least you're doing that now before you're married." Dave patted her hand consolingly. "That's a good sign that you two are adults, willing to compromise and accommodate the other's point of view. Now about the youth group," he winked at them both as they sat on either side of him, mouths hanging open in consternation.

"I just know you and your honey here will make good team leaders for the kids. I've arranged for them to go to Tyndale's farm on Friday night and play capture the flag, and I thought you two might like to come along and watch." He beamed down on them happily. "Next week you're on your own."

As the hefty minister lunged to his feet, Gillian glared at Jeremy. Do something, she telegraphed, and breathed a sigh of relief as he, also, stood up.

"I don't think Gillian, er, that is, Miss Langford and I, well, we don't exactly know just how to, well, deal with…"

He stopped abruptly when the reverend slapped him soundly on the back and bubbled with laughter.

"Course you don't, son," Dave chortled happily. "But you're smart young folk with lots of schoolin'. I have every faith that God will lead you in your dealings with these young people. Anyway, it will be good practice for when your own come, eh!" He chuckled with glee at their surprised faces.

"Meet you at the church in half an hour," his jovial voice chided them. "Don't be late." He surged through the room toward the front door, sniggering to himself as he went. "Well, well. A wedding. Haven't done one of those in a while."

Gillian sank onto the sofa, her knees buckling under the strain as she stared up at her intended. "Could you please stop this freight train?" she asked helplessly. "I think I want to get off."

She heard his hiss of disgust as Jeremy moved in front of her. The silver in his eyes glittered at her like steel, and his mouth was pursed in a hard, straight line of blame.

"Well, it's just a bit late for that, Miss Langford," he accused. "Especially now that the whole town thinks we're about to be married, *honey!*"

"Look," she began, anger poking at the way he was hinting that this was all her fault. "I was only trying to spare your aunt. She was just a little confused, and I didn't want to make it worse."

He shoved his hands in his pockets and glared furiously at her, his mouth grim.

"Well, you've made it much worse," he complained bitterly. "Now we've got the minister planning our wedding."

Gillian felt the chill of those cold gray eyes move over her with disgust as he said, "I don't want to get married. And especially not to a woman who is so obviously the opposite of everything I could want in my wife." His hands clenched and unclenched at his sides. "If I wanted one, that is. Which I don't."

Gillian felt tears of anger press against her eyelids, but there was no way she was giving in. Not with *him* standing there watching.

"Believe me," she enunciated clearly, determined that he would hear every word. "If I ever chose to be engaged again, which I won't, it certainly wouldn't be to some old-fashioned, stuffed shirt from the Middle Ages."

He glared at her for so long Gillian thought his eyebrows would be completely lost in his dark mussed-up hair. His words when they came were soft and menacing.

"Better to be old-fashioned than an airhead with no sense of responsibility. Good night!"

"Good night!"

He turned without a second look and stomped his way to the front door, collecting his suit jacket on the way. Gillian was smugly amused to see that somehow during the evening his tie had loosened and several shirt buttons had come undone. Jeremy Nivens also had taco sauce on his pristine vest, she noticed with satisfaction. Some of the superiority disappeared as she glanced in Hope's mirror and noted the state of her own disheveled appearance.

"Just a minute," she cried as he strode down the steps. At her words he stopped dead in his place and waited for her to catch up.

"What are we going to do about the youth group? Pastor Dave is expecting us to take over next week. We're supposed to be there tonight."

When he looked at her, Gillian flinched at the anger emanating from his frosty gaze.

"Just another situation you've entangled us in, Miss Langford." His face was carved in those hard, bitter lines that had been missing for a while tonight.

"Well," she murmured quietly, "are you going to tell him that you can't do it?" She waited expectantly for his answer.

"No," he bellowed, sending her reeling in shock. "I let him go away believing I would help, and I will. I'll set up a six-week Bible study for them."

Gillian stared at him, frowning.

"A Bible study," she murmured quizzically. "They usually do something fun on weekends. The Bible studies are on Wednesday evenings." She peered at him curiously.

"Very well, then." Jeremy jumped over the side of the car and vaulted into the seat with a move Gillian had only seen in the movies. It was proof positive that there was a lot more to the man than she had suspected, when he could make a move like that so easily.

"You plan their events," he muttered angrily. "I'll plan the food." He drove away without a single grinding of gears while she stood there staring after him. Jeremy Nivens was going to provide the food? As she walked back into the house, Gillian grimaced. What would the youth of Mossbank have to eat at their weekly get-togethers? she asked herself. Toast and jam? Or his American version of tea and crumpets? She dismissed the thought as uncharitable and not worthy of her and raced upstairs to change into her jeans and sneakers. If she was going to do this, and it looked like she was, she couldn't afford to be late for the first night.

To say that the youth group meeting that evening was a success would have been an overstatement of the facts. Two boys got into a disagreement after one of them twisted his ankle racing around in the bush behind the house, searching for the flag.

Several of the girls had declined to join in the roughhousing, opting instead to jump on their host's trampoline. Unfortunately, the combined weight of five bouncing teenagers had sent one of them toppling over the side where she'd hung suspended while Gillian and Jeremy tried to disentangle her sweater from the hook it had caught on.

That would have been enough, but Pastor Dave insisted on announcing their "engagement" to the assembled throng and then forcing each one to promise that they would keep it under their hats. The youngsters clustered around them excitedly. The girls wanted to see her ring while the boys stood back with Jeremy and muttered "Good luck."

She was up to her neck in alligators, Gillian admitted when one of the girls spotted the emerald on her right hand and demanded to know if that was her engagement ring. Strangely enough, it didn't hurt nearly as much as she'd thought, to tell them about Michael.

"It was," she murmured softly, perching on the log someone had placed around the fire pit. "But Michael died shortly before we were to be married. I wear the ring to remind myself of the happy times we shared."

"That must have hurt pretty badly," Rosa Almirez whispered, placing her hand on Gillian's arm.

"Yes, it did. More than you could imagine."

"How did you get over him?" Janet Sivers asked.

"Well, at first I tried to get away from all the things that reminded me of him and the plans that we had." A movement beyond the circle of girls caught her attention, and she noted Jeremy and the boys moving closer to the fire. "I was really mad at God for letting him die, and I thought He'd done it to spite me. I decided I'd move to Mossbank and teach here."

"I'll bet you thought you'd never find anyone else to love," Marisa Clairns murmured, her eyes dreamy. "And then Mr. Nivens came along."

"Not exactly," Gillian agreed, her eyes drawn to Jeremy's darker ones. "I decided I would never get married. That I would learn how to live on my own, without anyone else." She saw Jeremy's dark eyes narrow as he glanced down at the group around her.

"I was determined to do things my own way until God began working in me, and now I'm beginning to realize that

He only wants what is best for me. I have to remind myself that it's not my will but His that needs doing."

"But don't you feel sort of—" Blair Jenkins shrugged her elegant shoulders "—like a traitor?" she muttered at last. "I mean, Michael was your own true love. You can't just replace him."

Gillian smiled and patted the girl's soft, blond head. "God gives us special people in our lives to teach us things, Blair. I'm not ever going to forget Michael, and no one can take his place in my heart." The words came out with a force meant to reassure Jeremy of her good intentions. Instead he stood back from the group, looking down on her.

But his face was a closed book, and she refused to beg him to understand. Her private feelings about her fiancé were none of his business. She was only telling the girls in the hope that it would help them deal with their own futures.

"Well then, how can you marry Mr. Nivens?" Desiree demanded, her highly made-up face accenting the ring that pierced her eyebrow and glinted in the moonlight. "You're saying that you don't love him."

Gillian chuckled, pleased by the girl's astute mind, but just a little worried about the direction the conversation was taking. "No, sweetie. I'm saying that people have different places in our lives. You have brothers and sisters, don't you, Desiree?" She watched the young girl nod uncertainly. "And do you love one of them way more than all the others or is there enough room in your heart for all of them to fit comfortably—maybe even one more if it comes along?"

"Well, right now I'm not feeling a lot of love toward Zane," Desiree admitted, motioning to her older brother who was standing near Jeremy. "He read my diary, without my permission I might add, and I'd like to smack him upside the head." The other girls all giggled in appreciation, darting looks of condemnation at the red-faced youth. "But I get what you mean. Sort of like there's always room for one more."

"Yeah. Like love means different strokes for different folks," Blair added smugly. "And there are all kinds of love."

"That's exactly right," Pastor Dave said, smiling benignly. "And that's what we want to talk about tonight—God's love for each one of us."

The kids gathered round their pastor, sitting close together on the logs and listening with interest as he outlined God's special enduring love for each one of them. Gillian stayed where she was, relieved to have the focus off her for now.

"You see, guys," the pastor continued, "it's like there is no beginning and no end to the love God has for us. And it is always the same, not changing like Desiree said her feelings did when her brother wronged her. God's love is always there, always holding us up, always waiting for us. All we have to do is accept it."

As she listened, Gillian felt herself allowing some more of the pain and anger and frustration of Michael's death to slowly drain away. She would never understand why he had to die, she realized. But that wasn't important.

What was important was that God had not abandoned her, left her to face life on her own. He would be with her through the good and bad times. She just had to trust in that. And believe that some good would come out of it.

"God can't love us all the same," the pastor continued. "You and I have different life experiences, different needs for Him in our lives. What you need from God is different from what I need. That doesn't matter." He grinned a beaming smile that included the whole group. "'Cause God already knows that, and He's just waiting for me to ask Him for help."

As she glanced around at the teenagers, their faces upturned as they listened to their pastor, Gillian said a silent prayer of thanks for the new life she'd been given. *I don't know much about teenagers, God,* she murmured under her breath. *But if You'll help me out, I'll do my best. Even if I have to work with cranky old Jeremy Nivens.*

She watched, smiling, as the teens jostled for position in the lineup for chips, pop and hot dogs. They were a good group, and they needed some direction. Maybe this was one area she could do some good and help herself out of the doldrums while she did.

It was worth a try, wasn't it?

"It was a lovely meal, Hope. A perfect end to our day of shopping in Minot. And I've never had poached chicken au naturel before." Charity glanced at the leftover colorless, odorless, tasteless meat that Hope had prepared, and with a roll of her eyes, decided to change the subject quickly. "How is your Christmas project going?"

Hope poured out two cups of decaf and carried them across to the table. Her mind was busy arranging Flossie's encounter with Jeremy. It wouldn't do to be too overt…subtlety, that was the key. She sipped her coffee absently as she considered the upcoming banquet. Maybe she could arrange to have the two seated together.

"Hope?"

"Yes?" She stared at Charity's frowning face with perplexity. "Is something wrong?" she asked.

"Only the fact that I've asked you the same question three times without response." Charity looked askance at the fourth teaspoonful of sugar Hope had laced her coffee with. "And when did you start eating white sugar?"

Neither of them had a chance to say more, due to the pounding on Hope's front door.

"It's me, dear," Faith's happy voice chanted. "And Arthur. Don't worry, we've let ourselves in." She breezed into the kitchen, breathless and ruffled, with the red-faced grocer trailing close behind.

Charity shoved a chair toward him. "Sit down, Arthur, for heaven's sake. You look like you're about to have a heart attack." She watched his chest heave up and down for a few moments before demanding, "Did you run from the store?"

Arthur shook his bald head negatively as he wheezed and gasped for air. It was Faith's bright chipper voice that filled them in.

"Of course not," she protested, laughing as she flopped into the one vacant chair. "We raced each other here from my house. Arthur came for dinner." She raked her hand through her tumble of gray curls and grinned mischievously at the two women. "And he's got the most wonderful news."

Her bright green eyes sparkled as she patted Arthur's rough hand. "Go ahead, dear. Tell them."

Poor Arthur looked confused, glancing from Faith to Hope to Charity. His mouth was moving but there was no sound coming from it, and Faith was clearly losing patience with him.

"Oh, never mind," she said at last, her hands fluttering madly. "I'll do it myself." She took a deep breath and with a beam of satisfaction told her friends the good news. "Arthur says my Jeremy and your Gillian are engaged. Isn't it wonderful!"

Her two closest friends stared at her as if she'd just told them she was going to marry Arthur Johnson herself. Their mouths hung open in amazement and disbelief.

"It's impossible," Hope muttered, shaking her head as if to dislodge whatever prevented her from understanding such a thing. "Why, they don't even like each other!"

"Of course they like each other. They were kissing on my patio," Faith said fiercely. She wagged a finger in Hope's face. "People who hate each other don't do that."

"It's impossible," Hope whispered, her eyes wide-open. "You must have imagined it."

"I'm sorry, Hope," Arthur offered, rushing to Faith's defense. "But she's not mistaken. I saw it myself."

"There must be some mistake. Gillian can't stand the man."

"Well—" Arthur shook his head ruefully "—perhaps she's changed her mind, because she sure didn't pull away when he wrapped his arms around her and kissed her back. And in broad daylight." His tired eyes sparkled. "That was some kiss."

Faith nodded, grinning as she sipped Hope's overly sweetened coffee. Suddenly her expression changed and she stared at the other two women before turning to Art.

"Maybe we shouldn't have told them," she murmured softly, peering into his strong, steady gaze. "After all, Pastor Dave did say it was a secret."

Hope shrieked in the most unladylike fashion they had ever heard from her. "The pastor knows?" She sank dazedly into the kitchen chair with a weak groan.

Charity shuffled over to fan her friend for several moments, but there was no change on Hope's shocked face.

"Oh, my good Lord," Hope said over and over.

Charity helped the slender woman to her feet, issuing orders as they moved out of the kitchen.

"Faith, you and Arthur see to those dishes. I'm going to get Hope lying down in bed before she falls down. Then we'll all go home and leave her to sort this out in peace."

As they stumbled up the stairs together, Charity was already busy organizing the future for the little boy she'd met in Art's store and the jobs she had all lined up for him. It would be her first step in her own Christmas goodwill toward men project.

Chapter Five

Gillian slowly drove her aunt's car back into the small town at eleven-thirty that night, savoring the peaceful stillness. Where else in the world could you get such a wonderful feeling of security? she asked herself. The sky was bright and clear, its myriad stars perfectly visible in the black velvet expanse. She saw two figures chasing each other around the merry-go-round in the park, and Gillian found herself unintentionally watching them. It looked like fun—a carefree lighthearted romp that sent puffs of air out of their mouths to condense in the cool night air.

Gillian peered through the windshield. It couldn't be… Jeremy's Aunt Faith and Arthur Johnson? A smile curved her lips. Now there was a couple who knew how to enjoy life. She felt a tiny glow of pleasure cascade through her. It looked like her idea for a special Christmas project had been a good one. The older couple seemed to get along well together, and she had no doubt that Art would see Faith safely home, relieving Jeremy's anxiousness.

Ah, life was good. Well, except for one little problem. That silly pretend engagement. It seemed like the whole town knew about that now and believed the entire fabrication.

Sighing, Gillian slipped her car into gear and headed for

Hope's. Maybe after a good night's sleep she would come up with some new idea to put a stop to all this, she told herself wistfully. Maybe.

Hope was sitting in front of the fire, busily crocheting another of the delicate white stars she sold as ornaments at the Christmas bazaar. She looked up as Gillian stepped through the door, setting her work carefully on her lap.

"Hello, dear. You're a bit late." Her tone was mildly reproving, and Gillian stared. It didn't sound like her aunt at all.

"I may be from now on," she told her quietly, sinking into the armchair with relief. "The youth group showed absolutely no inclination to go home tonight. Once they get talking, they can go on and on."

"Was Jeremy there?" her aunt asked softly.

"Jeremy? Why, yes. He's agreed to help with the group, after all. How did you know?"

Hope's pale blue eyes were narrowed in disapproval when she glanced up from her handwork. "Arthur and Faith stopped by this evening," she murmured. "They told Charity and me that you two are now engaged." Gillian felt the probing intentness of her aunt's stare. "I do wish you'd told me yourself, dear. I'm not sure this is the time to go barreling into another relationship with a man you barely know and have said repeatedly you despise."

"It's not that I despise him, Hope. Well, not really. He just…"

"Please don't think I'm trying to interfere in your life, Gilly." Hope cut through her halting explanations. "You know I feel very strongly about women making their own decisions in this life. It's just that it's so sudden. And unexpected."

Gillian grimaced. "You can say that again," she muttered. She tried to explain, as quickly and briefly as possible, exactly how the situation had erupted from Faith's strange memory.

"She was upset from the fire, and I thought she was just confused, so I went along with it. Then Jeremy rushed in and began demanding answers, and she continued talking as if we were the hottest new pair since Anthony and Cleopatra."

Gillian paused for breath, the remembrance of that time on the patio causing a tide of red to flush her cheeks. Jeremy had kissed her; in anger, it was true. But still.

"But, Gillian," her aunt protested. "Arthur knows about your engagement. Faith said Pastor Dave told them. Apparently the whole town has been informed."

Gillian groaned, letting her aching head fall into her hands. She couldn't have managed Faith's delusional afternoon with less aplomb if she had tried. Now everyone would think they were engaged and intended to stay that way.

"It's going to look ridiculous if we announce that our one-day engagement is now off," she muttered, rubbing the tender spots on her scalp. "I should have nipped it in the bud instead of playing along and teasing him, calling him endearments. No wonder she thinks there's something going on." She heard her aunt speaking through a fog of dismay.

"Calling him endearments?" Hope's voice was squeaky with shock.

"Never mind, Auntie. It was a very bad joke and I'm paying for it now." She stood, tiredly massaging the throbbing pulse in her temple. "I'm going to bed. I'm so tired I can hardly stand."

She moved slowly to the stairs and then stopped.

"Hope?"

"Yes, dear?"

Gillian tried to arrange the curious facts of the evening in her mind. Something didn't seem quite right.

"Does Faith suffer from Alzheimer's?"

"I don't know, Gilly." Hope's voice was soft and pensive. "Her memory has been getting worse for a while now, but it usually involves forgetting where she's left something or not turning something off. This is completely different." She switched off the lamp and followed her niece up the stairs. "Why?"

"Oh, just something I was wondering about. Good night, Hope."

"Good night, dear. You know," Hope said, stopping at the door to her room, tears glistening at the corners of her eyes. "I've been praying for Faith for months now, asking God to heal her," she murmured. "She's been my friend for so many years now, and I can't bear to think of her forgetting all the wonderful times we three have had together. I can't imagine going to visit her one day and Faith not knowing who I am."

Gillian patted her aunt's shoulder. "God gave you Faith when you needed her all those years ago," she consoled her aunt. "I can't imagine that he's going to abandon you now."

Hope brushed away the tears and smiled her wide, cheerful smile as they hugged each other. "Thank you, Gilly. I'm sure you're right. He never gives us more than he knows we can deal with."

But as she lay in bed, the night sounds quiet around her, Gillian replayed the afternoon's events through her mind. She distinctly remembered Faith saying she had made the rouladin because beef was Jeremy's favorite dish.

How was it then that the older woman had claimed, only minutes later, that she and Arthur intended having a quiet meal together? She had even said there wouldn't be enough for Jeremy and almost ordered him to eat with Gillian.

Something about the incident bothered her, and as Gillian snuggled her head against the pillow, she wondered if Faith Rempel was as confused as everyone believed. Maybe she was just a little bit, well, crazy?

Either way, Gillian was going to have to talk to Jeremy Nivens *again* and try to sort out the whole engagement thing. And the nursing-home issue. Slightly barmy or not, Faith wasn't the type who would do well in the restrictive atmosphere of a nursing home.

Gillian closed her eyes and refused to think about it anymore. The whole thing was too preposterous to believe. She'd come to Mossbank to learn how to survive as a single woman after God had taken her intended husband and left her on her own. She'd had no intention of even dating anyone again, let alone getting engaged. And certainly not to the likes of Jeremy Nivens. Not ever!

As she lay in bed, her Bible open in front of her, Gillian reread the verse she'd underlined that morning. "If your faith is as large as a mustard seed," she mused, pausing on the text. It seemed as if God was asking her to trust in him, to believe that he would manage it all for the best.

"I'll try to believe," she whispered in the private darkness of her room. "But, please, God, could you help me sort out these strange encounters he and I keep having? Maybe somehow we could learn to be friends, with Your help."

Gillian had just applied pale pink polish to the last toe on her right foot when the doorbell rang.

"Blast it," she muttered, trying to stand and keep her toes elevated while retaining the puffs of cotton she'd placed between them. The bell rang again. "Come in," she yelled, but there was no response. In a jerky, halting gait she walked on her heels to the door and yanked it open, glaring at the man who stood outside.

"Yes," she demanded rudely, furious that Jeremy had caught her with her hair in a towel, her toes separated by blobs of white and clothed in her rattiest old sweats.

She watched his eyes widen as they took in the thick,

brown crusty layer of clay that covered her face, leaving just her eyes and mouth untouched. His blue-gray eyes widened even more as they moved down over the yellow knit sweatshirt that hung sloppily, exposing one shoulder, and the ragged joggers with the tears in both knees. But they stayed fixed on her elevated, white-cushioned toes the longest.

"Oh," he said.

The silence stretched between them.

"Is that all you came to say?" she asked perversely. "Thanks so much for sharing it with me."

"I guess this is a bad time to call," he muttered, his eyes riveted on her shirt front.

Gillian could have laughed at the ridiculous statement but she bit down on her lip. She moved slightly back on her heels trying to balance herself without falling backward.

"Do you need a doctor?" Jeremy asked.

Gillian stared. Was it possible that Faith's mental problems had been passed through the family to Jeremy? she wondered.

"Er, no, thank you." He looked relieved, she decided.

"It's just that you've cut yourself," he murmured, staring at the spatters of bright red on her sweatpants.

"It's nail polish," she told him, turning away from the door. "Come on in. I've got to sit down. Standing like this for more than two minutes is a real pain."

He followed her in to stand in the middle of the room, watching as she flopped onto the sofa and began to remove the rolls of cotton from between her toes.

"They're dry now," she answered the curious look in his eyes.

"Your toes?"

"The nail polish."

"Oh." He stood there gaping, as if he had never seen a woman with painted toenails before.

It was very disconcerting, Gillian decided, overly conscious now of the tight clay mask on her face, pulling her skin ever more taut as it dried. There was nothing for it, she was going to have to go wash her face.

"Excuse me a moment," she told him hurriedly, her skin a dried and barren wasteland under its cake of hard clay. "I'll be right back. Have a seat." She dashed out of the room without a backward glance.

Jeremy looked around, his eyes carefully observing that it was impossible to follow her orders. Every seat in Miss Langford's living room seemed to be covered with something. Clothes of every vibrant shade lay scattered here and there. He didn't recognize many of them, but something brown, tossed haphazardly on a nearby chair, caught his interest.

He picked up the note on top and read "Sally Ann." He recognized the suit as the one she'd worn in the schoolyard one fateful afternoon. If he recalled correctly, and he did, her skirt had blown up, exposing those long, slender legs and catching his class's attention. He wondered why she was giving the suit away. It was a much more suitable color for teaching than many of the other garments he noticed lying around.

Jeremy's attention caught on the bits of silk and lace he saw sprawled over the little side table. Although he averted his eyes as soon as he realized what they were, he couldn't shake the feeling of voyeurism at the sight of her delicate, lace-trimmed slips. They, too, were in bright peacock shades that he was coming to realize were part and parcel of Gillian Langford's dynamic personality.

"There, now." Gillian surged back into the room, her face clean and shining from the scrubbing it had received. The hard brown gunk was gone, and her lovely skin glowed with vitality. Her hair was free of its towel and lay against her head in tiny damp, wispy red curls that glimmered with golden highlights.

"Oh, dear. I'm so sorry. I was doing a bit of mending, and I'm afraid I've left everything all over."

Jeremy watched as Gillian scooped armloads of clothes up into her arms and whisked up the staircase with them. She showed little outward embarrassment when she picked up the sheerest, silkiest nightgown, but he could see a tinge of pink behind the spattering of freckles on her high cheekbones.

"There, now. Have a seat."

She was puffing slightly from all the stairs, and Jeremy watched her with interest. She sat there, calmly waiting for him to say something as he searched his memory for the reason for this visit.

"I hope you haven't suffered any repercussions from our supposed engagement," she said finally, covering the gap in conversation.

His brain snapped to attention. The engagement; that was it. He wanted to talk to her about their engagement. "I think we have a small matter to discuss," he muttered, and immediately wished he had shut up. She was right, Jeremy decided. He did sound like a stuffed shirt sometimes. But it *was* rather difficult to disengage yourself from an engagement that had really never been.

"That is, er, we should come to some agreement about our intentions. Not mine, but…" his voice trailed away. There just wasn't any delicate way to ask for an unengagement, he decided glumly.

"Oh, I see," she said with a grin, twisting her feet under her. "You want to weasel out of the nuptials. Is that it?"

"I never 'weasled in' as you so elegantly put it," he blustered. "You're the one who told my aunt that we would be married." He stopped because she was vehemently shaking her head.

"No," Gillian corrected him. Her golden-red curls glistened in a shaft of sun that poured through the window. "Your aunt told *me* we were getting married. I thought she might still be confused by the accident and went along with it."

"Well, obviously we can't continue the charade," he told her, picking off the white hairs from his slacks. The more he picked, the more there were.

"What is this, anyway?" he demanded finally, holding a handful of the white fluff out. He missed her answer because his nose twitched just then, and he couldn't suppress the loud sneeze that erupted.

"Cat hair," she told him smugly. "Mrs. Daniels was here and she brings her cats wherever she goes. Gee, I hope she didn't get it on my new black wool. It picks up everything."

Jeremy was beginning to feel like Alice falling down the tunnel. Everything was whirling and changing around him, and it seemed he had no influence over anything. It was not a pleasant feeling for a man who thrived on controlling his own universe, he decided.

"If you don't mind," he began sharply, "I'd like to get back to the matter at hand. The engagement," he prodded, when her eyes stared back at him blankly.

"I don't see that there's much we can do at this point," Gillian said quietly.

He stared at her.

"We're going to look like lunatics," she told him briskly. "If we get engaged one day and break up the next." Her shiny head shook decisively. "No, I think it's far better if we just let it stand for a while. Once the preparations for Christmas begin, no one will notice if you and I are no longer engaged."

Jeremy couldn't help it. Good manners forbade it, and yet

for the second time in one afternoon his mouth hung wide open as he stared rather stupidly at her. "Do I understand you correctly, Miss Langford?" he murmured. "You wish the inhabitants of this community to believe that we two are engaged, until such time as the novelty wears off, and then you propose to quietly dispense with the subterfuge?" He shook his head. "That would be lying, Miss Langford, and I do not approve of lying."

"Oh, get over yourself," she muttered rudely.

Jeremy pretended he hadn't heard it. "And what on earth would I do with the engagement ring, once you decided you no longer needed it?" he demanded, glaring at her in his most severe form.

"Oh, great," she chirped, clasping her hands together happily. "You mean you'll go along with it?"

"No, I don't mean that at all." He glared at her. "I'm trying to look at this situation rationally and with some forethought."

It was hopeless, Jeremy decided. The woman hadn't a serious bone in her shapely little body. For some strange reason he suddenly thought of her fiancé, Michael, and wondered what the man who had put up with all this nonsense had been like. He would have given a great deal to ask the man some very pertinent questions right now.

"No, of course I won't go along with it," he muttered. "It's ridiculous. The board would be down my throat."

"Oh, the board!" She kissed her fingers into the air. "Ned's the chairman, and I don't think he'd care one iota what we do in our spare time. And we don't need a ring. I could say that we're having a special one made, or that we haven't decided on one yet or something." Her big iridescent green eyes narrowed, and Jeremy felt his pulse pick up. "Besides, we couldn't disappoint your aunt, now could we? After all, she was so happy about us."

"There is no us!" He felt his temper exploding and poured every effort into containing it. "Why do you insist on carrying on with this ludicrous situation? We have nothing in common, so I very much doubt that anyone would be surprised at the sudden breakup."

He watched her face, studying the mobile features with interest. She was a curious mix, he decided. Like a coltish young girl galloping through life. And yet he knew that she was no teenager.

"Well, then, what about your aunt?" she demanded. "How can you disappoint her like this? She's so excited right now. She thinks you're finally going to settle down and be happy."

Jeremy would have interrupted then, but Gillian, it seemed, wasn't quite finished. He watched as her expression went from tenderness to indignation.

"I can't believe that you would actually send that woman to a nursing home," she grated, green eyes sparkling with indignation. "Faith will be heartbroken when she learns you think she's so incompetent that she has to have full-time care."

"Then I'll just have to deal with that, won't I," Jeremy returned evenly. He should have stopped there, but he felt obliged to answer the condemnation evident on her lovely face. "I love my aunt, you know. And I'm trying to protect her as best I can."

"By locking her up?" Gillian demanded. "You know she'll hate that!"

He sighed, controlling his temper with difficulty. That was something new, Jeremy admitted. Until he'd come to this little town he'd seldom felt anger, let alone had to control it. He'd lived his life on the basis of rationality—every decision he'd made had been carefully weighed as to the best possible outcome and benefit, and Auntie Fay was no different.

"It's my duty to see that she is properly cared for," he reiterated quietly. "Since I cannot be there all the time, I have to find another solution. The nursing home is the best resolution to the problem."

"There is no problem!" Gillian's voice was raised in anger, and Jeremy fought his own temper with difficulty. "Faith is perfectly fine on her own. So she burned something, so what? Lots of women burn a meal or two in their lifetimes." Her eyes shot little jade daggers at him. "You would know that if you had ever cooked anything," she muttered snidely.

"It's not just the fire," he admitted finally, knowing she wouldn't give up until he'd said it all. Gillian Langford bore a striking resemblance to a bulldog with a large juicy bone when she got herself into this mode. "Today I found some ice cream she'd forgotten in the back of her car. It had melted into the upholstery and took quite a bit of time and energy to clean up. Faith doesn't even remember buying it."

"So what?" Her narrow shoulders shrugged inelegantly. "I've bought things and forgotten them at the store after I've paid for them. That doesn't prove I should be put away where no one will pay me the least bit of attention. If she goes into a home, Faith will undoubtedly become more confused and forgetful from the stress of all the changes. She needs familiar surroundings."

Jeremy sighed. He didn't feel perfectly satisfied with this decision himself. It certainly didn't help to have to argue it all out with a woman who couldn't understand the fear that rose in him when he realized that he could have lost the one person in the world whom he most wanted to take care of.

"Look," he offered at last, keeping his tones even and calm, "Auntie Fay isn't the issue here, right now. What I came here to discuss with you is this preposterous engagement. I can't continue to live a lie. We are going to have to tell the truth. If we look ridiculous, so be it."

He shifted in his chair uneasily, wondering if he wasn't a

fool to divest himself of the most beautiful woman in town. He'd never had much to do with the fairer sex, but even Jeremy knew that Gillian Langford was something special when it came to the female of the species.

"I suggest that we speak to the pastor tomorrow after church." He forced the words out, anyway, unwilling to acknowledge the dull sense of loss he was feeling. "We have to do the right thing," he repeated to himself. "We can't keep living a lie."

Gillian chose that moment to jump up from her chair. "Then we'd better come up with a plan as to exactly how we're going to handle this," she said quickly. "It won't be easy. The whole town knows about us by now. You think of something while I get us a drink." She stared at him until he nodded, then moved to slip past his chair. But her pink toes seemed caught on the tassels of the rug, and she lost her balance.

Jeremy watched wide-eyed as Gillian reached out for something that wasn't there, teetered in midair for nanoseconds and then landed with a flurry on his lap. He reached out protectively to hold her slim shape steady.

It was sheer unfortunate circumstance that the three elderly women happened to walk in the door at that precise moment. He saw Gillian's aunt Hope study them suspiciously through astute blue eyes. She took note of the way his arm was curved around Gillian's waist and the way she dangled rather inelegantly on his lap…as if they had just finished some heavy-duty necking, he considered sourly.

"Oh, piffle!" Faith's high voice twittered in the yawning silence, drawing everyone's attention to her. Gillian took the opportunity to stand, freeing herself from his embrace, her eyes quickly slewing away from his.

"We should have given them another few minutes. Hello, young lovers," Faith trilled gaily.

Gillian met Jeremy's dark, forbidding gaze with her own and clearly heard the frustration in the words he whispered. "Oh, brother. Now look what you've done!"

Gillian hurried into the small church, checking for early arrivals as she did. D-day! And *D* was for *denial*...as in engagement.

"Hello, dear," Faith Rempel murmured. "Arriving a bit early, are you?"

"Hello, Mrs. Rempel." Gillian felt herself flushing at the glint of knowing in the older woman's eyes. She'd seen the same look yesterday when the three older women had busied themselves, leaving her and Jeremy alone and embarrassed.

Gillian slipped off her heavy, black wool coat and hung it up with more care than was strictly necessary.

"I'm supposed to play the organ today, and I was hoping to get in a few moments' practice before Sunday school."

Faith nodded benignly.

"I know, dear. Jeremy's already here. Go on in. You'll find him behind the piano."

Faith turned away and immediately began chatting with another elderly woman who had just come through the door. Gillian didn't hear a word they were saying; all she could hear was the loud and forceful notes of the doxology resounding around the high ceilings of the sanctuary.

She stepped through the doors, tilting her head to one side as Jeremy switched tunes and began a lilting but complicated rendition of Beethoven's "Hymn to Joy" from the *Ninth Symphony*.

Jeremy Nivens was good, Gillian admitted. Very good. He played the baby grand with firm authority and yet careful attention to detail. The fortes were steady and decisive while the pianissimos were delicate, light touches that communicated a depth of feeling for the songs. And through the entire rippling melody, she heard not one wrong note.

Sucking in a breath for courage, she walked slowly down the aisle, slipped off her shoes and took her position behind the organ, switching it on and setting the worn knobs just the way she wanted. He looked startled to see her there, but merely nodded his dark head at her.

"I was going to try number two hundred next," he murmured, waiting until she found it.

Gillian nodded, relieved to find that she knew the song. In fact, "Count Your Blessings" had always been her mother's favorite song, and she'd heard it repeated in poem form often over the years. The organ was simple to manage, and even though she hadn't played for months, it responded to her every request, matching the piano and Jeremy's notes beat for beat.

"You're very good," she told him when the last chords had died away. "I had no idea you could play."

He grinned back at her, a slight mocking note to his smile.

"Probably thought I was too old for music, right?"

Gillian grimaced ruefully at the remark, knowing she'd asked for it with her own uncharitable remarks weeks ago.

"I'm sorry," she offered quietly. "I should never have said a lot of what I did."

"Even if it was the truth?" He took pity on her after a moment and explained that he'd begun taking lessons when he was four.

"I've always loved the piano. At school the other kids used to have to pry me away from it. And of course we always had a school choir. It was good training in the classics, and there's nothing better than an old English church for a cappella singing."

He was flipping through several papers on the piano bench.

"I thought maybe this would do for the offertory," he murmured, handing her a copy of "All Creatures of Our God and King."

The sheet music was arranged for piano and organ and thankfully, Gillian noted, the organ section was fairly straightforward. "Could we run over it once before everyone arrives?" she asked, glancing up to find his dark eyes fixed appreciatively on her navy silk dress. "I'm afraid I haven't played in some time."

He shrugged. "Why not?"

The notes were carefully placed in several keys so that the total effect was one of building adoration for God's wonderful creation, providence and redemption as the harmony resounded throughout the joyous anthem.

"You play very well," he said, closing the lid as children began arriving for Sunday school. "I'm afraid that's all I can do for now, though. I've got that class the pastor landed me with, and they'll tear the room apart if I leave them for very long."

Gillian chuckled, straightening her dress as she slipped her feet back into her bright red heels. She picked up the matching leather handbag and walked with him to the Christian education rooms.

"They had better not," she chuckled, pushing a stray tendril off her cheek. "I have the room next door, and my girls are very well behaved."

His eyes widened in disbelief. "Don't tell me you were conned, too?"

"Not exactly conned," Gillian said, looking up at him with a pert grin. "Let's just say there was no opportunity to refuse." She tugged open the door to her class and motioned to the rows of seated girls who sat watching them and giggling behind their hands. "See, I told you."

Just then a paper airplane sailed out from the room next

door and there was a loud thump. Jeremy raised his left eye-brow at her and frowned. "And I told you," he muttered darkly, "they're wild, untamed animals. See you later." He was inside with the door closed before Gillian made her response.

"Yes. Later."

Later turned out to be only seconds before the morning service began and there was no time to do anything more than place her purse and Bible in a nearby pew and climb onto the organ bench once more.

The hymns the pastor had chosen were happy lilting ones that people sang when they wanted to praise God, and Gillian enjoyed hearing the small congregation join their voices in tribute to Him. The music included many of the same songs she had sung for years, and she managed to play them quite easily.

Jeremy, it seemed, wasn't quite so pleased. He frowned when Pastor Dave neglected to ask the congregation to stand for "This Is My Father's World" and "All People That On Earth Do Dwell." And he was almost scowling when junior church was canceled and the offertory held back to just before the sermon. Thankfully, however, his ill humor wasn't directed at her. Their number went smoothly, inspiring the pastor's kind remarks afterward.

As Jeremy sat down beside her in the pew, Gillian felt prickles of awareness as she heard the minister's next words. "They make a good team on the instruments, don't they folks. And I'm sure most everyone knows by now that these two are engaged, so Jeremy and Gillian will be teaming up together in the future, as well."

She closed her eyes at the murmuring and cheerful smiles directed their way. She ignored Jeremy's ramrod-straight backbone and the tense way he held himself in the seat. It was getting worse by the minute, she decided grimly. There was no way they could back out now without looking totally insane, but she still intended to give him the opportunity.

Gillian took a deep breath, opened her eyes and focused them on the minister. There was nothing she could do right now. But somehow, God would show her the next step. For the moment she intended to enjoy the morning message.

"Folks, I want to talk to you today about your neighbor," Pastor Dave began with a wide grin down at them. His eyes twinkled with mirth. "You know, I once had a neighbor who insisted on wearing his hair combed from one side of his head, clean over the bald spot on the top to the other side. He sprayed and patted and combed that mess and when a good wind came along, that hair stood to attention like a private saluting a colonel."

The audience laughed at the mental picture.

"He wore clothes from the sixties and shoes from World War II. I never had too much to do with the fellow. Always figured he was a little weird and if I got too near, some of it might rub off. Some folks might say it already has."

Gillian sat in her seat, nervously aware of the man seated next to her as the crowd laughed at the pastor's joke. From time to time, Jeremy's shoulder brushed hers and she felt a tingle of awareness. When it happened, she would shift slightly and refocus on the minister. It happened that she was shifting quite a lot.

"But you know, dear ones, that one day I really needed a friend to help me out and that fellow was the only person around. I had to swallow my pride and ask his help even though I'd avoided talking to him in the past."

The minister's voice was solemn and quiet in the stillness of the sanctuary. Even the children sat silent, listening.

"Well, it turned out that Duncan was more than willing to help me out of a tight spot. In fact he went beyond help. He went the second mile. And as we talked that day, I began to realize that Duncan was on the verge of suicide. Everyone at the university avoided him or made fun of him, and he felt the stigma deeply." Pastor Dave cleared his husky voice.

"His average was nine on the Stainer Scale of Nine. He couldn't go any higher. He had no less than four prestigious job offers from companies that had responded to his impressive résumé."

Gillian felt Jeremy tense beside her as a baby cried out its discomfort, but as the minister began speaking again, her attention was fixed on the pulpit.

"But on that particular day Duncan was at the bottom of the despair trough. The one job he'd really wanted had been offered to someone far less qualified, simply because Duncan hadn't fit the company image for their top man. He wasn't tall, wasn't handsome, and he was bald."

Gillian noticed several of the members dabbing at their eyes.

"There wasn't much I could say. Duncan knew why he'd been rejected. And he was hurting. Badly. I could have told him it didn't matter, but that would have hurt him more, because to Duncan, it mattered. A lot." Pastor Dave smiled.

"Duncan wanted just one thing from me. He didn't want to be judged and found wanting again. He certainly didn't want pity. And he really wasn't interested in trying to become someone he wasn't." A silence of expectation floated in the room as every eye focused on the minister.

"Good old Duncan just wanted acceptance from me. He'd already made up his mind that if he was rejected once more, he'd kill himself. And I stood between him and that decision."

Pastor Dave looked around at the congregation and smiled at them. "What we're talking about here is acceptance. A little charity. I'm happy to say that I didn't miss it that particular time, but I wonder how often we Christians actually are able to bypass the outward appearance and accept the person inside who is desperately crying out for our attention."

His words went on and on, but Gillian was focused on what he had said about accepting other people for who they are. Some part of her conscience nagged her about that phrase; poking and prodding until she was forced to acknowledge that she hadn't always accepted people for who they were. Especially lately. Especially the man seated next to her.

But then, there was such a lot about Jeremy Nivens that needed correction. Even now he was sitting there impatiently checking his watch every few minutes, as if that would remind the pastor that the service usually ended about this time.

Gillian came out from her reverie just in time to hear Pastor Dave's final admonitions.

"We have to learn to accept people for who they are, without trying to tamper with their personalities. This week let's all see if we can pass around a little of that unconditional acceptance that Christ gave to us."

Gillian moved to the organ and played the last hymn, her thoughts still whirling madly. When the pastor had moved to the foyer and half of the congregation had left their seats, she looked at Jeremy and, noting his nod, ended on the last verse. He got up from the piano immediately, closing the lid carefully.

"Jeremy," she murmured quietly, knowing she had to make the first move. "I'll go with you to talk to Reverend Dave after everyone has left. We can clear up this misconception about the engagement then."

He raised his dark eyebrows as he stared at her in disbelief. "Are you deranged?" he demanded furiously. His eyes glared down at her like chips of cold, blue-gray ice. "He's just announced the happy event to the entire congregation. Here comes someone now. No doubt a congratulatory word."

He frowned in distaste. "It appears that we have little choice but to go along with this for now, Miss, er, Gillian. We'll go for lunch together and discuss the situation then."

Gillian kept her voice low as Lavinia Holt surged toward them, a red-faced Flossie in tow. "But my aunt is expecting…"

"Oh, bother the aunts," he exploded, grasping her arm in his and urging her forward. "They have done quite enough." He bent his head to her ear in a manner that suggested a lover's intimate conversation but was, in reality, a direct order. "Do not invite that Flossie woman to come with us. I have had quite enough of her company for a very long time."

Lavinia burst upon them then, and it was impossible to question him further, but as Gillian glanced past Jeremy's black-suited shoulder, she caught a curious gleam of smug satisfaction in her aunt's eye.

Now what, she asked herself, *is that all about?*

Chapter Six

The restaurant teemed with families and friends enjoying the delicious brunch arranged so colorfully on big mirrored plates. Gillian wasn't sure how, but Jeremy had managed through sheer power of personality to procure the most secluded table in the house. She allowed him to take her coat before sinking into the chair and glancing around.

Good! There was no one she knew nearby.

"What would you like to have for lunch?" he asked her, frowning as he studied the lineup at the brunch trolley.

"We didn't have to come here," Gillian murmured, glancing around at the highly polished silver and sparkling glasses. "We could have talked just as well in the park." She risked a look at his glowering face and smiled. "You could have *kicked* something there."

Jeremy's eyes opened wide but he was denied a reply as the waitress showed up. They decided on soup and salad.

"And I'd like a slice of apricot cheesecake for dessert," Gillian said, smiling. "It looks too good to resist. Do you want some?" She glanced at her companion.

"No, thanks," he replied. "I'm not one for desserts. I will have some coffee, though. Decaf, please." When the waitress turned to leave, he leaned back in his chair and stared at her. "Well, Miss Langford, how do you propose to resolve this situation now?"

Gillian felt some of her good humor dissipate while struggling to maintain the smile on her face. If she had hoped for a friendly, uncomplicated lunch, it was obvious that Jeremy had no such intent.

"Why do you insist on calling me that?" she hissed. "You know my name, and people are going to think it a little strange if you call your fiancée 'Miss' all the time."

"Miss Langford, this is not…"

"It's *Gillian,*" she grated.

"Gillian," he started again. "This situation is not of my making, and I assure you that I do not intend to allow it to go on for one second longer than necessary." Jeremy rubbed his chin.

It was obvious that he detested saying the words, Gillian decided. "Don't worry," she told him impishly. "I'm not all that demanding. Flowers once in a while. A meal now and then. Maybe a kiss or two under the moonlight." His eyes glittered with some emotion she couldn't quite define and Gillian wondered why she'd added that last, when she had no intention of being kissed by this man again.

"Miss, sorry, Gillian," he began, "I don't think…"

"Kidding," she told him hastily. "I'm kidding."

"Oh. Too bad," he added. Gillian thought she detected the hint of a teasing smile on his lips for just an instant. She didn't know what to make of his reply. It wasn't quite the answer she'd expected.

Silence yawned between them until the waitress brought their soup. It was Gillian's favorite, beef barley with chunks of colorful vegetables floating in the thick savory broth.

"This is excellent," she murmured, breathing in the aroma. She saw his handsome face glower at her across the table. "What's the matter?"

"Nothing," he told her. "I hadn't realized they'd put in peas, that's all. I ate enough peas at school to cure me of them for a lifetime," he muttered dourly. "In fact, all the food I ate at school was pretty bad. Perhaps that's why I enjoy Aunt Faith's cooking so much." He patted his washboard stomach with a grin. "Everything she makes is a temptation."

"Ah," Gillian grinned. "You don't look as if you need to worry about your weight." She studied his broad shoulders and wide strong chest, then caught herself and stared down into her soup.

"I intend to have a good, long life," he said sincerely. "Which is why I watch what I eat."

He sounded so smug that Gillian couldn't help saying, "Dull, but long."

He flushed at that, glaring at her as she dipped a cracker into her steaming bowl. "My life is not dull. Not at all. I enjoy my work—I like an organized approach." His eyes sparkled with glee at her crinkled nose and just to tease her, he deliberately moved the cup and saucer an inch to the left.

"But don't you find it sort of, well, boring, to have everything so…programmed? I'll bet you even know what you're having for dinner tonight."

He glanced up, startled. "What's wrong with that?"

"Nothing," she agreed. "It's just that there's no opportunity to try something new…to enjoy something completely spontaneous." She saw his dark eyebrow rise mockingly.

"I do believe that I've had enough spontaneity for one week, Miss—Gillian. It's not every day that a man finds himself engaged to a woman he barely knows and then hears the news proclaimed from the pulpit."

Gillian blushed. "Well, okay. I get your point." She pushed the soup bowl away and leaned back in her chair to study him. "But that was sprung on you. You didn't really relish the change, if you understand what I'm saying."

Jeremy shook his dark head. "I'm afraid I don't," he told her truthfully. "We all have hopes and dreams, but we can't stand around, waiting for them to come true. We need to have a plan and then follow it." He glanced up, his eyes glowing blue. "Take you, for instance. You had your future all mapped out and then something changed. I'm quite sure you didn't embrace the change," he muttered. "I'm sorry. I don't want to hurt you by bringing up the past."

"It's okay," she told him quietly. "You're right, I didn't expect Michael to die. And it was very hard to accept. But I'm learning that God has a plan in everything that happens. I might not like it, but I can't be happy until I accept it and learn to move on." She swallowed the lump in her throat and continued.

"It's getting easier to talk about him now, especially with the kids in the youth group. They're so eager to explore life, to find out the boundaries." She blinked up at him. "That's how Michael was. There weren't many things he wouldn't try at least once, just to find out what it was like."

"What kind of things?" he asked as the waitress brought their salads.

Gillian thought for a moment before a memory slipped into her mind. "Like bungee jumping. He did it, you know. Off a bridge." Gillian wiped away a tear. "I was so scared, but Michael thought it was wonderful. Like skydiving."

"It is pretty dangerous," Jeremy told her. She could hear the disapproval in his voice.

"I guess it is. But Michael always said that God would take him home when He, God, was ready. And until then, he intended to live." She glanced down at her emerald ring; the one they'd chosen together. "I don't think he ever expected to go so soon, but since he did, I'm glad that he got to do some of the things he loved."

Jeremy said nothing, merely staring at her. She felt his

scrutiny but refused to look away. She had nothing to hide. When he spoke, his voice was pensive.

"Perhaps, if he'd taken a little more care, he would have had more time with you. I believe that God has natural laws that we humans aren't supposed to break."

Gillian sat a little straighter, studying him with a frown.

"Why do you always speak of God as if He's some kind of glowering judge, waiting to punish us?" she demanded. "I don't believe He's like that at all. I believe God wants us to do what's right, but when we goof up, He's not standing there with a whip, ready to apply the forty lashes."

"If He didn't want us to obey him, He wouldn't have given all the rules," Jeremy countered.

"The rules are guides, Jeremy. No one is perfect. God knows that. And he's prepared to forgive us. After all," she continued softly, "God is all about love. In everything."

Jeremy began saying something and then stopped abruptly, his face registering amazement. "Good grief," he muttered. "She's followed me here." Gillian was about to turn around when he said, "No, don't look. Just pretend we're a newly engaged couple having a perfectly amiable conversation."

Laughter bubbled up inside her. If only he could see the humor in their situation. "We are newly engaged," she said with a chuckle. "And the conversation was amiable. I thought." Then all words left her as Flossie Gerbrandt stood beside her, smiling a fatuous grin of adoration at Jeremy.

"I'm sorry you had to leave so soon the other evening," Flossie exclaimed in a whispery voice. She brushed her hands over her brightly colored skirt. "I was really enjoying your stories about England."

"Yes," Jeremy murmured. "I enjoyed it, also. But I had quite a bit of schoolwork to finish. Perhaps another time."

Flossie's eyes were wide with curiosity as she glanced from Jeremy to Gillian in surprise, obviously wondering why he hadn't been spending his evenings with his fiancée. There was nothing to do but step into the gap he'd created, Gillian told herself. And warn him about next time. With a tickle of delight, she wove her hand into his bigger one and patted it in true loverlike fashion.

"He means we'd both like to have you over for an evening," Gillian put in graciously. "Perhaps over the holidays."

"That would be nice. When are you getting married?"

Gillian watched Jeremy's eyes as he inadvertently swallowed a mouthful of the steaming coffee. It must have gone down the wrong way, because he began coughing.

"Oh, we're not sure yet, Flossie," Gillian said. "Everything's been moving so fast. We're trying to think of the best possible time, and since both of us work, well, you know what it's like."

Gillian smiled, to take the sting out of her words, recognizing the look of adoration that Flossie directed at her fiancé. Jeremy would have to act his part as her adoring fiancé well, if he didn't want to hurt this woman's feelings.

Flossie finally left a few moments later, and Gillian let the silly smile slip from her face. "You're going to have to do better than that if you want people to believe this engagement is the real thing," she lectured, dipping a fork into her cheesecake. "Mmm-hmm, you really should try this. It's delicious."

"The whole thing is preposterous, and we have your aunt to thank for this current situation."

Gillian felt her eyes open wide with amazement. "Hope?" she squeaked, staring at him. "You're blaming Flossie on Hope?"

Jeremy bristled. "Of course I'm blaming her. She set the whole thing up, after all. It certainly wasn't my idea to have dinner at Flossie's house."

Gillian shook her head in confusion. "I don't get it," she

murmured. "Why would Hope try to pair the two of you up? Flossie is the one who will get hurt. Unless you really care about her..." She raised one eyebrow inquiringly and accepted his lowered eyebrows as a *no*. Gillian tried to ignore the little flutter of relief in her midsection.

"I certainly have not encouraged her. She's a nice enough woman, just so painfully shy that I hesitate to even speak to her. She needs to be included in more fellowship events." Jeremy eyed the cheesecake with an envious glint in his eye, glancing away only when Gillian pushed the plate toward him.

"Go ahead," she offered generously. "Try it. I think you'll like it."

"I can't," he murmured. "They've taken away my fork."

"Here, you can use mine." Before he could change his mind Gillian had sliced off a bit of the delicious dessert and was holding it to his lips. "I haven't had anything contagious in weeks now," she teased.

With a sigh of resignation, he took the small bite in his own mouth, rolling it around to savor the wonderful flavor. Just when she thought he would agree about how good it was, he surprised her.

"Probably eighteen grams of fat in that slice," he muttered, carefully wiping his lips with his napkin. "But delicious none the same. More, please?"

Gillian was surprised by the glint of humor in his eyes and was about to add her own pithy remark, when they heard a little boy speaking to his friend nearby.

"Well, maybe I do gotta be an angel, but I sure aren't playing no harp. I'm gonna play the drums!"

Gillian giggled at the note of pride in the squeaky voice and turned to see if she could identify the source. As she did, her eyes fell on a small table in the far corner of the room.

Faith Rempel sat staring as her companion, Art Johnson, who spoke in obviously worried tones, his forehead creased.

"Oh, look," she said to Jeremy. "There's your aunt with Art. Looks like they're really interested in something. I think they make a wonderful couple."

"*'Couple,'*" Jeremy echoed bitterly, setting his teaspoon against the saucer with more force than was strictly necessary as he glared at the two. "They're not a couple. He's just trying to inveigle himself into my aunt's good graces. He obviously wants something."

"Why would you say that?" Gillian demanded. "He's been a good friend to her lately, taking her for walks and having dinner with her. I think it's wonderful that she has some companionship. You don't have to worry so much about her now. Wouldn't it be wonderful if they fell in love?" Her voice died away dreamily as she stared at the elderly pair across the room.

Seconds later she felt Jeremy's strong fingers close around her arm. "My aunt was married for over thirty years to the same man," he informed her angrily, spots of color dotting his cheekbones. "I hardly think it's likely that she would find someone to fill my uncle's place. Fall in love indeed!" He glared at her.

"I'm sure she did love her husband," Gillian agreed calmly. "But just because she's loved one man, doesn't mean she can't love another. Your uncle is gone and Faith is still here. I think it would be wonderful if she could find someone to share these last years with." She didn't add that she hoped Art's presence would keep Faith out of the nursing home.

"Ha," he crowed triumphantly. "You say you think my aunt should get involved again, but you follow a different set of rules for yourself." His eyes gleamed at her. "Your fiancé died, but you still have your whole life ahead of you. Surely you want to find someone to grow old with?"

Gillian tried. Nobody could say she didn't work extra hard to stifle the response that came bubbling up from her subconscious. But it didn't help. The words spilled out helter-skelter, anyway, destroying the smile on his smug countenance. "Some might say I've taken that step a little too early," Gillian said softly. "I mean getting engaged so soon after moving here, *and* to my boss."

He sighed then; a deep, wrenching sigh that admitted the hopelessness of his situation. "Does anyone win with you?" he asked with a small laugh. "Ever?" But there was a sparkle in his eyes and a determined set to those broad shoulders that told her he wasn't totally dismayed.

She could have been depressed by that look, except that Jeremy Nivens was tall, dark and very good-looking. And perhaps the push-pull sense of challenge between them was more exciting than she'd ever admit. And she suddenly realized that she wouldn't mind losing a battle or two to him once in a while if it meant he'd relax that rigidly controlling stance of his and let her see what went on behind the depths of his blue-gray eyes.

"Come on," she invited, gathering up her purse. "It's almost time for choir practice. They're going to start on the Christmas cantata today."

"I had intended to finish some paperwork this afternoon," he muttered in her ear as he held her coat out. "I'm not sure I'll have enough time for choir this year."

"Sure you will," Gillian said gaily, threading her arm through his.

"No, I'm sure that I—"

"If you don't," Gillian told him quietly, "Verda will have you building sets for the Sunday school pageant. They're doing a five-act play."

Reluctantly he steered them toward the church.

"I guess I can just fit in practice time," he muttered, his breath catching at the sound of her merry laugh.

The same thing happened an hour later when Flossie asked Gillian to sing a duet with him. Jeremy felt his whole body come tinglingly alive as her clear contralto tones ran over the sweet pure notes.

It was just another facet that he was learning about Miss Gillian Langford, he admitted. She had a beautiful voice, obviously well trained, as she sustained the last note for eight full counts. He felt his own voice ring true on his notes when the time came for his tenor part in the song.

"Oh, perfect," Flossie breathed when they finished the song in harmony. "You sing wonderfully together. You'll have a real ministry with that after you're married."

Jeremy felt that same old tinge of regret creep up on him. Gillian Langford was a beautiful, talented woman, whom any man would be proud to acknowledge as his soon-to-be bride. But she just wasn't right for him.

He wanted someone less, well, colorful. Someone who wouldn't draw people's attention when she walked through a room. Someone who didn't always try to change the status quo. Someone who followed the rules instead of making up her own. Someone who was content to follow the path *he'd* chosen, instead of veering off into little side journeys that took a completely different turn from the events he wanted to occur in his life.

His eyes moved over her slim, graceful form as she stood talking to several couples in the foyer. Her green eyes flashed, bringing her whole face alive and setting off the glints of reddish-gold in her hair.

Jeremy wanted someone less, well…his mind sought for the right word. *Dynamic,* he decided. That was it—a woman who was more calm and stable in her reactions. Those were the assets he was looking for in a woman.

Against his will his eyes were drawn back to her generous smile as she chuckled at some joke an elderly bald-headed man murmured for her ears alone.

No, he told himself. Gillian Langford wasn't at all suitable.

Was she?

"I didn't do nuthin'!"

Red-faced and belligerent, seven-year-old Roddy Green glared at his teacher with all the aplomb of a confident politician. It would have been convincing, too, if Gillian hadn't seen him slip a handful of elastic bands into his pocket.

"Roddy, we are supposed to be discussing Thanksgiving, and the pilgrims who had the very first Thanksgiving in our country many years ago…and all the things we have to be thankful for." She fixed him with her sternest look while removing his stash of projectiles.

She would have liked to rub the throbbing spot on the back of her neck, but that would be a sure sign that he'd gotten to her; Roddy could read adult reactions like a book.

"I don't got nuthin' to be thankful for," he muttered angrily, stabbing the toe of his filthy sneaker into the mat.

"I don't have *anything*," Gillian corrected, holding on to his arm when he would have ducked away. "And you have lots to be thankful for. How about your home and your parents and food in your tummy and a warm coat for the winter?"

To her amazement he burst into tears, yanking his arm out of her grip and dashing through the door in a flurry of action. Fortunately Gillian had an aide present in her room on Wednesdays, and mere seconds elapsed before she grabbed her coat and headed out after him.

Roddy was sitting in a little grove of trees just beyond the school yard. Technically it was off-limits to the students, but she wasn't about to discuss that now.

"Roddy? What's the matter?" Gingerly she placed her hand on his bony shoulder, leaving it there when he didn't flinch away. Gillian waited while he gulped and sobbed, dashing his sleeve across his face before glaring up at her.

"It's sumpthin' I can't talk about," he told her. "I promised my mom I wouldn't go blabbin'." He sniffed sadly, and new tears welled in his big sorrowful eyes.

"I certainly wouldn't want you to do that," Gillian murmured agreeably, slipping her arm a little farther around him. "But sometimes talking things over with a friend can really help. I'd like to be your friend, Roddy. Would that be okay?"

She waited breathlessly for his answer, sensing somehow that this child needed help. He peered up at her through the hank of dark, unkempt hair that hung over one eye. His look was skeptical, but at least he didn't pull away.

"I know how it is," she commiserated. "Every so often things just get too big for us, and even praying about it seems hard. That's when it's nice to have someone to talk to." She breathed her own prayer for heavenly guidance before tipping his grubby chin up toward her.

"Can't you just tell me a little about what's wrong? I know something is bothering you, because you haven't been doing your work as well as before. And today you weren't even listening during story time." Gillian glanced around the school yard. "I didn't see you playing soccer at recess, either, Roddy, and I know that's your very favorite."

"I…I was tired of playing that baby game. 'Sides, I don't got no ball to play with. The other kids don't like me to play with them. They say I'm dirty."

The words came out on a tiny half sob of pain, and Gillian felt her heart shatter at the cruel words. She didn't have a chance to say anything because suddenly the words were pouring out of him.

"I know I need to get cleaned up, but I haven't got time. I gotta get supper for my brothers and help my ma get them to bed. Then it's my job to wash all the dishes." He said it with a sort of fierce pride. "Since my dad ain't there no more, I'm the man of the family."

He looked fearful, as if he had revealed some secret. Gillian murmured something soothing.

"I'm not s'posed to tell anybody 'bout my dad goin'," he muttered. "I didn't even tell Miz Flowerlady an' she said she's my special friend."

Gillian frowned thoughtfully.

"You mean Mrs. Flowerday?" she asked quietly. When he nodded, she pretended a previous knowledge of the relationship. "Yes, she's a really good person to have as a friend. Besides that, she can bake cookies like you wouldn't believe."

"I know," Roddy agreed, eyes glowing. "I go past her place sometimes, and she gives me some. I'm s'posed to be doin' jobs for her, but I can't. I gotta help my mom till she gets better."

It got sadder and sadder, Gillian decided, swallowing past the huge lump in her throat with difficulty. She straightened her shoulders briskly. Roddy definitely didn't want her pity.

"Well, my goodness," she said. "You are a man to be able to do all that." She stared at her hands, thinking madly. "I guess in the morning, what with your brothers and all, you don't have much time to make a lunch do you?"

He glanced at her sheepishly.

"I forgot to get some more peanut butter," he muttered. Gillian guessed that there probably wasn't any money for it.

"Well, Roddy. The thing is, our class will be having some homework for the next few weeks, and it's going to take some extra time. Maybe on Saturday you could bring your brothers to my place while your mom rests. Then you could have time to do some homework."

"Oh, no," he gasped, staring at her in consternation. "I couldn't do that. My mom would be really mad!"

"But, Roddy, she would be able to rest much better, don't you think? And I'm going to be at home all day. I'd like to have visitors. You could just bring them over in their stroller for a little while, couldn't you?"

He looked doubtful.

"Well," Gillian murmured, hating to push. "You talk it over with your mom. And I'll make some gingerbread men from my aunt's secret recipe just in case you can come. Okay?"

He took a long time in replying. "I guess."

Gillian smiled and got to her feet.

"In the meantime," she said nonchalantly, walking back toward the school with him. "I have a shirt and a pair of overalls that I bought for my nephew for his birthday. I found out that he's too big for both of them. Since I can't take them back, why don't you try them? I'd sure hate to just throw them out."

"You mean blue jean overalls," he breathed, peering up at her with huge, awestruck eyes.

"Yep," she grinned. "The real thing."

"All right!" he cheered, racing ahead. Seconds later he was back in front of her. "Uh, thank you," he murmured.

"That's quite all right. I'll get them at noon when I go home for lunch. Okay?"

He nodded, obviously thrilled.

"Now how about if we go back and finish our drawings?"

He cocked his shaggy head to one side. "Y'know," he muttered, holding the door wide for her to go through, "I don't like drawing pilgrims and turkeys. They're too hard."

Gillian grinned and led him back inside. *Back to normal,* she thought. *Almost.*

An hour later she was determinedly dragging the principal from his office.

"Come on, Jeremy. We have to hurry. I only have an hour." Gillian tugged open the door of his car and slid inside.

"Er, what, exactly, is this about, Miss—" he stopped as she gave a low growl of warning. "I mean, Gillian."

"It's about a little boy who's carrying the weight of the world on his shoulders," she muttered, leaning over to glance at the speedometer. "Can't you step on it?"

"I'm already doing forty," he told her. "And why are you dragging me downtown, anyway? I'm not involved."

"Oh, yes you are," she told him, grinning. "I want you to go to Frobisher's and get a pair of running shoes while I pick up some overalls at Hanson's Department Store."

"Why do you suddenly need new shoes at lunch hour on a Wednesday?" he asked crankily, peering at his watch. "At this rate, I'll never have time to eat. I'm starving."

"I don't need shoes, Roddy does. Here's the size. I want those new white ones with the black streaks on the side. And a pair of black socks," she added as an afterthought. As soon as Jeremy slid to a stop she was out of the car. "I'll meet you back here as soon as you get them."

"But, but…"

She left him sitting there "butting." There was no time to waste if she was going to pull this off. She also had to get a phone call through to Charity before lunch was over. Jeremy wasn't likely to give her any time off during school hours, she decided grumpily.

Within moments, Gillian had her fingers on a pair of the coveted overalls. She bought a pair a little larger than she thought he would need, just in case her guess was off.

Anyway, they'd probably shrink in the wash. If they ever got washed.

A red-and-black-plaid shirt in warm brushed cotton matched very well. On an impulse she tossed in the denim cap that hung nearby. Ten minutes later, with all the tags snipped and in a plain brown bag, Gillian hurried back to the car.

Jeremy was leaning on the front fender, shoe box in hand as he gazed at the colorful display in the local café. Mouth-watering burgers, delicious sandwiches with crunchy pickles and golden steaming pies with rich cherries oozing out filled the windows in glorious Technicolor.

"Did you get them?" Gillian asked breathlessly. Without waiting for his answer, she tugged the shoes from the tissue-filled box. "Have to get rid of this stuff," she muttered and handed him the box and paper. "Here."

"Wait a minute," he grumbled, staring at what she'd given him. "It's not as if he will wear the things for very long, anyway. We'll soon be knee-deep in snow." He peered down at the runners she was shoving into her bag. "Do you know how much they charge for those things?"

"No," she murmured, intent on arranging everything neatly in her brown bag. "And I don't care. Money's not an object right now."

"Since when?" he grumbled. His stomach protested loudly, bringing Gillian's laughing glance back up to meet his glare. "I'm probably going to starve to death, you know. You had no right to give my lunch away to that scruffy child. Auntie Fay made those roast beef sandwiches just the way I like them. She even put in a piece of her special carrot cake. I love that cake." He closed his eyes in remembrance.

"Far too much fat for a man your age," Gillian informed him pertly. She grinned at him happily. "Anyway, he needed it more than you. I suspect he hasn't been eating properly."

She nodded at the café. "Let's go in here and have a nice nutritious low-fat salad. We've got half an hour before we have to go back."

Once they'd placed their orders, Jeremy tilted back in his chair and stared across the table at her.

"Why was it we needed to make this rush trip again?" he asked, frowning as the lunch-crowd volume grew.

"Sssh! I want to keep this between you and me," she hissed, glancing around to make sure no one was listening. When Gillian was satisfied that no one had heard his comments, she leaned toward him, beckoned his head nearer and explained.

"So you see, I've got to get someone over there to check up on the mother. Maybe she needs help. I know I would. Twins are no easy task!"

Jeremy shrugged. "You could always call in Social Services," he said, crunching into a cashew that had lain on the top of his chicken salad. "They have people trained to handle these situations."

Gillian snorted. "We don't even know if there is a 'situation' as you put it. And who do you think Roddy will suspect when those outsiders come rushing in? *Me,* that's who. Besides, his mother asked him not to tell their woes to the whole town. She's probably embarrassed or something."

"And your solution is?" His face was full of skepticism.

"I'm going to get Charity Flowerday on the case. Apparently she's already made some overtures toward Roddy. If anyone can figure out a way to help that family, Mrs. Flowerday can."

Chapter Seven

"Hello, Hope, dear. How are you? Frightful weather, isn't it?" Charity Flowerday bustled through the door and shook off the thick layer of wet snowflakes on her shoulders. "I was hoping to speak to Gillian. Is she home?"

"No. She and Jeremy are working late at school—preparing for the school Christmas pageant, they said." Hope shook her blond head with disdain. "I love this coat of yours," she murmured, stroking one hand over the muskrat hairs. "Do you think other people, outside of Mossbank, I mean, still wear fur coats?"

"I imagine." Charity smiled, slipping her feet from her galoshes. "I loved them myself. There is nothing like the warm cosiness of mink or fox."

"I know," Hope said with a sigh. "Especially when it's forty below and there is a stiff north wind. Of course, you know, most folks have cars nowadays. They drive wherever they're going."

"Well, there is that of course," Charity agreed. She sank into the soft, plushy armchair and sighed at the warmth coming from the fireplace. "But I think the reason furs have gone out of vogue these days is because there was such a fuss about animal rights and such." She stared into the glowing coals thoughtfully before resuming her train of thought.

"I don't think anyone in my generation ever thought of that. I know I didn't. We simply wanted fur because it's so warm. Now I see these movie stars marching around, carrying signs and such, making everyone else embarrassed to even admit they own a fur coat, let alone wear it in public."

They sat there for several seconds before Hope sighed again, a deep, heartfelt, tired breath of air that came from the depths of her very soul.

"Why, Hope, what's the matter?" Charity stared at her friend curiously, wondering at the tiny frown that pleated Hope's smooth forehead. "Are you worried about something?"

"Someone," Hope replied in a dull flat voice. "Gillian."

"Gillian? But why, dear? She seems so happy these days. Why she was full of vim and vinegar when she asked me to check out little Roddy's situation. And Jeremy was there, too. Bought a pair of shoes for the lad, I believe." Charity beamed across at her friend, genial benevolence casting her generous features in a less-harsh light.

"*That's* exactly what I'm afraid of. They're doing far too many things together. I'm afraid Gillian is growing attached to him." Hope stabbed the needle through her cross-stitch fabric viciously and tugged it through the other side without regard for the fine fabric.

"But surely that's good. After all, dear. They are engaged." Charity's tired eyes opened wide when Hope jumped to her feet.

"It's pretend," Hope insisted. "Why are you all acting as if it's the greatest thing when you know as well as I do that it's only a temporary misunderstanding?"

"Well," Charity murmured, lifting her half-completed afghan from her bag and knitting furiously. "It doesn't look like it's temporary anymore. She was kissing him that day, remember. And they have been spending an awful lot of time together."

She ticked the occasions off with a click of her needles. "The youth group, choir, the instruments at church, Roddy, and now the Christmas program." She shook her head, smiling from ear to ear. "Where there's smoke, there's fire, my mother always said. Seems to me that there is a lot of smoke between those two. And I'm glad. They're good for each other." Charity placidly knit another few rows before sensing that something was wrong. "Hope?"

"Do you *dare* say that they are falling in love?" The words came through tightly clenched teeth. "Don't you dare."

"But, Hope," Charity protested, laying aside her handwork. "I think it would be a wonderful thing if they grew to love each other. Jeremy is a good foil for Gillian's natural exuberance. And she's a catalyst for change in his life. I think God has done very well by those two young people."

"It's too soon," Hope protested angrily. "Far too soon after Michael's death for her to know her own mind. Why, she hasn't even grieved him properly!"

"Oh, my dear." Charity placed her arm around her friend's narrow shoulders and squeezed them. "How can you say that? There is no set period of mourning. And God's timing is always right. If He has brought them together, we should do all we can to help them on their path."

"And if He hasn't?"

Charity smiled at the doom and gloom in her friend's voice. "If it isn't God's will that Gillian and Jeremy pursue this relationship, then He will direct it that way." She patted Hope's shoulder before resuming her seat. "It's our job to pray for His direction in their lives, and it's His job to direct."

"I suppose," Hope answered halfheartedly. "But I so

wanted someone special for *Flossie.* That girl deserves a medal for the life she's led with that mother of hers."

"I think," Charity giggled girlishly, flushing a faint pink, "that God is working in that area, too. I noticed Lester Brown talking to her last Sunday. He seemed fairly smitten."

"Oh, pshaw! Lester Brown is ten years older than Flossie," Hope protested. "And a widower, to boot."

"So what?" Charity sniffed airily. "He's a good, kind man who treats Flossie as if she were a queen. And he *doesn't* live with his mother. In my books he's okay."

Hope was about to explain all the reasons why Lester Brown was totally unsuitable for her protégée when the front door flew open and Faith bounded through.

"Oh, my," Charity breathed.

"Lord love us," Hope said.

"Oh, piffle," Faith exclaimed. "Now I've gotten all this snow inside your lovely hall, Hope. Sorry. It's just that I really must sit down for a moment."

With a whoosh, Faith plunked down onto a nearby chair and scrunched her eyes tightly closed. She had on her snowsuit; the one in her favorite shade of pale pink. Thick snow encrusted the heavy mittens lying at her feet in a pool of melting snow.

"Oh, thank goodness," she said, blinking at them several moments later. "For a moment there, everything was spinning round and round. It's much better now." Her bony fingers reached up to touch the area just above her hairline, disturbing the wild disorder of her hair. "Just here, it seems to be a bit tender," she told them.

"Where have you been?" Hope demanded, picking up her mittens and wiping the floor in a swift economical movement.

"What have you been doing?" Charity asked at the same

time, peering over her glasses at the disheveled woman. "You look like you fell face-first into a snowbank."

"I did!" Faith's eyes glowed brightly in her ruddy face. "And I hit my head on the teeter-totter. I think it's okay now, though. I couldn't have been out for that long."

"Faith Rempel, do you mean to tell me that you were out in all this snow, by yourself, knocked unconscious?" Hope's scandalized tones were squeaky with disbelief.

"You have to go out in the snow to cross-country ski," Faith told them simply. She smiled happily. "It was wonderful—all that fresh white snow. I fairly flew over the trail. Fresh powder. That's what the kids call it." She wore a pleased, proud look on her face as she imparted the information.

"Fresh powder, indeed!" Hope glared at the older woman in frustration. "It's supposed to get quite cold tonight," she grumbled. "What would you have done if you'd been stuck in that snowbank overnight? Hmm?"

"I would have wished my friend Hope was there with some of her yummy hot chocolate." Faith peered up at her hostess wistfully. "Please?"

"Of all the silly, extravagant, overblown ideas! Men!" Gillian's voice rang out, clear and angry. "Hope, I'm home." The three elderly ladies glanced at each other and then winced as the front door slammed shut.

"I can hear that, dear. We're just going to indulge in some of my infamous hot chocolate. Would you like some?"

"Oh. Hello." Gillian stood at the entryway, hands clenched at her sides. Her gaze rested on Faith's bemused face for several moments before she declared in frustration, "Jeremy Nivens is a horse's patoot!" Then, turning, she stomped up the stairs to her room.

"Well." Charity smiled, resuming her knitting at lightning speed. "That certainly clarifies matters."

"What do you mean, Charity?" Hope stared at the tiny woman's complacent figure. "She's furious. Shouldn't I go and talk to her?"

"Oh, I don't think so, dear." Faith shook her salt-and-pepper head negatively as she eased one arm out of her snowsuit. "When a person gets into that state there's only one thing to do—let them sort it out for themselves."

"What state?" Hope looked disbelievingly from one to the other of her nonchalant friends. "What state?" she demanded again, an edge to her normally soft tone.

"Gillian's in love," Faith murmured with a coy grin. She looked for confirmation to Charity who merely nodded.

"Deeply," she said before her needles resumed their clackety-clack sound in the silent room.

"He's crazy. Totally out to lunch. Bonkers!" Gillian viciously stabbed the carrots on her plate with each angry word. "He thinks he can just order something and it will be done."

"Who, dear?" Hope inquired mildly, as if she didn't know.

"Jeremy pigheaded Nivens, that's who!" Gillian glared at her aunt. "And don't you dare try to smooth it over. This time he's gone too far."

"Gillian," her aunt began, aghast. "I would never take his side over yours. You know that. Now, calm down and tell me what the problem is this time."

"The problem," Gillian said between clenched teeth, "is that Mr. Nivens feels that our JFK Elementary should put on a play for the parents this year. A four-part play that involves all classes, extensive costumes, six massive sets and hours of practicing."

"Well, that sounds lovely, dear. I think the parents will enjoy seeing their children on stage as part of the school body. In my day we could never afford the time out of the classroom for such an elaborate affair but then…"

Gillian cringed as her aunt hit on the main point of contention between herself and the principal. Her ire surged up once again as she cut Hope off in midsentence.

"That," she grated, "was exactly my point when I looked over what he intended. It's almost Thanksgiving, Hope. There is hardly enough time to prepare a class recitation, let alone a four-part play."

"But, surely if you scheduled practices for after school and Saturdays, you could fit it all in?" Hope crunched thoughtfully on her carrots. "I mean, obviously the parents will help. And I don't mind sewing some costumes."

"Ha! After school and on Saturdays, you say. Wonderful! Fine idea! Except that Pastor Dave was by today to inform me that Jeremy thinks it would be a great idea for the kids of the youth group to go skiing a week from Saturday."

"Oh, how wonderful. I'm sure they'll enjoy that." Hope brightened considerably at the news, failing to notice the red suffusing Gillian's already-flushed face.

"Yes, it's *fantastic.* Except that I had already promised my Sunday school class that we would go to the city and do some Christmas shopping that day. Now what are we supposed to do—change our plans for *him?*"

The gall of the man, Gillian fumed. She wasn't about to tell her aunt how Jeremy had practically ordered her to go along with his play idea—right in front of the other teachers! Engagement or not, he had no right to pull rank in such a despicable manner.

The youth group thing was merely icing on the cake. Proof positive that they could never, ever work together. They were supposed to function as a team with the kids—in tandem, planning each outing jointly. But now, apparently, he'd gone ahead and booked the ski hill and even rented skis without even consulting her. It was…infuriating, she decided at last. But it was also just like something Mr. Jeremy Nivens would do. Why, she had a good mind to— The doorbell rang just then, cutting off her nasty thoughts.

"I'll get it, Hope. You finish your meal." Gillian pulled the door open with a wide, plastic smile that quickly cracked when she saw the tall, lean man standing outside. "What do you want?" she demanded, furious that he would confront her here, in her own home. Was there no refuge?

"I hope I'm not disrupting your meal," he said politely, stepping through the door without waiting to be asked.

"Yes, you are," Gillian said curtly, snapping the door closed. "But then, what's new? You have a tendency to proceed like a bull moose."

"Is something the matter, Gillian?" he murmured softly, his innocent eyes peering down at her. She couldn't fault the note of concern in his low voice. "It's not still the play, is it? I tried to explain how easy it would be, but you stormed out before I could say anything."

Gillian flopped down into the armchair and glared at him.

"What is there to say?" she demanded sharply. "You *advised* us that we would be doing the play. Don't kid yourself that there was any free choice involved."

She watched as he sat down opposite her on the sofa. He sat perched on the edge of the cushions as if ready to take flight at any moment. The smooth note of concern had evaporated from his voice and a frown had narrowed his eyes.

"Okay," he muttered. "What's the problem this time? What have I done wrong now?"

Gillian stared at him, outraged that he'd even ask such a thing.

"You know blessed well," she spat out, her newly manicured fingernails digging into her palms.

"No," Jeremy said wearily, raking one hand through his

usually neat hair. "Actually I don't. But I have a feeling you're going to tell me."

And Gillian did. Clearly, concisely and without sparing her words.

"It's a good thing we're not actually engaged," she finished, holding her tears back with difficulty. "I'd call the whole thing off, if my intended husband pushed and bullied people the way you do."

"I didn't know about your plans, Gillian. You never mentioned that your class was planning an outing. And you could have. The Sunday school superintendent specifically asked everyone about their Christmas plans last week."

"It wasn't planned then," she told him sourly. "And that still doesn't absolve you of planning youth group activities *without* me."

He sighed a deep sigh; long, drawn out and full of frustration. It whistled loudly through the silent room. Belatedly, Gillian wondered where her aunt had gotten to.

"I didn't *plan* anything," he protested angrily. "As usual with regard to us, the pastor is a little off the mark. The ski hill merely called back with the rates and advised me that they had a cancelation and that I could book it now and cancel later if the time wasn't suitable. I thought it was a good idea to book it just in case.

"If you're that much against skiing, we can cancel right now." His chin jutted out in that hard, determined line that bespoke his disgust with the whole sequence of events.

"What I'm against is people trying to order me around. I am not some subservient species, Jeremy Nivens. I do have a brain, and I can think for myself." Gillian crossed her arms over her chest and glared at him.

"Oh, for goodness sake," he muttered, surging to his feet. "This is ridiculous. I thought perhaps we might have a civil conversation for once, but I see that's impossible. Again." He brushed past her to snatch up his coat. "We'll have to find some other time, when you're not so irrational, to plan future youth meetings."

Gillian grabbed his arm as he strode toward the door. "That's what you're here for? To plan youth group meetings?" Gillian stared at him, wondering if all her faculties were working. "Very well, then," she said briskly. "Let's begin." She swept back into the living room and tugged out a pad of paper and pen. She'd show him who was irrational, Gillian decided grimly.

"Now, then. This Saturday we have that scavenger hunt, right? And next Friday? Or were you going to cancel that and have it Saturday instead?" She sat perched on the edge of the sofa, pencil at the ready.

"Will you stop acting like some eager-beaver secretary?" he murmured. "We agreed we would be partners in this. If you don't want to go skiing on Saturday, why not say so?"

"It is not that I don't want to go skiing," Gillian enunciated clearly. "I quite like skiing. The point is that I have made other commitments. Don't you ever do anything with your Sunday school class?"

He stared at her.

"That bunch of hooligans? I don't think so. I had to ask Mr. Johnson to help me out on Sundays just to keep them all in line. You saw what they're like."

Gillian stared at him as a new idea popped to life. It might work, and it would offer a perfect way out of the present impasse.

"Why not invite them to go skiing?" she asked softly. "They're too young for youth group, and yet they are desperately searching for their own niche in the church. Maybe an excursion of their own is just what they need."

"It certainly isn't what I need," Jeremy groaned. "How in the world would I get them there, together and in one piece? Without going insane, I mean?" He gave her a sour look that told her he was not enamored of the prospect.

"I've already chartered a bus," Gillian told him excitedly. "It's only half-full because I hadn't gotten around to telling the girls they could invite a friend on this shopping excursion. Your aunt is coming with us. If Mr. Johnson came with your boys, it would be great." She grinned at the thought of the preteens' pleasure in leaving their elders behind.

"I don't know," Jeremy muttered thoughtfully, studying his toes. "Downhill skiing can be dangerous for someone who doesn't know the rules." He rubbed his chin. "I have taught others, of course, and I was once a member of the ski patrol."

Gillian knew what was coming and blurted it out, just to prove she had a head on her shoulders. "You'd need permission slips from the parents, of course," she said smugly. "My girls have already handed them in. And they'll have to cover the cost of their equipment and food."

He raised one eyebrow. "I'm happy to see you've taken such precautions," he told her. One long finger rubbed at the cord pulsing in his neck. "That still leaves Friday night and the youth group, though. What will we do about that?"

Gillian grinned. Here it was; opportunity just waiting for her. "Snowmobiling," she crowed. "The Reids invited us to use their farm whenever we wanted. They have two machines and I've counted six others that I think would be available. Mrs. Reid even said she would be happy to make hot chocolate afterward."

Gillian waited for Jeremy's response. It was halfhearted at best.

"I don't know much about snowmobiling," he murmured, staring at her curiously.

"But I do," Gillian told him gleefully. "I've ridden one hundreds of times. I learned when our family moved to Canada for two years. The Canadian prairies are one of the best places in the world to ride a snowmobile."

"Isn't it rather, er, dangerous?" he asked quietly. "I've heard stories of people being killed."

Gillian nodded solemnly. "If you go too fast, it is dangerous," she agreed. "But maybe Mr. Reid would mark out a trail. I know they have a huge meadow that is completely unfenced. Aunt Hope and I used to go berry picking there. We could simply follow the trail."

Jeremy looked less than thrilled with the idea, but he offered no concrete resistance to her plans. They discussed several other things before he got up to leave.

"I hope this has resolved some of the tension between us," he said, pulling on his overcoat once more. Blue twinkles sparkled in his ever-changing eyes. "Although I don't know how you could accuse me of being unwilling to cooperate," he muttered, shoving the buttons through their buttonholes willy-nilly. "You arranged everything for the snowmobiling. I had nothing to say about it."

"Well," Gillian murmured, feeling pleased that they were back on speaking terms, at least. "We each have our strengths, I guess. Mind you—" she handed him his gloves "—I'm still furious about that silly play you've chosen for the school. For the next few weeks we'll be doing nothing but practicing."

Jeremy shook his head, chuckling as he stepped out the door.

"Please don't start that again. It's already past eleven, and I'm on supervision bright and early tomorrow morning. Besides—" he grinned at her across the sparkling snow "—it won't be that bad. You'll see."

Gillian watched him walk down the path. He was almost out the gate before he turned back.

"By the way," he called. "How's the Green situation?"

"Charity is on the case," she called back.

* * *

"Hello," Charity Flowerday beamed up at the emaciated woman who had answered the door. "I'm looking for Roddy. Is this where he lives?"

"Why, yes," the woman whispered, pausing to cough raggedly into a handkerchief. "I'm his mother. But he's at school." A piercing cry rang through the air. "Oh, dear. I have to go."

She whirled away so quickly, she didn't notice Charity squeeze inside through the door. By quickly divesting herself of her coat and galoshes, Charity just managed to follow the woman into the kitchen. On the floor sat two identical two-year-olds, one banging on the other one's pot.

"Oh, what lovely babies," Charity exclaimed, reaching down to touch one tousled brown head. "What are their names?"

"Oh, you startled me!" Mrs. Green put a hand to her chest. "I didn't realize you'd followed me."

"And I'm sorry I did that," Charity said. "It was very rude of me, of course. But I wanted to talk to you about Roddy, and I knew you didn't want to stand chatting at the door. Especially with these two big enough to get into everything." She waited silently until the woman had finished yet another bout of coughing.

"My dear Mrs. Green," she murmured, resting her hand on the woman's thin arm. "You sound as if you're ill." She peered assessingly at the wan complexion and the tired eyes.

"I'm very tired," the other woman admitted. "I'll just get the twins down for their nap and then I'll rest." Slowly she removed two half-full bottles from the old refrigerator in the corner. "Come on, Charlie, Patrick. Time for a nap."

The boys stood quickly enough, eyeing Charity as they toddled over to their mother.

"No bed," muttered one of the tykes, grabbing the bottle out of his mother's hand, ready to toss it across the room.

Swifter than an eagle, Charity slid the object out of his grasp and returned it to his mother. She held out her own hand.

"Come along, my boy. When mother says it's nap time, we have to obey. Mother needs a nap, too. She's very tired. Here we go, now." She nodded encouragingly at Mrs. Green and was relieved to find the woman understood her signal. Seconds later the boys were in bed, happily sucking down their milk.

"Now, why don't we sit in here. That's right, you just put your feet up on the sofa and rest. I sometimes chatter on, so you'll be sure to tell me, won't you." Charity smiled, noticing the droop of the woman's eyes.

"Something about Roddy, you said." Mrs. Green yawned delicately, trying to hold her eyelids up with apparent difficulty.

"Oh, Roddy. Such a lovely boy. Comes to see me, you know." Charity babbled away, her eagle eye noticing just when Mrs. Green nodded off. "Just loves my cookies, he does." She kept up the monotonous babble until she was sure the other woman was asleep. Then, tiptoeing out of the living room, she gently closed the door to the kitchen and opened her purse.

"Such a wonderful thing, these cell phones," she murmured, punching in a number on the keypad with little difficulty. "My Melanie always did think of the most wonderful Mother's Day gifts. Of course, it probably comes from working in the nursing home. So practical." She spared a thought for Faith's possible admittance into that home and winced as the woman's voice came on the line.

"Hello, Faith? This is Charity. Charity Flowerday. Yes, dear, that's the one. Now listen carefully. I have a job for you."

Three hours later Gillian found all three of the women sitting around the Green kitchen table enjoying a cup of coffee.

"But where's Mrs. Green?" she asked curiously, shushing when Hope told her to. "I need to talk to her about Roddy's costume for the Christmas play," she whispered.

"Don't you be bothering that sickly woman with the likes of that," Charity muttered, folding the last basket of laundry Faith had lugged in from her car. "She's worn to a frazzle with those two."

"Those two" sat on a blanket on the gleaming floor, Faith between them, munching on a cookie.

"I think you should check those squares," Charity murmured just loudly enough for Faith to hear. The older woman got to her feet and looked into the oven. "They look lovely, Faith, dear."

"Everything looks real nice," Roddy murmured, staring around his home with interest. His finger slipped over the bright red vinyl on the kitchen chairs. "Where'd these come from?"

"Why, Roddy Green," Charity pretended surprise. "These are your very own kitchen chairs. I just washed them and used a bit of sealing glue on them."

Roddy didn't look convinced, especially when he saw the bit of leftover vinyl sitting on the counter, but his attention was caught by the wonderful spicy odor wafting through the house. He sniffed several times and then licked his lips.

"Gingerbread," he cried, causing everyone to hiss "Shhhhh."

"Roddy, I think the twins want to play outside now. I brought over a little sleigh for you to use. I think they'll both fit into it." Hope watched in admiration as the seven-year-old slid the two toddlers into their snowsuits without difficulty. "My, you are good at that," she said.

Flushed at the kind words, but happily chewing on his own cookie, Roddy ushered the twins out the door. With a shriek of laughter they plunged face-first into the snowbank and rolled in it excitedly.

As soon as the children had left, Charity stood to her feet.

"Now, ladies, this woman needs help. Her husband is off looking for work in the city, and she's been left alone with hardly any money and three young 'uns, to boot. We've done all the cooking and cleaning we can for now, but she's got to get to a doctor or these children will be orphans."

"I'm not that sick," a weak voice from the doorway murmured. "I can still care for my family."

"Of course you can," Charity murmured. "But first, Hope here is going to take you down to see Dr. Dan to get something for that cough. Don't worry—" she held up one hand, forestalling the protests they all knew were coming "—we'll watch the children till you get back."

It took a round of introductions and a few moments of heavy-duty persuasion, but finally Anita, as she had told them to call her, pulled on her worn wool coat and headed for the door. Her face brightened considerably when her hand found the loose change in her pocket. She'd forgotten all about it, she murmured. Maybe she could afford some medicine, after all.

Once they'd left, Charity turned to Gillian.

"That girl needs a warm winter coat—maybe nothing fancy, but something warm. And some gloves and boots. Can you handle that?"

Gillian nodded, a little stunned by the overwhelming need of Roddy's family. "Yes, I think so. I have several bags of clothes in my room that I was going to give away. She's more than welcome. I'll go get them right now." She scurried out of the kitchen.

"Faith, you get on the phone to Jeremy," Charity said. "I want him to look at this furnace. Something's not working right. This house is too cold for those young children." She pulled a pan of golden Santas and stars and Christmas trees a little nearer and began decorating each with colored icing. "Then, of course, we've got to get some groceries here. I couldn't haul over near enough."

"Arthur would help," Faith squealed happily. "He'd bring over whatever you needed."

"Of course," Charity said, beaming. "While you talk to your nephew, I'll make a list."

Gillian heard the two of them chuckling merrily as she tugged on her boots and buttoned up her jacket. The meager confines of Roddy's home had shocked her. They didn't even have the bare necessities in this house. And that coat of Anita's!

As she pulled on her warm leather gloves, she thought again about those red, worn fingers that Anita had tried to hide in her tattered gloves. And a picture of the lovely new navy coat she'd just purchased for herself floated guiltily through her mind.

She didn't need it, Gillian reflected. Not really. Her white melton was barely two years old, and there wasn't a mark on it since she'd had it cleaned. She thought of the matching red leather gloves and the red woolen scarf she'd purchased especially to go with the new coat. Anita had the kind of blond fairness that would suit the dark color, she thought. And the red would give her pale skin some color.

When you do it unto the least of my brothers, you do it unto me.

It was a verse she had read in her private Bible study that

very morning. Had God meant her to help out Anita with her new coat? Surely her white one would do just as well?

A little voice whispered inside her head as she plodded through the snow-clogged streets, *Would you have Jesus wear the white or the navy coat?*

She scurried onward, knowing what she had to do. It wasn't that much of a sacrifice, Gillian told herself, snuggling against the fur collar of her jacket. She would still be dry and warm in her other coat. She jumped as a car horn sounded behind her.

"Where are you going?" Jeremy asked, his dark head catching snowflakes as he leaned out the window. "I thought everyone was at the Green house."

Gillian stepped over the snowbank and slipped into the seat beside him. "They are," she told him, rubbing her hands in the warm air coming from the heater. "I'm on my way to Hope's to pick up a few things for Anita, that's Mrs. Green, while she sees the doctor. Apparently that's why Roddy's been so unkempt." In a few short sentences, she relayed the whole sad story. "Faith was trying to reach you when I left. Something about checking the furnace."

"I don't know anything about furnaces," he told her grimly. "Why don't they just get a repairman? And if it's dangerous, I certainly don't want my aunt involved!" He glared at her as if the whole situation were her fault.

"Look," she said, exasperated by his attitude. "This is a family that needs help. Christmas is supposed to be a time for giving. Can't you spare a few moments to give a little to someone else for a change?"

Jeremy swallowed his retort as he noticed the flash of ire in her sparkling green eyes. All right, he had sounded uncharitable. But blast it, anyway, it had been a day to forget, and he had no wish to add anything else.

"Okay. We'll go to Hope's and you can get what you need,"

he said acquiescing. "Then I'll drive you back and take a look at this monstrosity. But I'm warning you, I don't know anything about furnaces or repairing them. Absolutely nothing."

Jeremy watched as she jumped out of the car once they reached her aunt's. She moved like lightning, he decided. No wasted effort; no pretense. Just get the job done. He liked that about her. He followed her inside.

But as she slipped off her jacket and bent over to unlace her boots, Jeremy decided there were certainly other assets about his pretend fiancée that he had overlooked. Her hair, for one thing. It burst out of her cap like fairy dust suddenly set free. He mocked his poetic thoughts even as he watched the light sparkle off the soft curls that stood out around her head from the static electricity.

"There," she said, straightening as she tugged her royal blue sweater over her hips. She waved him in. "I'm going to be a few minutes so make yourself at home."

And sure enough, a few moments later she was trying to manhandle a huge black garbage bag down the stairs.

"Here," he offered, meeting her halfway and taking the weight in his arms easily. Jeremy set it down in the middle of the living room and straightened to find her directly in front of him, mere inches away. His breath caught in his throat at her luminous beauty, and he reached out to touch one glistening curl that had strayed across her eyes.

Gillian stood perfectly still, allowing him to move the strand as she stared back at him. Her eyes were wide-open, innocent. Her lips rosy and shiny as she gently swiped her tongue across them.

It happened so quickly that Jeremy decided later he couldn't have stopped himself even if he'd wanted to. His hand curved around her chin as he leaned forward and pressed his lips against her full mouth. He moved his mouth against her gossamer-soft one and felt Gillian's shiver of response.

She didn't move away. She didn't even open her eyes to chastise him. Instead, her head tilted just a little to allow him greater access. Jeremy took that as a yes and wrapped his other arm around her slim waist as he deepened the kiss. She stiffened for just a second, and then her arms were draped around his shoulders and, hallelujah, she was kissing him back.

When Jeremy finally pulled back he found Gillian's clear, wide gaze fixed on him.

"Why did you do that?" she murmured, her fingers pressing against the lapel of his jacket.

"Because you're very beautiful and I wanted to." He smiled, feeling more lighthearted than he had in years. "Didn't you want me to?"

As Jeremy stood silent, Gillian blushed a deep, startling rose. She lowered her gaze, long golden lashes hiding her eyes from him.

"Actually, I did," she whispered in a voice so soft he barely heard it.

"Good," he muttered, tugging her against him once more. "Because I'm going to do it again."

Gillian's strong arms slipped around his neck as she pulled his head a little nearer. "Good," she echoed breathlessly.

Less tentative, more demanding on Jeremy's part, this kiss asked more questions, which he noticed she willingly answered. It could have gone on and on, but the telephone rang, abruptly breaking their silent communication.

Jeremy let his arms fall away and stepped back as she moved toward the phone. His eyes intently followed her, noting the swift rise of that wonderful color to her cheeks and the way her eyes glanced at him and then skittered away

when she saw him watching her. Jeremy smiled to himself
and sank onto the nearby sofa.

Gillian wasn't any less affected by this new intimacy than
he was. Good, because he fully intended that there would be
more. He had this ridiculous insatiable craving to touch those
lips once more; to trace the planes of her beautiful face and
nibble on her earlobe. It was crazy. It was wonderful.

It wasn't like him at all.

"That was Hope." Gillian stood by the phone, twiddling
the cord between her fingers. "She wants us to bring some
of her raspberry jam over." Not once did she look at him.

Jeremy stood and walked over beside her rigid form.
When he placed his hand on her shoulder, Gillian lifted wide,
startled eyes to stare at him.

"I'll say I'm sorry, if you want," he told her, allowing the
smile to tug at the corners of his mouth. "But I'd be lying.
I'm not sorry I kissed you." He grinned. "And sometime, at
a more convenient time, I fully intend to do it again."

His heart sank as Gillian just stared at him, as wide-eyed
as a doe. Then, just when he was sure all hope was gone, her
eyes began to glow with that inner light.

"And I fully intend to kiss you back," she told him, smiling. "But right now we've got to get back to the Greens'."
And leaning over, she teetered on her tiptoes as her lips
grazed his cheek. "Later."

It was a promise, Jeremy decided. One that he'd hold her
to, hopefully *sooner*.

"What is all this stuff?" With a grunt of relief, Jeremy
stuffed the last bag into his backseat and tilted the driver's
seat back in its usual position. "We should have called a
mover."

"Mostly it's clothes I bought to get you off my back," Gillian told him pertly. "You did spend the first few weeks of
September telling me how inappropriately I dressed, remem-

ber? I blew a big chunk of my wages buying black, navy and neutral-colored clothes."

He snorted. "I never said any such thing. I merely suggested—"

Gillian held up one hand. "You know what..." she told him, frowning fiercely, "don't go there. We'll only end up arguing some more, and I think we've gotten beyond that these past months."

He nodded, edging closer to her.

"Far beyond that," he agreed, slipping one arm around her waist.

He watched, not totally amused, as Gillian ducked away from him and climbed into the car, eyes brimming with laughter.

"We have work to do. Remember? The Greens," she chided, watching him frown.

Jeremy shifted gears easily and moved the car slowly away from the curb, enjoying the rub of her shoulder against his in the small confines of the sports car. Gillian sat with a huge box on her lap.

He kept careful watch as she handed it to Mrs. Green and noted the glow on her lovely face.

"Oh, but it looks new," Anita protested, lifting the expensive wool coat from the tissue.

"It is," Gillian said.

"But you can't give away your new coat," the woman protested folding it back into the box with a sigh of regret.

"Well, if you don't want it, I guess I'll have to find someone else," Gillian told her, smiling. "I certainly can't wear it. There's something about the fabric that bothers my skin, must be allergies. I break out in a rash," she told them.

Of conscience, Jeremy felt like adding, for he had seen her remove the tags from the coat and gloves at Hope's and knew full well she could have returned both to the exclusive shop she'd gotten them from. He'd also seen her press her cheek against the soft cashmere and sniff the new leather.

But now, as he watched her give away the lovely clothes and saw the smile of joy cross her face when Anita tried them on, he felt a pang of something deep inside.

Yes, Gillian Langford was a sight to behold. She might wear bright, colorful clothes, and she certainly was hot-headed. And no one could argue that wherever she went, heads didn't turn to notice the stunning auburn hair. But today he had seen something completely different; something that had him realizing he really knew very little about the beautiful woman everyone thought he would marry.

Today he had seen deep inside, to the generosity and kind spirit that was just as bright and just as glorious as her outward beauty. And suddenly he wanted her to turn that loving, caring smile she was bestowing on those children on him. He wanted to be the recipient of one of those dazzling grins and return one of her spontaneous hugs.

So when she sat down next to him at the dinner table with the aunts, Arthur Johnson, Anita and her children gathered around to say grace over the savory stew and fresh biscuits, Jeremy reached under the crisp, white tablecloth and clasped her hand in his. And when she glanced at him in startled surprise, he bent his head near hers, eyes twinkling, and whispered for her ears only, "After all, we are engaged! Remember?"

Chapter Eight

"All right, children!" Gillian tried to keep the Christmas spirit in her voice, but it was difficult to do when the surrounding din had nearly reached ten on the Richter scale. "Choir, I want you to try that last number once more."

Obediently, the kindergarten and first-graders lined up, albeit helter-skelter. She looked around for her pianist, but Jeremy was busy trying to get the members of the cast into costume and ready to go on stage. Puffing her bangs out of her eyes in resignation, Gillian straightened the last little girl into line and then sat down at the piano herself. Although she had never even seen this music before, she decided to give it her best shot. Someone had to!

"All right, children, here we go. One, two, three, four. 'City side....'" And indeed, off they went. Off-key, off tempo and in no particular order.

Half an hour later Gillian sank onto the staff-room sofa, thrust her feet up onto a nearby chair and blissfully sipped at her coffee. She needed this. It had been a Friday to end all Fridays.

Around the room the other teachers were packing up to go home for the weekend, but Gillian ignored them as she closed her eyes and dreamed of Christmas holidays; of mornings spent lounging lazily in bed; quiet solemn afternoons of uninterrupted reading. They opened in startled awareness, when she felt the cool press of masculine lips against hers.

"Jeremy," she gasped, straightening in such a rush, some of the cooled coffee slopped over the mug and onto her white corduroy pants. "You can't do that in public!"

"It isn't public," he told her, grinning as he waved a hand around the empty staff room. "Everyone has gone home. Long, long ago."

"Oh." She yawned. "I'm dead."

"It has been a trying week," he admitted, lifting the mug from her hands and sipping from it. For some reason, the gesture sent tingles of awareness through Gillian's body that heightened when he sank down beside her and placed his arm along the sofa back behind her.

"By the way," he told her, playing with a curl escaped from her neat chignon. "That last song you were doing with the choir?"

"I know," she groaned, tilting her head back and feeling his hand rub her scalp. "Don't remind me. It was awful."

He laughed. "Yes, it was. Part of the reason it was so awful is because you were doing it in a different key. I transposed it into five flats. It's easier and the kids can hold pitch better." He chuckled at her groan of dismay. "And the other problem was that you had the wrong boy singing the solo."

"No wonder he didn't know the words," she exclaimed, glaring at him. "You might have said something." The words died as he leaned closer and brought his lips to within inches of hers.

"I thought I just did," Jeremy murmured before moving closer.

Gillian wanted that kiss; had waited days for it. And nothing and no one was going to stop her from enjoying it. Long moments later she laid her head on his shoulder and murmured, "This is nice. I could just go to sleep."

"I don't know why not," Jeremy murmured, brushing a gentle hand across her hair as he stood to his feet. "As long as you've got the snacks ready for tonight, your time is your own."

Gillian narrowed her eyes and peered up at him.

"What snacks?" she asked warily, rising from the sofa as a tiny feather of dismay wafted through her mind. "What's going on tonight?"

"Snowmobiling. Have you forgotten?" He tugged her by the arm over to the coat stand. "Go home and rest. You'll need it."

Gillian felt all the old anger begin to rise anew. "But why is it my responsibility to arrange the food?" she demanded. "You are supposed to be part of this 'team.' It wouldn't hurt you to help out once in a while." She saw the tightening around his mouth, felt the sizzle of electricity in the room as his eyes darkened and his brow furrowed.

"Just a blasted minute here," he muttered. "You distinctly told me that our hosts would provide the hot chocolate. I'm sure you said that you would look after the snacks. In fact, I could almost swear to it."

Gillian bristled. "There is no swearing on school property," she told him self-righteously. "And don't go all grim and nasty just because you imagined something that never happened. I got the snacks last time, you get them this time." She snatched up her coat and thrust her arms into it angrily.

"I can't. I've got a parent coming in this afternoon," he told her, glancing at his watch. "In about five minutes, actually. I'll barely make it to the church on time as it is."

"Well, my time is important, too," she told him, frowning.

"I know that," he sighed with long-suffering forbearance, irritating Gillian to no end. "But just this once could you help me out and pick up something for them? Donuts, chips and dip—they'll inhale anything."

"For your information," she flung, knowing it was sheer tiredness that was making her so cranky, but feeling justified anyway, "I *have* helped you out. On numerous occasions. With no thanks for my efforts. It's about time you did some of the work you're so eager to dish out. The rest of us are tired of being your peons." She angrily marched out the door without a backward glance.

But halfway down the hall Gillian remembered that he expected her to supply the food. "And pick up the donuts or whatever yourself," she called grumpily. "I'm going home to soak in the tub."

Let his high-and-mighty bossiness fill those bottomless pits called children for once, she told her nagging, reprimanding conscience. *It surely is about time he took on some of that job.*

Still, as she lay in Hope's big tub with the soft subtle fragrance of rose-scented bath oil drifting around her, she couldn't help but wonder what kind of food Jeremy would bring.

"As long as it isn't egg salad sandwiches," she muttered, frowning as she dipped her head under the water.

There was a surplus of youth and a shortage of cars that evening, and it wasn't easy to find a ride to the farm. Even now Gillian was sure the good reverend wondered why Jeremy wasn't driving his fiancée to the event.

"He's probably going to be late," she told Pastor Dave. "Tonight Jeremy is supplying the food."

"Oh, boy," a teenager groaned from the backseat. "I hope you know what you're doing, Gillian. He doesn't like normal junk food, you know. He always says there's too much fat in chips and too much sugar in pop."

"Yeah," Marissa's voice chimed in. She giggled. "I never noticed that he applied the same theory to pie, though. Mrs. Rempel told my mom that whenever she makes pies, Jeremy pigs out. I watched him at the church supper at Thanksgiving and it's true! He had *three* pieces."

Gillian smiled, recalling the night in question with mirth. Jeremy had been scandalized that there was only one kind of salad available. And he'd rudely labeled the gravy as "artery-clogging fat." But when he'd passed the pie table, his eyes had glistened with avaricious glee.

The kids from town sat twittering in the back, whispers whizzing back and forth between them. Gillian grinned, knowing all that exuberance would soon be outside in the fresh air. They were a good bunch of kids; full of mischief, but caring.

Jeremy was already there when Pastor Dave's car rolled down the lane into the farmyard. He stood in the middle of the path, talking to several of the men who had brought snowmobiles for the kids to use. As everyone tumbled out of the car, Gillian took her time, studying the situation as she strove to think of something to overcome the angry words of earlier.

When she looked up, however, Jeremy's eyes met hers. To her surprise they were glowing with excitement. He grinned and motioned her over.

"Mr. Reid has made a trail for us. It follows through the woods, goes through a couple of fields and ends up back here. And there are more than enough snowmobiles for everyone to share." He rubbed his hands with glee. "It's all worked out very well."

As if he had some part in that, Gillian grumbled to herself as she nodded and shook hands with the men who had so graciously loaned their machines.

"Thank you very much. We really appreciate this. And

the kids will be very careful with them, won't you?" Gillian glanced around at the group of grinning faces, glistening with good health, and listened as they called their thanks to the men.

Mr. Reid, Pastor Dave and the other men organized everyone on a machine, some in pairs, some singly. One by one, they were shown the controls, told the dangers and warned to stay on the track. It was only as they came to the last one that Gillian noticed she and Jeremy had been paired. Apparently this was not to his liking for his face had grown pale.

"I think I remember most of it," she told a smiling Mr. Reid. "It's been a long time, but some things you don't forget easily."

Gillian snapped on her helmet and turned, only to find Jeremy's huge eyes staring at the black leather seat with something remarkably like fear. She held out his helmet, and when he didn't immediately take it, slid it on his head herself. "I'll drive first since I've been on one of these before. You just hang on to me."

It wasn't what she wanted. In fact, the less contact she could have with this disturbing man, the better. But the rest of the group was sitting, waiting. It was obvious they didn't sense Jeremy's fear, and something, some regret for the way she'd spoken this afternoon, made Gillian want to keep it that way.

"You lead, Tim," she called out to the oldest Reid boy. "You already know the way. The rest of us will follow, but not too closely. Jeremy and I'll follow behind everyone else to make sure no one is left stranded. Okay?"

They all nodded their agreement.

"No stopping on the trail, Gillian," someone called out teasingly. The other kids chimed in, making their catcalls loud and embarrassing.

Gillian slid down her visor and pulled up her gloves,

hoping that no one would notice the red stain she felt flooding her cheeks. A stop on the way was the farthest thing from her mind right now. When she waved her hand, Tim started off down the track, the others following at an evenly spaced distance.

"Climb on," she told Jeremy quietly. "We'd better get going."

"Perhaps it would be best if I stayed here. Just in case someone is needed..."

Gillian flipped up her visor and glared up at him, hoping anger would do the trick. "Are you crazy?" she demanded inelegantly. "I'm not taking that bunch into the bush on my own. If anybody stays, it's me. Now either you get on, or you go by yourself."

He did, but it took several moments for him to adjust himself to the feel and slope of the seat, and by that time the rest of the group had long since moved out of sight. Gillian took her place in front of him and gunned the engine twice before taking off. He slammed into her from behind as they flopped over a mound of snow, and seconds later she felt his hands around her waist.

The evening was a lovely, clear, crisp one with thousands of stars twinkling brightly overhead. Gillian breathed in the fresh air with relish, bounding along in the cold, but snug in her warm ski suit. Jeremy had righted himself somewhat. However, his hands still clung to her tightly, sending tingles of awareness all through her body. She had to expend considerable effort to concentrate properly on her driving.

You haven't thought about Michael for days.

The thought came from out of the vast blue-black of the sky above, and it sent Gillian reeling. She had come to this small town to grieve and to dwell on her loss and the past; to live a future full of regret. And yet, a few short months later she felt more alive than she had in a long time. Why, even tonight the wind seemed sharper, the air fresher, the pain less bitter.

How is this possible, Lord? she questioned. *Didn't I really love Michael, after all? Was it only infatuation, to be forgotten so quickly?*

She thought of the strange new feelings that rose up within her whenever the man behind her came near. Somehow her day brightened perceptibly with his presence. It didn't matter that they didn't always agree. And she had long since forgiven him for the slights she had first felt. But what about now? What about when Jeremy touched her, kissed her, as he'd done earlier today. Was that love?

Gillian was jolted out of her reverie by the tapping on her shoulder. She slowed down and glanced behind, tilting up her visor as she did. "What's the matter?" she asked curiously. "Are you too cold?"

He shook his head.

"You don't like it, do you?"

"No, that's not it. It's just that, uh, I was wondering if, that is—" He stopped for a moment and then it all came tumbling out in a rush. "Do you think I could learn to drive this thing?"

Relief swept over her. He wasn't going to be a party pooper, after all. "Of course." Gillian pushed herself upward and swung one leg over to step into the snow. Immediately she sank in the white, fluffy snow to well above her knees. "Whoops." She giggled, grabbing his outstretched hand. "I forgot about this part."

Jeremy slid up into the driver's place and with his help, Gillian finally clambered back up onto the running board, huffing and puffing at the exertion made more difficult by the thick layers of clothing. Quickly she explained the controls and then urged him to try them out.

"We're losing sight of the others," she murmured, watching the last machine round the bend. "If we're not behind them, they'll tease us endlessly."

Jeremy grinned, snapping his helmet back into position and gunning the engine. "Yes, ma'am." He saluted.

Seconds later Gillian felt her head jerk backward as he hit the accelerator a little too fast. They whizzed down the trail and around the bend and came upon Reva and Tim.

"You're too close," Gillian yelled, but evidently Jeremy had already figured that out as he jerked abruptly off the trail, over a small mogul and smacked down on the other side with a thud that sent them both through the air to land on the ground behind the now-quietly purring snowmobile.

Gillian lay there staring at the stars, wondering if they were in the sky or her head. She felt winded and dazed as she tried to remember why she had ever suggested this. There were voices now; lots of them. Someone tugged off her helmet, and she could make out a number of children from the youth group gathered around.

"Are you okay? Anything broken?" Hands whipped up and down her legs and arms, checking briskly for injuries.

"Jeremy," she gasped, sucking oxygen into her starved lungs.

"Is fine. How about you?" He was sitting beside her, grinning as if he had just completed the Grand Prix for snowmobiles.

"Okay, I think. Oooooh!" She rubbed a spot on her left hip gently, feeling the tenderness with each movement she made. "I'm going to have a bruise there, though."

"What happened, anyway?" Reva asked, staring down at Jeremy. "Didn't you hear Gillian tell us not to go too fast? You were really moving."

Gillian looked at Jeremy and noticed that he'd removed his helmet. His dark hair stood out wildly around his pale face and there was the beginnings of a bruise on his temple. But he was grinning from ear to ear.

"I just never expected it to respond so easily," he murmured. "It was great. I can hardly wait to try again."

Gillian groaned as she got to her feet with his help.

"I can," she muttered. "I can wait quite a while."

"Before you go roaring off again, I think you'd better check your machine, Jeremy," one of the older boys snickered. "You might have to dig it out of that snowbank you hit first."

Jeremy whirled around in dismay, glancing first right, then left, looking for damage. The entire group burst out laughing when his relieved gaze finally landed on the softly purring red machine sitting quietly by the trail.

"You guys," he said. "You had me worried there for a moment. I thought I'd really done some damage."

"Only to me," Gillian grumbled, moving to take her place on the back of the snowmobile. "Come on, guys, let's move. This is when I could really use some hot chocolate."

One or two of the girls teased her about her aging status, but within a few minutes they were back on the trail, moving at a sedate pace.

"No more bronco riding," she warned Jeremy. "If you intend on doing that again, you do it alone."

He grinned at her, holding up his right hand. "I promise."

They wound through the forest, filling the silence with the roar of engines. Jeremy flicked the lights off for a moment. It was very dark, eerie, but for the shafts of bright moonlight that lit up a glade here and there. Every so often Gillian felt the tingle of fresh snow on her neck as an evergreen bough sifted down some of the light powdery covering that balanced on its branches.

And then they were out of the woods and into the open meadow covered by a blanket of snow. Mile after mile they crossed, sometimes weaving away from the path, but always returning to it again. Up ahead, some of the group was stopped, and Jeremy slowed to find out the problem.

Twelve teenagers lay flat on their backs in the snow, waving arms and legs rhythmically.

"Come on," Tim and Reva called. "It's great."

Jeremy studied them curiously before glancing back at Gillian.

"What, exactly, are they doing? Or shouldn't I ask?"

"They're making snow angels, of course. I can't believe you haven't done that before." When he shook his head, she sighed and pointed. "Watch the snow when they get up."

They sat silent as Tim pulled Reva out of the snow. And sure enough, there in the smooth, puffy whiteness was indeed the outline of an angel. Quick as a wink, Gillian turned and shoved as hard as she could, tumbling Jeremy into the snow.

"Hey," he protested, but it was too late. Gillian had already flopped down beside him and was tugging on his arm.

"Like this," she instructed.

They had almost finished when a pelter of snowballs caught them square in the face. Scrambling to their feet, they completely destroyed the imprint as they balled-up some snow and fired at the group now surrounding them.

"You're outnumbered," someone shouted as a huge ball of soft snow hit Gillian smack on the mouth. "Give in!"

"Never," she shouted back, chucking snowballs even faster. It was only seconds later that she noticed Jeremy was no longer there. Turning, she saw him sprawled in the snow while several boys laughingly washed his face.

"Hey," she yelled, tossing several missiles at them. It was a mistake. Within moments her attackers had doubled their effort and she could only flounder through the deep snow toward her machine when they gave pursuit.

"Your turn," the girls chorused, mock-threateningly. It

was only through the cleverest bargaining, fierce warnings and promising things she could never deliver that Gillian escaped the same fate.

At last, tired and laughing, the entire group mounted their snowmobiles and headed off for the Reids' home. When they trooped into the house, Gillian's nose twitched at the delicious odors emanating from the kitchen. What in the world had Jeremy come up with for supper? she wondered.

"Pizza," several boys hollered, smacking their lips in delight. "All right!" They high-fived one another in eager anticipation. Even the girls were casting mouthwatering glances toward the kitchen.

"Why, you're just in time," Mrs. Reid said, smiling. "Mrs. Rempel and Mr. Johnson just now dropped off these things. They're still hot."

As the kids jostled one another for a slice of pizza and a cup of hot chocolate, Gillian nudged Jeremy in the ribs.

"That's cheating and you know it," she teased. "You were supposed to bring something *you* made for this group of ravenous wolves. I'm going to have to speak to Faith about this."

He grinned, tweaking her nose.

"Don't you dare," he whispered. "You already know how much I cook and how well. Besides—" he watched the pizza disappear with worried eyes "—I'm starved."

"Hey, Jeremy," one of the teens called out. "You're not eating any, are you?"

Jeremy stared at the girl, his forehead furrowed. "Why not?" he demanded.

"Far too much fat in this stuff," she chirped, and proceeded to stuff the rest of the piece into her mouth.

"So, I'll take a walk later or something," he muttered, snatching up one of the most heavily loaded slices.

Giggles burst out of the girls, and the guys openly guffawed him.

"Opt for the 'or something,' Gillian," they teased. "Just don't get on a snowmobile with him."

And to Jeremy's obvious embarrassment, the youth group, in garbled bits of conversation, told the Reids all about his snowmobile prowess, or lack thereof. That prompted a discussion on being grateful. Since it was only a week after Thanksgiving, they all had a great time talking about things to be thankful for. Everyone joined in on the subject; no one was left out. Mr. Reid then gave a short devotional about showing thanks as well as saying it.

And suddenly the evening was over.

Gillian felt proud of their group. The kids had handled the machines and themselves with respect in spite of the naysayers at church who had repeatedly reminded her of her foolishness in thinking of such a thing for the youth group.

And one of those very people was present right now, she noted, arching one eyebrow at Jeremy. In fact, he had been the loudest of them. How was it that suddenly he couldn't seem to stay away from the machines?

Gillian watched curiously as he finished a short discussion with Mr. Reid, half ran over to the bright red racing unit that Tim Reid had been driving and jumped on. Seconds later he went whizzing past her, obviously intent on making for the open field.

Gillian watched as he zigged and zagged across the snow. A number of the youth were going home by snowmobile, and she waved and called goodbye to them, smiling at their remarks about the maniac on the red snow machine. When at last he got off, Jeremy's face was flushed with the cold. But nothing could dim the glow in those blue eyes.

As everyone filed back to the cars, Gillian felt a hand tugging on her arm. She turned in surprise to see Jeremy's solemn figure behind her.

"I'll give you a ride back, Gillian," he offered quietly.

"It's all right," Gillian said just as quietly. "I came with the pastor. I can go back with him."

"He's not coming back out here," Jeremy told her. His hand moved to her back, urging her toward the cars. "I'm taking everyone who rode with him, as well as my own crew. Come on. I need to talk to you, anyway."

Gillian went because she assumed they would say whatever needed to be said on the way back. She hadn't counted on the wealth of giggling passengers crowded into the car.

"I don't think there's enough room," she told him, eyeing the mass of wriggling bodies.

"Sure there is," he told her blithely. "We might have to squeeze at bit, but we'll manage."

Gillian ended up squished next to Jeremy's lean body, sharing a corner of his seat, with her legs tucked in the space between the seats. His arm across the back of the seat allowed her more room. It also send shivers of awareness over her.

"Are you okay?" he murmured in her ear, reaching to twist the key.

"I think so. Changing gears might be a little difficult for you, though," she said, wondering if he would return his arm to its place behind her after moving it to the gearshift by the steering wheel.

"Well, if *you* shifted, it would be easier," Jeremy agreed.

Gillian straightened.

"Me? I can't drive a stick shift," she told him, panic stricken at the thought. "I'll wreck your transmission."

"No, you won't," he said confidently. "And even if you did, it's still under warranty. Want to try it?" His eyes sparkled down at her. "Come on, Gillian. You're always telling me to take a new risk."

She tried to absorb what he was telling her and ignore the tingles of awareness where his arm brushed her shoulder.

They putted off down the road as Gillian tried to figure out the intricacies of the five-speed manual transmission wondering why anyone would buy a car that didn't shift itself down or up or whatever.

The teens laughed outright at her tentative attempts, and when the car stalled in the middle of the farmyard, they only laughed the harder.

"You gotta shift with more authority," one boy offered knowledgeably from the backseat. "Act as if you know what you're doing."

"But I haven't a clue what I'm doing," she told them as the gears ground once more. "And it's obvious that I am no authority on this particular subject. Why don't they make just one gear?"

Jeremy chuckled in her left ear.

"Come on, Gillian," the two teens in the front seat chorused. "Try to remember. You can do it."

As Jeremy pressed the clutch down, Gillian tried once more to find second. Without notable success.

"Here," Jeremy murmured in her ear. "Like this." His hand covered hers, and the gearshift slid smoothly into place, and the car raced ahead. "It's not really that difficult."

Gillian shifted away from him a little, wishing suddenly that he'd purchased a bigger car. It was embarrassing to be squished up against him, but at least all the others were equally crowded.

"Sorry," he murmured, as his arm brushed against her once more. "I guess I should have told Pastor Dave that we would need his car to get back to town."

"Where did he go, anyway?" she asked curiously. "I didn't even see him leave."

Jeremy shook his head.

"Nor I, but Mr. Reid told me there's someone out here that he's been asked to visit. He was going on from the Reids and he wasn't sure how late he'd be." He helped her shift into a higher gear and then leaned back comfortably. "I told him that we'd agreed we could both handle the youth group from here on in."

"You mean you guys are gonna be the leaders?" Desiree asked from her perch in the backseat. "Cool."

"All right!" Two boys high-fived each other, grinning. "Say hello to the good times."

Gillian grimaced at Jeremy before twisting her head around.

"What are some of the things you'd like to do?" she asked the group as they huddled together over the front seats. And immediately wished she hadn't, as all sorts of totally ridiculous suggestions flowed from the excited teens.

"And for sure we could have a bridal shower for you, Gillian," one of the girls suggested. "It would be so much fun. Just think of the decorations, Emily. And my mom makes a really good punch. It's even red and we could make little heart ice cubes."

Gillian felt her heart sink to her shoes. This ridiculous, pretend engagement was beginning to get to her. And she certainly wasn't sitting in as the bride for the whole church to shower. Even Jeremy's mixed-up old aunt couldn't ask that much of her.

"I don't think there's any need to plan that far ahead," she heard Jeremy stammer, and she grinned at the nervousness in his voice. "Let's just take one youth group meeting at a time."

"I vote we have a cookie bake before Christmas," Gina chirped. "That way we could make up little trays of baking for the seniors in our church and the community who don't have anyone to make them home-baked treats."

Gillian jerked her head around and found Jeremy's face just inches from her own, his glittering blue-gray eyes staring into hers. His mouth was a heartbeat away from hers, and she could smell the chocolate on his breath as he sighed a deep, hearty sigh of resignation.

"Auntie Fay," he muttered, helping her shift into third.

Gillian nodded her head and left her hand where it was, nestled under his. She relaxed against the curve of the leather seat and allowed his body to support her.

"Absolutely," she whispered. "It's all her fault, anyway."

Their eyes finally broke apart when one of the teens began singing a familiar chorus. Thankfully everyone joined in, and no one noticed the surreptitious looks Gillian and Jeremy cast each other. Looks that Gillian would have liked to ponder a little longer, if she'd been alone.

Chapter Nine

It was growing late by the time they dropped the last passenger off at home. Gillian had long since claimed the passenger seat in the front, a move that did have some merit. For instance, the thick curving leather bucket was much more comfortable than her former position squished between Jeremy and the wriggling teens.

Of course, she did miss Jeremy's arm around her shoulder. But on the other hand, she was no longer so terribly tense—waiting and wondering if and when he would touch her.

"You know, it will soon be Christmas," she murmured, staring out at some of the houses people had begun to decorate. "It's my very favorite time of the year."

"It's not mine," Jeremy snorted. "All that consumerism and hype about giving. If people thought about that a little more during the year, we'd all be happier. And why is there so much emphasis on parties? Some people hate parties."

Gillian gritted her teeth and swallowed down the response that begged for release. He probably hadn't had many good memories of Christmas to resurrect from his childhood, she reminded herself.

"I'll bet you're one of those people who never do your shopping until the twenty-fourth," she joked. "And then you get all cranky and upset when everything is picked over." It was an intriguing thought and she dwelt on it for several long moments. Until his voice broke through her reverie.

"I don't shop at Christmas," he informed her coldly. "If I decide to give anyone a gift, I simply write out a cheque."

Gillian stared in disbelief. "Nothing?" she asked on a whisper.

"Not one single thing," he confirmed vehemently.

She was startled and rather dismayed, but not for anything would she let him see her feelings.

"This does not bode well for our future together," Gillian advised him finally, smiling rather sadly. "I absolutely insist on my fiancé giving me a gift rather than a cheque. Money is so impersonal."

There was silence for a few moments. Christmas carols played softly in the background on his CD. Gillian was lost in her own plans for Christmas until she heard his voice.

"What did Michael give you last year?" he inquired quietly. Gillian jerked her head around to stare at him, but could read nothing on that implacable face. "I'm sorry," he murmured. "If it will hurt you to speak about him, just forget it."

"No," she told him in amazement. "It doesn't hurt. Not really. Not anymore. And it's rather nice to remember the past sometimes." She turned to smile at him. "Michael gave me a gold locket. We had our pictures taken in one of those booths, and he cut them out and put them inside."

"Was it later that you were engaged?" His tone was mild and Gillian could find nothing that gave away his true feelings although she scrutinized him closely.

"Yes. Michael asked me to marry him on my birthday in March. We'd gone out for dinner, you see." The memories were flooding over her now, warming her with a love from the past.

"Michael had frozen my ring in an ice cube. After I said

yes, he proposed a toast." She chuckled. "I was complaining about there being something in my drink. He got really red and flustered when I asked him to call the waiter over for a fresh one."

Jeremy smiled. It was the kind of silly romantic gesture he would expect of someone Gillian Langford would get engaged to. And it was totally unlike anything he himself would ever do. If he wanted to get married, that is.

But his plans didn't call for marriage. Not yet. He had given himself three years at JFK Elementary. Three years to make good and move on. He had planned it for so long; a move to something bigger and better; more satisfying.

For as long as he could remember, Jeremy's focus had been straightforward and deliberate. He fully intended to become headmaster of a very prestigious boys' academy in England before he turned forty. That meant proving himself as an educator in the States, and JFK was merely a stepping stone along the way. He had no intention of becoming encumbered with a wife until he was thirty-five, and then she would be exactly the opposite of the woman seated next to him.

He grinned to himself as he thought how silly it would be to imagine that Gillian Langford would be content to stay home and be a mother. She was a dynamic, charismatic woman who thrived on other people and the challenge of her work. He'd seen that very clearly these past few weeks.

"Did you want children? You and Michael, I mean," he blurted out, trying to picture her with her own towheaded little ones.

Her glistening autumn-colored head whirled around; green eyes wide with shock. "Uh, pardon?"

Jeremy wished that he had somehow rephrased that, but it was too late to worry about it now. Besides, he really wanted to know. To see if his idea fit the picture.

"I just wondered if you had planned on children," he repeated, more softly now.

"We never really talked about it," Gillian told him seriously. She was still peering at him through the gloom of the car interior. "I suppose I'd always thought in terms of a boy and a girl, but probably not right away. We were both just getting settled in our careers, and Michael's law practice was building up nicely."

Silence reigned for a few taut moments. Jeremy could see her fiddling with the end of her scarf. Suddenly her head tilted up, her green eyes meeting his with a question.

"Why did you ask that?" she murmured.

Jeremy couldn't help it; he flushed to the roots of his hair. It was an innocent enough question. After all, he'd been probing the depths of her former relationship, why shouldn't she question him?

"Would you like to have children?" Jeremy heard the hesitancy in her soft voice as she posed the question.

"Six," he stated clearly. "Not too far apart. And I don't care if they're boys or girls." He waited for her reaction.

"Why six?" she asked quizzically. "Is there something magic about that number?"

"So they won't be alone," he muttered, wishing he'd never brought the subject of children up. He lifted his chin. "I'd like to have a houseful of family. And a wife that stayed home with them," he told her sharply. "I don't much care for day cares and babysitters."

"Well," Gillian sputtered. "With six children, it probably wouldn't pay for her to go out to work anyhow." She sat quietly for a few moments, obviously considering his words. "I don't think you'd like that at all," she said finally. "It's a pipe dream that you've carried because you were an only child."

"On the contrary, Gillian," he told her, angrily gripping the steering wheel in frustration, "I've thought about it long and hard, and I can assure you that is exactly what I want. At thirty-five, I'll be fairly well set in my career and ready to take on a wife."

"You mean you've even got the year picked out when you'll get married?" She sounded stunned.

"A person owes it to himself and his future family to have these things organized and planned for a satisfying future." He heard the defensiveness in his own hardening voice.

"But think for a moment, will you?" Gillian protested. "Just think about this rosy, idyllic picture for a good long moment. Six children—running around, leaving their toys everywhere, arguing. Laundry, clothes, bicycles on the driveway, activities to chauffeur them to."

"I've considered all that," he told her coldly, wishing she would just stop talking. But Miss Gillian Langford was shaking her head in dismay.

"I don't think you've thought about it at all. Not realistically, anyway," she stated clearly. "You're a neatness freak. You like everything organized right down to a T. You want everyone to follow your specific set of rules and do things your way."

"And?" He deliberately fixed her with his coldest look. It didn't faze her in the least, of course. She just kept right on jabbing at him with his words, destroying his dream.

"Look, Jeremy. Kids need more than other kids around to play with. They need to feel loved and cared for and free to be kids." She shook her head. "Think about the kids at school for a moment. Some organization is good, and it's necessary when you are dealing with that many children. But sometimes they need to just sit alone and dream…to spread out their toys and build that space station of the future."

"Discipline is the key," he reiterated acidly. "If they know the rules and learn to follow them, their lives will be much happier."

Gillian shook her head at him again, more vehemently this time. "Don't you see?" she argued. "There is more to it than that. In the Old Testament, there was a strict and stringent code of rules that took a whole sect of the population just to study them! Nobody could keep them all, there were so many. But God changed that. He made the regulations dealing with the body less important and the state of the heart far more significant."

She reached across the car and placed her hand on his arm. Jeremy felt the tingle of awareness at her touch ripple all the way up his arm.

"Don't you see?" she burst out, impassioned. "What all of us need are not more rules. We need love—unconditional acceptance that tells us that no matter what we do, someone will always love us. Just because they do, and not because we did or didn't keep ninety-five percent of the rules this week."

"You're always denigrating responsibility and the role of personal accountability for one's actions," he countered. "But that is exactly what is wrong with society today. No one is responsible for anything. If the rules are too difficult, change them or throw them out."

He might have known she wouldn't give up, Jeremy thought in frustration. She never could let his opinion go without challenging it.

"Not at all," Gillian protested grimly. "I'm merely saying that there is more to raising children than a whole ream of rules they have to follow. What you are proposing sounds more like a military academy than a caring, loving home."

"And what you're proposing is a laissez-faire approach that has everyone running around wildly amok, here and there, doing his own thing. If you think about it rationally for a moment, you'll realize that—"

She interrupted him. Again!

"You always claim rationality when someone doesn't agree

with you," Gillian charged angrily. "I am quite rational, thank you very much. And I'm also human enough to know that all people, but especially children, need love to nurture them through the hard knocks of life." Her emerald eyes glared at him, flashes of light from the dashboard reflecting in pinpoint stabs. "Haven't you ever done something just for the sheer pleasure of it?"

"Actually, I—"

She cut him off again. "Yes, you have," she grinned, eyes sparkling now as her hands flew through the air emphasizing her point. "Tonight. On the snowmobile. You let go and really had fun. You raced that machine around Mr. Reid's yard like a kid with a new toy." She studied his burning cheeks, wondering at his reaction.

"You're thinking of buying one, aren't you?" she crowed.

"Well, what if I am?" Jeremy sputtered, angry at her easy perception of him. He'd made it a practice over the years to hide his emotions. How did this woman manage to read him so easily? "There's nothing wrong with me owning a snowmobile, is there?" he challenged belligerently. "I am an adult—solvent, and in my right mind."

"I'm not so sure about that last part," she said, laughing out loud at his dark look. "You did fall tonight. Maybe you hit your head."

"Now, just one minute," Jeremy began. That was as far as he got.

"I just want to know one thing," Gillian asked pointedly.

"What?"

They were parked in front of her aunt's house, and Jeremy could afford the time it took to study her jubilant face. It did not reassure him. He leaned back in his seat and gathered his composure about him like a cloak. "Well?"

"When you were dashing around on that machine at the

Reids'," she began, unable to hide her pleasure at his discomfort.

"I was not dashing," Jeremy protested. To no avail.

"When you were *dashing around*," she repeated, grinning from ear to ear like a teasing Cheshire cat. "Did you think about the noise you were making? Noise that most likely bothered the neighbors or the Reids' cattle?"

The woman was watching him closely, and Jeremy strove to keep his face devoid of emotion, even though his mind was reeling with the possible consequences of his hasty actions.

"Did you pause to consider the damage you might be doing to that crop of winter wheat that had sprouted under the snow?" Gillian had the nerve to laugh at his aghast look. "And, last of all, did you happen to think about the rest of us, standing around in the cold, waiting for you to finish your joyride?"

"I, um, I didn't realize..." Jeremy didn't quite know what to say. It was ridiculous to think that a man in his position had behaved so childishly, without forethought for his actions.

"The answer is no." Gillian snorted in amusement. "And that was because you just let go, for once in your life, and enjoyed the moment." She licked her finger and stroked a number one in the air gleefully.

"I was just—"

"Being a kid," she cheered. "I know. Wasn't it great to let go of all the old *shoulds* and *should nots* and just have some fun?"

Jeremy felt her fingers thread through his and squeeze gently as if she were trying to reassure him that such exploits were perfectly natural.

"That's why kids are kids and parents are adults," she told him, frowning slightly. "The kid has to have the freedom to try new things, yes. And the parent has to set up the boundaries, reasonable boundaries, to make sure that no one gets hurt. But no one has the right to take away the freedom of childhood."

Jeremy eyed her dubiously. Some of what she said made sense, there was no doubt. But there was still the matter of responsibility; he had no intention of abandoning his opinion on that!

He was about to remind her of it when Hope's front door flew open and the older woman scurried down the walk toward his car. She had no coat covering her thin shoulders. Instead she trailed it along behind, yanking on a soft knitted hat as she moved. Her face was pinched and white. Jeremy pressed the button to unroll Gillian's window and called out a greeting.

"Is anything the matter, Miss Langford?"

"You have to go to Faith's immediately," Hope gasped, sliding adroitly into the seat behind Gillian's. "Arthur just phoned. She's fallen. Off the roof."

"The roof," Jeremy gasped, slamming into first. "What in the world was she doing on the roof?"

"I don't know," Hope whispered miserably. "Arthur just said he had found her lying in the snow."

"Oh, my God!" It was a prayer that Gillian silently endorsed as he drove the short distance to his aunt's home. They found Arthur kneeling on the front lawn, cradling Faith's head in his lap.

"She's alive," he called out to them excitedly.

"Of course I'm alive, you silly man," Faith said, rising awkwardly to her feet. She was a bit shaky, but her hand was firmly enmeshed in Arthur's, and her smile of adoration was for him alone.

"Auntie Fay, what in the world were you doing on the roof?" Jeremy demanded, searching the tired, faded eyes. "You might have been killed!"

"Oh, piffle," the older woman protested, walking slowly across the lawn and up the steps to her front door. "I won't be going for a long time yet, Jeremy. The Lord has too much for me to do." She pushed open the door after brushing Arthur's cheek with her cold lips. "Come along in, my dears," she said merrily. "It's so nice to have company. I'll make tea."

"No, Auntie, you won't." Jeremy angrily brushed Arthur's hand off his aunt's shoulder and ushered her into the nearest easy chair. "I want you to sit down there until I check you over. You've had a nasty fall and you should rest." His hands moved carefully over her arms and legs, and finding no damage, he got to his feet and stood glaring down at her.

"I'll make her a hot drink," Hope murmured, scurrying from the room.

From the corner of his eyes, he could see Gillian sink down onto the sofa. He knew the feeling; he felt like his rubbery legs wouldn't hold him for much longer, either. His frown deepened as Arthur seated himself near Faith and enfolded her hand in his, despite Jeremy's scathing glance.

"I still want to know what in the world you were doing on the roof," her nephew demanded from his position across the room. It was the only seat left, and he had to take it. Fear and shock still raced through him at the thought of his beloved aunt lying helpless in the snow while he'd been out. Joyriding like a pubescent teenager!

"Putting up the Christmas lights, of course, dear," she told him placidly. "I do it every year. Blue ones, thousands of them. Of course, I don't actually put them up."

Jeremy sighed in relief at that news and immediately sucked in his breath in dismay when she continued.

"Actually I just take out the burned-out bulbs and put in new ones." She smiled happily at him. "Next week I'll put up the manger scene. You remember that. Your uncle made it years ago. It was the Christmas you came to visit us."

Immediately he was lost in the memory of that long-ago time when he'd flown across the Atlantic by himself so that he could spend Christmas with his own family. He'd been ten, he recalled, and they'd made him feel like he was their son. Uncle Donald had already started the crèche. By the time Jeremy arrived, there was only the rough-hewn manger to build and the donkeys to paint. He'd done it lovingly, with great care, because it mattered to Auntie Fay.

"Here you go, dear. Drink this up now and you'll feel better soon." Hope handed mugs to everyone.

"What is it?" Faith demanded, peering into the cup. "I won't drink some silly herbal remedy, you know."

"It's peppermint tea," Hope told her, a smile playing around her thin lips. "Yours, not mine."

"Oh, good. I love peppermint tea." Faith sipped daintily from the steaming cup, her eyes cloudy with some far-off dream.

"Does your head hurt?" Hope asked softly, searching the older woman's face for some sign of injury.

"Of course not," Faith giggled. "I landed in the snowbank, silly. Just had the wind knocked out of me. It was actually rather fun. For a few moments I was flying, just like the birds."

"Do you finally see why she has to go into a home?" Jeremy hissed from his position behind Gillian. He felt all the old anger and frustration at the situation rise up inside. Why did it have to be his aunt who was senile? Dear old Auntie Fay who wouldn't hurt a flea?

"No, I don't!" Gillian scowled back at him. "She's perfectly fine. Arthur was here and he looked after her. Nothing has changed."

"Everything has changed! She could have been killed." His face whitened at the thought of life without Auntie Fay.

"You could have been killed when you took that trail too

fast tonight," Gillian flung at him. Her eyes were like chips
of jade. "You weren't. Neither was she. Relax." Her finger
poked him painfully in the chest. "And *you* do those bulbs
next time."

He couldn't believe she would compare the two. One had
no bearing on the other. "But don't you see, if she had been
properly supervised, Auntie Fay would never have even gone
up the ladder, let alone fallen."

Gillian rolled her eyes. "And if you hadn't gone snowmobiling, you wouldn't have tipped into the snow. Life is full of
risks. Would you rather have not taken the risk, and missed
the enjoyment of the ride?"

Jeremy felt all the old familiar frustrations he had always
experienced with this woman rise up and clutch him around
the neck. The thought of Auntie Fay lying there in the snow,
dead or dying, sent his heart into his mouth.

"I have to keep her safe," he said huskily. "I can't let something like this happen again. She can't die. Not now."

"She'll die in a nursing home," Gillian whispered fiercely.
"Even if you keep her body preserved and intact, her soul
will wither up and die if she's forbidden the enjoyment she
finds in life. It would be like a prison. How can you do that
to her?"

"How can I not?" he retorted angrily.

A burst of merry laughter across the room drew their
gazes to the happy group seated in front of the fireplace.
The flames crackled merrily, their warmth filling the room,
Jeremy noticed. He wondered if that would be the next thing
he'd have to deal with: a house fire. Firm resolve strength-
ened his backbone as he made a mental note to call the gas
company and have the thing disconnected.

"What are you two whispering about?" Faith asked, her
face wreathed in a happy smile.

Jeremy would have answered her then; would have laid

it all out plain and clear right there in front of everyone. But as usual, Gillian interrupted him.

"We were just discussing the trip into the city tomorrow," she said quietly. "I think I'd better get home so I can get some sleep to prepare for twelve hours with a bunch of preteen girls. Good night, Faith. Have pleasant dreams."

"I always do dear," Faith said back, her gentle face glowing with joy. "And I'll be over bright and early tomorrow morning to accompany you. I'm looking forward to it." She rubbed her hands together with glee.

"Oh, but *you* can't go, Auntie Fay. Not after that fall. Why you'll overtax yourself and…"

"We're both going," Arthur informed him with a scowl. Jeremy was frustrated at being interrupted again. "We have to take those lads skiing, remember." He winked at Jeremy. "Besides, Faith says she feels fine." Arthur smiled at Hope and Gillian. "We'll both see you tomorrow morning."

"Yes, I'll pop on home now, too," Hope murmured, picking up her coat.

Good manners dictated that Jeremy leave then, also, since he had been the one to drive Hope and Gillian over. On the ride back, no one said a word. But the air was tense with things left unsaid, and Jeremy knew from the down-turned line of her lips that he hadn't heard the last of any of it from Gillian.

That was okay. He had a few last things to say on the subject himself. And he would have launched into it when Hope left them alone a few minutes later except that Gillian's usually brilliant vivacity was suddenly dimmed, and she moved sluggishly to take off her coat; her beautiful face drawn and weary.

Somehow, when she looked at him with those expressive eyes, her vibrant curls cascading around her shoulders, the words wouldn't come. And they still didn't when Gillian leaned toward him tiredly.

"Could you just hold me for a moment, Jeremy?" she murmured, wrapping her arms around his waist as she leaned her head on his shoulder. "I need a hug very badly just now."

"What's the problem?" he asked quietly, unsure of how to deal with this new situation.

"It's just that when I saw her lying there in the snow, for a minute, just one minute, it reminded me of Michael and I didn't know how I was going to deal with death again. It hurts, Jeremy. It hurts."

"I know," he murmured, brushing his hand over her bright hair. "It always hurts to lose someone special. That's why I want to take care of Auntie Fay."

But even as he said the words, he knew how ridiculous they were. Everyone died sometime. Faith wouldn't live forever any more than he would. They would all breathe their last and move on to meet their Maker. So why not enjoy some of what life offered right now?

And so he stood there, his arms around Gillian's slim figure, his chin resting on her silky hair, and held on to his pretend fiancée. And as he breathed in the light floral sweetness of her perfume, he wondered if he wasn't missing something in his categorization of the vivacious Miss Langford—some tiny missing piece that was essential to knowing the real woman under all that effervescent exterior. Something that had to do with the little girl hiding inside; the one who needed a hug from him when she remembered the bad things in life.

Chapter Ten

"'It came upon a midnight clear.'"

The voices rang out through the narrow confines of the bus as thirty voices joined in yet another Christmas carol. Gillian grinned with relief. So far their little group of pre-teens from the Sunday school had been as well behaved as any of the kids in the youth group they'd supervised.

The girls were thrilled that they were going to go shopping on their own, and the boys had good-naturedly decreed that they *might* consider taking the female of the species skiing next time.

If there was a next time, Gillian thought, a whisper of sadness hanging in her mind as she remembered Jeremy's decree of the night before.

She glanced toward the front of the bus where Faith sat beside a bedraggled-looking little girl. They were busy talking a mile a minute, and Gillian could only imagine what about. She had half an idea that the only way little Suzy Briggs had been able to come was because Faith had found her odd jobs to do around her house for the past two weeks. Gillian knew that Suzy intended to spend every dime she'd earned on gifts for her large and needy family.

Privately Gillian thought it would be nice for the girl to

spend a little on herself. Her fair hair badly needed a professional cut; it hung in shinglelike layers on her small head, straight as a stick and most unbecoming. The other girls all wore jeans and sweaters under their ski jackets but Suzy had on an old pair of baggy black trousers that were far too big for her and a short-sleeved wrinkled blouse in the ugliest shade of pea green imaginable.

"I think we'd better discuss the rules now," Jeremy murmured in her ear. "We're about five miles from the mall."

Gillian nodded and cleared her throat. She refused to look at him, afraid he'd see the condemnation in her eyes. It hurt to look at Faith and know what he had planned for her.

Memories of the night before and Jeremy's arms around her drifted across her mind. It felt so right; so good. And yet it wasn't. She could never condone his plans for his aunt. And even though she had succumbed to need last night, and leaned against Jeremy, drawing his strength into herself, Gillian had no intention of doing that again.

Why ask for more heartache? she told herself. Jeremy's ideas for the future and her own were so far apart, nothing could close the chasm.

She loved him; she knew that now. It was a love that had grown up in spite of her desire to mourn Michael. She had intended to avoid love, and instead it had sneaked up behind and conked her on the head.

But it was a futile love. They were worlds apart. She wanted children, all right, Gillian assured herself. But she wanted them to be healthy, happy individuals, not little robots that performed all the correct responses but took no joy in life.

And she wanted to live her future, not spend it being afraid of the next cataclysmic event. Most of all, she wanted a husband who would love her for herself. Jeremy wasn't the man for that. He had this preconceived stereotypical idea that she was some bubble-headed creature who couldn't be trusted to distinguish left from right.

"Gillian?" She turned to find his blue-gray eyes peering down at her. "We're almost there," he reminded.

"Yes, I know. Girls," she called out abruptly and waited for their heads to turn toward her. "We'll be arriving shortly. I just wanted to go over a few of the rules of this expedition. Number one—everyone stays in the mall. Nobody leaves without my consent. Number two—we all meet for lunch in the food court at noon. Number three—we all stick together in groups of two or three. I don't want anyone wandering off to do their own thing. Clear?"

When they all hollered their agreement, it struck Gillian as funny. Here she was, the person who had been trying to get Jeremy to ease up on his multitude of rules and now she was here, doing exactly the same thing. Evidently he noticed it, too.

"You see," he said with a grin, brushing a long strand of hair out of her eyes. "Rules are good."

"*Some* rules," she asserted. "Others are just excuses to impose your will on someone else. Come on, ladies," she called, grabbing her purse and leading the way. "On Dancer, on Prancer."

"We'll meet you back at this door with the bus at five," Jeremy called over the hubbub of noise as the girls jostled for position while Suzy helped Faith down the stairs. "Have fun."

"We will," they chimed in boisterous unison.

And they did.

It was a whirlwind of activity inside the mall and the girls quickly disappeared into the throng of shoppers, pairing off in groups of two and three. Faith was tugging at Suzy's arm.

"Come on, girl," she scolded, "we've got to get a move on if we're going to use that free coupon I have for Alfred's."

Gillian scurried along behind them, curious to see what was at Alfred's. It turned out to be a hair salon. And, wonder of wonders, they had an opening immediately for Suzy to use Faith's coupon.

"You go ahead, honey. Let them do their job. You'll be surprised at the difference it makes. I'm going to have a cup of coffee while I wait." Faith spent a few moments consulting with Alfred. "He says an hour. I'll be back then. All right?"

Poor Suzy nodded in a dazed fashion as the stylist with bleached white hair tinted purple on the ends escorted her back to the sink. She seemed fascinated by the curious assortment of colors on the back of his head and barely nodded when Gillian told her she'd stay with Faith.

"Nothing weird, Alfred, remember?" Faith's voice rang through the salon causing several heads to turn. But Alfred was unabashed. He grinned from multiringed ear to ear and tripped forward in his strange high-heeled shoes to pat Jeremy's aunt on the shoulder.

"You know me, Faith," he said in a normal tone that was totally unlike the high squeaky voice he'd used earlier. "You can count on me." He stepped back when Faith tried to slip a bill into his pocket.

"No way, Faith. I got my Christmas gift when you helped finance this place last year. The little girl's cut is on the house."

"Thank you, dear," Faith murmured, kissing his cheek. "You always were the sweetest child in my Sunday school class."

Alfred looked decidedly pained at that, Gillian thought, amused. But he bore it in good form, waving goodbye with his black-nailed pinkie.

"Now, Gillian, dear," Faith murmured as they walked away from the salon. The older woman slipped her arm into hers and beamed. "I have a couple of stops to make before we have that coffee."

In fact, they made ten stops in all. Gillian watched as Faith purchased a pair of jeans similar to what the girls on the bus had worn. They were in a size far too small to be Faith's, although the sweater that went along with them was in her favorite pale pink.

Then there were the toy stores, where they loaded up on a remote-controlled car, a video game, a road race set and two rather heavy construction machines. The ladies' store sold her an ivory sweater that was far too large for Faith and the jewelery store had a wonderful pair of earrings and matching necklace that Faith declared "just perfect." There were also several books, two nut trays, a pair of slippers and a man's sweater in a brilliant peacock blue.

"That's for Jeremy," Faith confided, grinning. "He wears so many dark colors, I think he might enjoy a change."

"Yes, I'm sure he would," Gillian agreed dubiously, glancing warily at the bright yellow slash across the sweater's front panel. She wondered if she had imagined the sparkle of delight in Faith's eyes when she paid for it.

"You know these are going to be too heavy to lug around all afternoon," Gillian said, hoisting the metal vehicles a little higher in her arms.

"Oh, my dear, how thoughtless of me. I've let you carry everything! We need a locker. Now let me think." Faith glanced around several times as if getting her bearings. "Over here, I believe. Ah, I was right." She grinned, delighted with her good memory.

Once the articles were safely stored, they hurried back to the salon to find a beautiful young woman waiting for them. Suzy's pale hair had been expertly trimmed close to the head in the back and sides. A straight fall the color of spun gold lay just above her ears.

"Oh, Suzy," Gillian breathed excitedly. "You look beautiful. Why, your eyes are just gorgeous!"

"Of course they are," Faith agreed. "Those great big baby browns were just hiding, waiting to be discovered." She scurried over to Alfred who was busily snipping another patron's hair. Gillian didn't hear what Faith said, but whatever it was, Alfred let out a shout of laughter and hugged the older woman tightly.

"Have a wonderful Christmas," he called out as they left. His voice was back to its strange pitch, she noticed absently.

"*Now* I need coffee," Faith declared.

Gillian heartily agreed and they treated Suzy to a milk shake. It was then that she noticed Suzy's beautifully manicured nails. Gone were the torn and dirty ends. They were perfectly filed and buffed to a gleaming natural shine. And the girl had just the tiniest bit of pale pink lipstick on, too.

Gillian shook her head in amazement. Dear sweet Faith, plain and ordinary as she was, had seen the hidden beauty in this girl as no one else had. It was obvious in the way Suzy now walked and talked, that her self-esteem had been greatly enhanced.

"Now, dear," Faith began, laying her hand on Gillian's arm. "Suzy and I have several things to do. And they're secret. We don't want anyone to know. So you just go ahead and do your own shopping. We'll meet you back here with the others for lunch."

Secretly relieved, Gillian argued only a little and finally left them in front of a shoe store contemplating runners for Suzy's brother. She'd been hoping to do some shopping herself and it looked like this was her opportunity.

Gillian swept through the mall quickly, choosing a gift for each member on her list with care. She was scurrying back to meet the others when she saw it.

A snowmobile helmet.

It was black with red flames on the side and the words "So Race Me" applied across the back. The visor was electrically heated, she was told, to prevent cloudy vision.

Gillian instantly decided that she would never find anything more suitable and purchased it without a second thought. Even if Jeremy never wore it, and she really hoped he would, he would be reminded of the one time in his adult life that he had let loose and just had fun. Her purchase meant a quick trip back to the locker area, and so she was late meeting the girls.

A quick look around the food court set her nerves jangling. No Faith. She counted the girls and noted with relief that they were all present. Where had the woman gone?

"Suzy," she asked, standing behind her. The girls stopped talking as they noticed the concern in her voice. "Where is Faith?"

"She said she wanted to get some of those specialty coffee beans," Suzy told her, glancing around. "She was right over… I don't see her, Gillian!"

Gillian felt the apprehension and disquiet that had plagued her all morning build to new heights as she surveyed the milling crowd.

"Please, Lord," she begged silently.

"There she is," Suzy called out with a gasp of relief. "Over there."

As she spotted her friend, Gillian felt some of the tension in her shoulders and neck ebb away. She looked toward Faith, assessing her from Jeremy's viewpoint and wondered how the other woman was doing. What she saw made her smile with delight. The tousled-headed senior was eyeing the Mexican stall next door with a decidedly greedy look.

"I'm starved," Jeremy's aunt announced cheerily.

Her words proved to be the perfect tension breaker. As they all laughed appreciatively, Gillian stuffed the nagging worry to the back of her mind. Of course it had been a good idea to invite Faith. The girls loved her, and she made no pretence about the obvious affection she felt for each of them. She sat munching on Mexi fries and admiring each girl's taste and choice.

"Well, girls," Gillian interrupted finally, glancing at her watch. "I think we'd better get back at it. There are only four and a half hours until the mall closes!"

Amidst the burst of laughter, Suzy moved to Gillian's side.

"I'll keep my eye on her this afternoon," she offered softly, her pretty mouth spread wide in a smile.

"Oh, Suzy, that's very sweet of you to offer," Gillian murmured, patting the girl's hand. "But you don't have to. You go off with the other girls and have a good time."

"I know I don't have to," Suzy answered. "I want to. And Mrs. Rempel has the best time of anyone I know."

"She does, doesn't she?" Gillian agreed, nodding. "How about this then—you get to shop with Faith until three. We'll all meet back here for a break, and then it will be my turn. Share and share alike, you know."

The rest of the girls agreed to return at three, and Gillian went off to do another round of shopping, this time for her parents. Her father was easy. Anything pertinent to golfing suited him just fine. But her mother was another story altogether, and Gillian was deep in a study of delicate crystal cherubs when she glanced at her watch and noticed the time.

Three-ten!

She was late and at the far end of the mall. With as much haste as possible she rushed through the crowd of shoppers, bumping and excusing as she went. The food court was jammed with other people taking a break, and she couldn't spot the girls anywhere. Fear rose, clutching at her throat as she scanned the tables in a systematic pattern, praying for help.

How could you take a bunch of girls and an old woman into this crowded mall and then let them go off while you calmly spent your time shopping, a little voice inside her head nagged. *You're supposed to be the one in charge; well, then, take charge! Find those girls!*

"Miss Langford?" Gillian wheeled around, puffing out a sigh of relief as she saw three of her group standing near.

"Where are you seated?" she asked breathlessly. "I couldn't spot you guys in this crowd."

"Uh, well, the thing is, Miss Langford." The tallest one shuffled and looked down at her shoes. Gillian felt her nerves tauten as she saw the dismal looks on their faces.

"What's the matter?" she demanded. Something inside her wound even tighter as she saw how white their faces were. "Where are the others?"

Only by extreme control could Gillian keep herself from shrieking at them. She searched the masses once more but there was no one she knew standing by.

"Mrs. Rempel is lost. Suzy's looking for her. She took the others to help."

Waves of foreboding washed over Gillian as she struggled to remain calm.

"But how could she be lost? Suzy was going to stay with her, she said."

Stop condemning the girl, she commanded herself. *Suzy wasn't in charge, you were.*

"Suzy said Mrs. Rempel wanted to rest for a moment. Suzy left her on a bench outside a music store. You know, those areas where husbands can sit and wait for their wives." Jessica waited for Gillian's nod of understanding. "Well, Suzy got held up at the cash register, and when she came out Mrs. Rempel was gone. We've been looking for her for fifteen minutes. If anyone finds her, they'll take her back to the food court and wait for the others. Is that okay?"

The young girl's uncertainty in the face of this disaster touched Gillian and she patted the narrow shoulder gently.

"Not just 'okay,' Jessica. Very well done. You girls have been a wonderful help. I know you all care about Mrs. Rempel, so let's concentrate on finding her, all right?"

They all nodded enthusiastically and paired off to search anew. Gillian strode through the mall, frantically winding up one aisle and down the other. She'd left one of the girls in the meeting place, and the security people had made an announcement, but a half hour later Faith had not shown up.

When the girls returned at four, tired and worried, and still without Faith, Gillian knew she would have to call Jeremy. The police would have to be alerted, and they would need to make another search before the mall closed.

"We need to pray, Miss Langford. Mrs. Rempel said she always prays when she's mixed-up or confused."

Gillian smiled. "You're absolutely right, Suzy, and I should have done that already. Let's pray now."

She shepherded the girls into a little circle, and they all bowed their heads.

"Please, Lord," Gillian murmured. "We're in trouble here and we don't know what to do. But we know that You know where Faith is and that You are there protecting her. Help us to believe and show us the right way. For we ask in Your name. Amen." When she glanced up she saw many of the girls wiping tears from their eyes.

"Okay, ladies. This is what we're going to do." She outlined her idea of starting at one end and proceeding through to the other. "Two of you will stand guard at the elevators and escalators. The rest of you go through quickly but thoroughly. Ask the salespeople for help."

"What are *you* going to do?" one of them asked her softly.

Gillian tried not to look as worried as she felt.

"I'm going to call her nephew and Mr. Johnson at the ski hill."

There was a low whistle.

"He's going to be furious. And Mr. Nivens gets really hot when he's angry." It was the understatement of the year, but Gillian refused to dwell on it.

"Can't be helped," she muttered, slinging her jacket over one arm. "We have to find Faith. That's the most important thing right now. Ready, girls?" They nodded and raced off to do her bidding.

It took forever to get the attendant to agree to call Jeremy to the phone. And eons passed before his low deep voice rumbled across the line.

"Gillian?"

"How did you know it was me?" she asked surprised.

"I just knew. Something's wrong, isn't it?" He sounded wary and just a little unsure.

Gillian took a deep breath, breathed a prayer and blurted it all out.

"It's Faith. We can't find her."

"What do you mean you can't find her? Surely you didn't let her go wandering around alone in her condition. Of all the harebrained, stupid…"

"You can holler at me later," she said, cutting him off. "Right now we need help. The girls and I have been searching for almost an hour and we can't find her anywhere. She was sitting on a bench, resting. And then she was gone."

"What? Grown women don't just vanish."

He sounded ready to lecture her again, and Gillian brushed a tear from her eye as distressing images of Faith in trouble ran through her mind.

Please, God, don't let her be in trouble.

"I don't have time for this," she told him briskly. "I need to help the girls look. Are you coming or not?"

"Of course I'm coming."

She breathed a sigh of relief and explained their arrangements if someone found the older woman.

"If you check the food court first, you'll know whether or not she's been found."

"Fine. I'll see you shortly." He sounded as worried as she was, and Gillian could only empathize with his anxiety. She knew how much he loved his aunt.

"Jeremy?"

"Yes?" His voice was brusque, and Gillian shivered, thinking of the terrible things that could happen to a woman on the street, alone.

"Please hurry," she whispered softly, clenching her hand into a fist. "I'm so scared." Tears flowed down her cheeks as she pictured dear, lovable Faith alone in the city.

"I'm coming. I'll find her," he assured her grimly. "Just hold on."

He arrived twenty minutes later, disheveled and gray with worry. Gillian rushed up to him and, oblivious to Arthur Johnson or the boys clustered round, wrapped her arms around Jeremy and hung on, needing the solid assurance of his strength. Although the girls had been back and forth several times, no one had found the elderly woman.

"It's all right," he muttered, brushing his hand over her hair awkwardly. "She's fine. I'm sure she just wandered off somewhere to relax for a few minutes. Or got involved in looking at something. We'll find her." His thumb brushed the tears from her cheeks, and then he gently set her away from him. "Now, tell me what you've already done."

Swallowing her sobs of worry and frustration, Gillian explained the systematic search of the mall that the girls had conducted.

"They're going from one end to the other again now," she told him. "So far nothing."

He thought for a moment and then beckoned the boys nearer. For once Gillian was glad of his rational, organized mind as he brought calm to the situation.

"Okay guys, here's the plan. We're going to start at the opposite end from the girls. Anybody finds my aunt, they bring her right back here. Okay?" They nodded. "Good. Away you go. Check in every fifteen minutes." He glanced at Gillian. "Is the mall Security in on this?"

"Yes, I alerted them a while ago. They've got several men looking for her with the girls. So far nothing."

Arthur stepped forward.

"I'm going to do some looking for Faith on my own," he told them. "I'll talk to some of the people here—see if anyone noticed her." He patted Gillian's arm. "Don't worry, girl. She's fine. God is watching over her. She's just forgotten the time."

With a smile and a wave he walked off toward an elderly man who sat snoring nearby.

"Miss Langford?" Gillian turned to find the security guard she'd contacted earlier striding toward her. "Any news?"

"No. No one's seen her. This is Mrs. Rempel's nephew, Jeremy Nivens. Jeremy, this is Peter Brown, the head of Security."

"Mr. Nivens, I'm glad to see you here. Miss Langford has been trying to do it all. She could use a little help." He turned to Gillian. "I've checked with Metro. Those hoodlums you reported seeing earlier today are in custody, so they aren't involved in this. That's a good sign. I have to admit I was worried about kidnapping for a while there."

"Kidnapping," Jeremy bellowed. "Why would someone want to kidnap my aunt?"

Mr. Brown explained briefly about the latest group of troublemakers who had recently been haunting the mall.

"Needless to say, we're happy that Miss Langford and her charges had no contact with the men."

"But she might have run into them later," Jeremy exploded, staring at Gillian in dismay. "I can't believe you would let her go off *shopping* under such circumstances. She was probably nervous and confused and needed watching." He glared at her accusingly.

Gillian felt the heat of her own anger rise up. She'd known he would find a way to blame her. Good grief, she blamed herself.

"Faith wasn't nervous or confused," she said, rebutting his erroneous conclusions. "She said she was hungry. We sat down together and ate lunch."

"Ah. So then you just let her wander off by herself. Good thinking."

"No, we did not *let* her wander off by herself. Although she is a grown woman and fully capable of deciding that for herself." Gillian bristled at the sarcasm in his voice.

"Auntie Fay wouldn't even be making these choices if she was in a nursing home. Someone *competent* would be caring for her."

The blue in Jeremy's eyes had frozen into a hard glittering glacier of reproach and Gillian wondered how she had ever thought she could rely on him when he had just made such an abrupt about-face. He didn't care about her, not really. She was just a convenience; there to blame everything on when he needed a scapegoat.

"I am competent," Gillian said between clenched teeth. "We were taking turns shopping with her. Suzy said Faith wanted to sit down for a moment. She agreed to wait there while Suzy paid for their purchases. When she returned, Faith was gone."

"My aunt should never have been left alone." Jeremy's low voice was full of scorn. "Someone with a more serious outlook on life would have recognized the precariousness of her situation."

Gillian whooshed out her anger on a sigh of frustration as she glared at the tall grim-faced man.

"Someone like you, you mean? Someone who wants to keep that wonderful woman jailed in a cell for old people. Someone who won't let her enjoy anything in her life without a watchdog there to make sure she won't take too much pleasure, have too much fun."

"If this is your idea of fun, Gillian, I'm afraid I have to agree. I would never have subjected my aunt to these crowds and confusion. Once again, your irresponsibility has landed someone else in trouble." His face was cold and hard with disdain as he frowned down at her.

Gillian felt all the pleasure and wonder she had known in his arms, the joy when his lips melted on hers, suddenly drain away. She should have known, she told herself. She should have known it couldn't last. He had an image of her that could not, no, would not be swayed. It really didn't matter what happened between them now. Jeremy had just proven his total distrust of her whole theory on enjoying life. And it hurt. A lot.

"We'd better get looking," she told him softly. "There's no point in standing here arguing anymore. You just can't, or won't, accept that your aunt is a thinking, feeling human being, who is fully capable of making her own choices in life."

"Someone made a choice here," he expostulated. His mouth curved bitterly. "The wrong one."

"You can't keep her fenced in, Jeremy." Gillian tried one last time to force him to see. "You'll only hurt her if you try." With that she walked away, joining three of the girls who were starting the search once more.

For over an hour they combed through the throngs of

people, moving here and there when they thought they spotted Faith, only to turn away disappointed when an unfamiliar face peered back. Several times Gillian sent one of the girls to check the food area, but there was no good news.

"Let's just check outside, along the parking area. Perhaps someone has seen her or knows where she might have gone." They had only gone a few steps toward the exit doors when Glenda pointed.

"Look," she gasped excitedly. "Mr. Johnson's found her."

And sure enough, there was Faith, beaming happily, her arm curved into Arthur's as they strolled across the mall.

"Don't ply her with a bunch of questions just yet, girls," Gillian advised them quietly. "She might be a little confused. And we'll want to get her to Jeremy right away."

"Hi, Faith. All done your shopping now?" Suzy's voice bordered on tremulous when Faith greeted the other members of the search party now seated at an empty table.

"My dear, I simply gave up. I decided to get a breath of fresh air. That's when I heard the church bells." She had a vague, faraway look in her eyes, but other than that, the older woman seemed perfectly fine.

Gillian breathed a sigh of relief as she whispered a prayer of thanksgiving. "I'm going to have Jeremy paged," she told Arthur. "Could you stay with her?"

The older man's faded eyes twinkled merrily. "I intend to keep her by my side for the rest of our lives," he confided.

Gillian whispered a word to the hovering guard and watched him hasten across to his office. Moments later the announcement boomed around the mall.

"I'm so happy for you, Arthur. You're exactly what Faith needs," she told him grinning. "But you might have an argument from Jeremy on that." Her face fell. "He wants to put her in a nursing home."

Arthur's face shone with an inner light, and Gillian noticed the gentle way he enfolded Faith's hand in his.

"Nothing is stronger than love," he told her softly, nodding his head toward the young man who was rushing down the aisle toward them. "Not even him. You just have to have faith." He grinned. "And Faith!"

Gillian watched as Jeremy hugged his aunt with relief. She listened to his questions and Faith's soft answers.

"Oh, piffle," she exclaimed in vexation. "I'm so sorry I worried everyone. I heard the bells, you see. And I wanted to explore the church a little closer. Oh, Jeremy, the choir they have there! It's like a group of angels." She closed her eyes in remembrance and drew a deep breath. "I could listen for hours."

"You did." Gillian laughed and ignored Jeremy's glaring eyes. "But I'm glad you enjoyed this excursion as much as the girls did. And I'm sure the guys had a wonderful time skiing, too."

"I did," John Vernon informed them. "But I was sure glad we had to leave early. My legs are tired!" The other boys concurred with varying degrees of grimacing, and Gillian smiled at them all.

"Well, I think it's time for supper. How about the rest of you?"

"Pizza," Suzy chirped. "But not here. We need some fresh scenery." Everyone except Jeremy, Faith and Arthur burst out laughing at her assessment of their worrisome afternoon. The older couple were too busy gazing into each other's eyes to hear the discussion, but Jeremy made his feelings known.

"I think we'd better wait to eat until we get home," he decreed. "It is a bit of a drive and I'm sure my aunt is tired."

"Why don't we ask *Faith* what she'd prefer to do?" Gillian murmured into the dismayed silence of the children. "We can't guess about her feelings. We should ask her."

"Thank you, dear," Faith murmured, glancing from Arthur to Jeremy. "As it happens, I'm starving. Those faritas we had at lunch were good, but there wasn't much to them. Pizza sounds wonderful."

"Fajitas, Mrs. Rempel. They're called fajitas. But I thought you had a taco salad?" Suzy peered at her friend in concern, obviously wondering about her memory.

"Oh, I did. And then I had the faritas. And Mexi fries." Faith beamed at the young girl. "Such small portions they give," she complained, rubbing her stomach.

Chapter Eleven

"I'm sure I don't know what I'm going to do about this quilt project for Faith and Arthur's wedding," Charity Flowerday complained to Anita as they sat together beside the quilt frame assembled in Charity's front room. "Every other year I've made a quilt for someone as a special project. But this year my hands are too stiff to do more than a few stitches here and there."

"Why, I'll help you, of course," Anita murmured, her eyes brightening as she stared down at the colorful blocks. "I love to quilt. And the boys do sleep for a while each afternoon."

"Thank you, dear. That would be a great help." Charity patted the slender white hand gently and smiled vaguely. "It's not just the quilt that's bothering me, of course. I had so hoped and prayed that Faith would be happy this Christmas."

"But I hear Mrs. Rempel is getting married on Christmas Eve. I'm sure she couldn't be happier. She just glows."

"Harrumph! That's the problem right there. She and Art want to get married, and it would be a wonderful match, but that silly old Jeremy is putting a spike into the works. I declare, if I were a little stronger, and that man a little smaller,

I'd put him over my knee." She nodded toward her best china teapot sitting on the table.

"Pour the tea, would you, Anita? I just want to soak in a little more of this lovely warmth, and then I'll put the heating pad away."

"Are your hands very bad?" Anita asked, her forehead furrowed with concern.

"Yes, today they certainly are. This time of year is usually good for me. Once that cold weather sets in, the arthritis seems to settle down. But with all this warm, cold, warm, cold, they ache constantly." She grimaced. "Now I'm not going to bore you with all the ugly details of getting old. You're far too young and pretty for that."

They sat sipping the strong, fragrant tea and munching on the shortbread Anita had baked only that morning.

"Did I tell you that Sean's coming home next week?" Anita asked, her face a happy reflection of the good news. "He's managed to save quite a lot while he's been in that camp up north. There was nothing to spend it on." She frowned as she replaced her cup on the saucer. "Of course, the work is over now, so we'll have to make it last. There's not much work for him around here."

"Anita! That's wonderful news. I know how lonesome you and the boys have been and what a big load you've been carrying on those small shoulders. We'll just have to pray that the Lord will provide something around here for him." Charity's face grew thoughtful. "And it wouldn't hurt to throw in a word or two for those two," she murmured, jerking her head toward the window where Jeremy and Gillian stood outside arguing.

"They'll be there all day if one of us doesn't let them in," Anita said lightly. "I've never seen two more opposite people. They argue over everything."

"Yes, it's sad, isn't it? I remember a time when the two of

them had begun to get along quite well. Faith's plans only seem to have helped draw the battle lines." She shook her head sadly. "I never really understood how they came to be engaged, but now that they are, I do wish they could find some common ground."

"They have," Anita chuckled, rising from her seat on the sofa. "Their common ground today just happens to be in the street outside your door. I'll go get them, shall I?"

Without waiting for a response, the slim, elegant figure disappeared toward the front of the house. Charity clicked off the heating pad and sat staring at it bemusedly.

"I just have to find a way, Lord. Anita and her family are coming along fine now, and it's time I focused on Faith. She deserves happiness, Lord, and I know Art will make her very happy." She sipped her tea absently, staring down at her swollen ankles. "It's just that Jeremy's putting so much pressure on her right now. It must be so distressing. Could you just give me a sign, some little signal that this will all work out?"

"Excuse me, Mrs. Flowerday." Jeremy Nivens's low rumbly voice filled the tiny room.

"Of course, dear. Please come in, won't you? Anita, do we have any more tea?"

"Um, we don't really want any…."

"I'd love a cup," Gillian's bright voice broke in. "I've been slaving over this ridiculous concert for ages. My feet are killing me."

"Of course they are. Do sit down, Gillian, dear. How is the school pageant going?"

"Wonderfully!"

"Awfully!"

"Well, there seems to be some disparity of opinion here," Charity chuckled. "Which is it?" She could feel the spark of tension as her two guests glared at each other.

"It *was* going all right," Gillian began. "The kids were

starting to learn their songs and the glee club has come along really well."

"And thank you so much for making those cummerbunds and ties," Jeremy told Anita, accepting the tea from her with a smile. "When we get them all dressed in white shirts and dark slacks, they'll look wonderful."

"I enjoyed sewing them," Anita murmured. "It was nice to be able to repay you for all you've done."

"The choir bit sounds lovely," Charity murmured, glancing from one to the other. "We've haven't had a children's choir here for ages. Why were you arguing?"

"Because Gillian claims she can't get all the children to learn their parts in a week, and that's all we've got left." Jeremy scowled across at his fiancée and Charity smothered the grin that twitched at her lips as Gillian glared back.

"And?"

"He wants to do *The Nutcracker Suite,*" Gillian wailed on a note of pure frustration.

"Do you mean the ballet?" Charity gasped, dumbfounded by his aspirations.

"Yep. Costumes and all. I just can't do it all and cover my lesson plans, too. There's too much work." Gillian's face was flushed with anger. *"He—"* she stabbed a finger in Jeremy's direction "—thinks I'm whining and not trying hard enough, but I just can't do any more. I promised to help Faith with the wedding, and that takes a lot of time, too."

"A wedding that shouldn't even be taking place," Jeremy grumbled. He glared at Charity. "What's the rush, anyway? It's not as if they're two young lovers. They've known each other for years."

"Which is why they don't want to waste any more time," Gillian hurled at him. Charity watched her green eyes blazing with indignation. "You've thrown up every barrier you can to their happiness. Shame on you. Why can't you be happy for her?"

"Because she's wrong!" He slammed the teacup down on the table in a manner that had Charity worrying about her Royal Doulton china.

"She's not wrong. She's deliriously happy!"

"She's delirious, all right," Jeremy agreed with grim concern. "Yesterday I found her out on the front lawn golfing!"

"What's wrong with that?" Charity asked, hiding her dismay behind a facade of well-being.

"At twenty-five below? In three feet of snow? I'd say it's enough to have her committed."

"You wouldn't." Gillian's face had paled to an alabaster white that frightened Charity. "She was trying out an idea I had for youth group next week—snow golf. She's not crazy."

"Well, before any of this goes any further I'm taking her to that old fellow, what's his name?" Jeremy thought for a moment. "Dr. Green, I think it is. I want her to have a complete physical and then I'm going to speak to the man myself, just to make sure." He glared at Gillian defensively.

"You're just looking for a label so you can classify someone else's perfectly natural idiosyncracies on that chart of yours." But Charity could see the despair behind Gillian's brave facade.

Charity glanced from one to the other of the opponents and decided the Lord had given her a sign. This was going to be her Christmas project, no doubt about it. If she could keep these two from killing each other before Faith's wedding, she would have done everyone a favor.

"Jeremy, you wouldn't really have her committed, would you?" Gillian's voice was full of fear and foreboding.

"I've already seen the woman at the nursing home," Jeremy muttered, a tide of red coloring his cheeks. "Melanie something or other. She says that they have a bed open right now and that with Alzheimer's patients it's best for them to have constant care." His voice lowered. "I've come to suspect that's what's wrong with her."

His face grew red under Charity's dire look. "I don't want to do it, but she's going to need professional care. A lot of it. I know I can't manage it on my own. Not without quitting my job. The woman at the nursing home said such arrangements rarely work out best for the patient anyways."

"My Melanie?" Charity blazed angrily. "My daughter told you that?" She glared at him balefully. "I'm sure she didn't know exactly whom you were planning on getting into that bed, did she?"

Charity could see she was right. She struggled to her feet with difficulty. Moving slowly across the room, she came to stand in front of her best friend's nephew and fixed him with her most severe look as her cane rapped him twice against the ankle.

"Now you listen to me, young man, and you listen well. I am most distressed to hear such talk. Faith Rempel has been my dearest friend for more years than I can remember, and I will not have you destroying the happiness she's finally managed to find. After all these years she deserves to be with Arthur."

"But she's my aunt," Jeremy protested, surging to his feet.

"Sit down and don't speak again until I invite you to," Charity hissed through clenched teeth. He sat. "Faith *is* your aunt, although what she did to deserve such a miserable nephew, I can't imagine. Do you mean to sit there and tell me that you actually thought you might have your dear 'Auntie Fay' committed to a nursing home against her will, without her consent? This is your idea of love?"

"I wasn't really going to go through with that," he muttered, his face flushed as he stared at his hands.

Charity breathed a sigh of relief and sat down on the chair Anita had pushed close for her to use.

"I certainly hope not," she muttered. Her hand gripped the cane as she stared at him. "Judge Conroy is a friend of hers and I don't think you'd get it passed, but even the attempt would wound poor Faith so deeply." She poked her cane against his leg. "Don't you read your Bible, boy?"

"Yes, of course I do," he answered, his dark eyes glaring at her belligerently. "Every day."

"Well I suggest that tomorrow morning you start reading Paul's first letter to the Corinthians, chapter thirteen. If this so-called love that you feel for your aunt can't allow her the freedom to be who she is, what good is it?" She reached for her worn, large-print edition on a nearby table and flipped the onionskin pages with familiarity.

"Paul says that love is *patient,* love is *kind.* Love is never *selfish.* Love doesn't demand its own way." She glanced up, checking to see if he was paying attention to what she had said.

"If you *love* someone you will be loyal to him or her no matter what the cost. You will always believe in her, always expect the best of her, and always stand your ground in defending her. That's God's version of love, Jeremy. Is that the kind of love you feel toward Faith? Or is the kind of love you have the kind that demands its own way—the kind that sets you up as God...all knowing?"

She pushed herself upward and motioned toward the door. "I want you to go for a drive and think long and hard on that. You've always had Faith in your corner, cheering you on. And I don't think that's going to change just because she gets married. But can't you allow her this little bit of happiness?"

"It's not that I don't want her to be happy," he said sadly. "It's just that I'm concerned about her. She's getting more forgetful each day. I couldn't bear it if..." He let the words die away, unspoken.

"I know you mean well, son. I know you think you know what's best for her. But look deep into your heart and ask yourself if you're really giving Arthur a fair chance? And if you still feel justified, then you're going to have to accept that they don't agree with you and move on with your own life."

Charity grasped his arm with her arthritic hands and exerted enough pressure that he would look at her. "If you can't be happy for her, then at least get out of her way so that she can live her life the way she wants. You can still be there whenever she needs you, son."

Charity watched as he surged to his feet, her heart sinking as she realized he'd heard none of what she'd said.

"It's obvious that you don't understand the consequences of what you're asking me to do," he almost snarled. "I have only my aunt's best interests at heart. And I will be the one who has to pick up the pieces of this debacle."

"Really?" Charity appraised him with a shrewd glance. "Then there's obviously nothing I or anyone else can say to change your mind. We will just have to agree to differ on this subject! Good day."

She returned to her chair, silently issuing a few pertinent prayers to heaven to guide this obstinate young man. When she heard the front door close, she lifted her head to stare at her two remaining guests.

"That is one very determined young man."

Gillian laughed, albeit a little hysterically. "That's the understatement of the year," she muttered. "You should see him at school."

"I don't have to now. I've heard many reports of his work with the students. I haven't seen such dedication to imparting knowledge since your aunt retired." Charity fixed the young woman in her sights. "You love him, don't you?"

She watched the flush of red on Gillian's fair skin and secretly smiled to herself. *Ah, thank you, Lord, maybe there's hope here yet.* "That's no doubt why you agreed to marry the man."

"But I didn't! It was all a mistake, you see," Gillian explained breathlessly. "Faith got confused and called me his future wife. I thought it would be a good idea to play along—you know, not upset her." She grimaced. "Everything snowballed after that. Every time we decided to clear things up, something else happened. After the pastor announced it in church one Sunday morning, we decided to let it go for a while."

Charity shook her head tiredly. Youth, she reminisced. How very tiring it was.

"You see, we thought we could 'break up' just before Christmas. Everyone would be so busy with their Christmas plans that they wouldn't even notice, and when they did it would all be in the past. I never wanted to hurt anyone."

"Yes, dear. I understand all that. I think I've known there was something wrong between you for some time. But do you love him?"

"I didn't want to." Gillian stared at her hands, twisting them around and around. "He's not at all the type of man I want to marry." Her big green eyes stared at Charity, willing her to understand.

"In fact, I came here mourning Michael. I never thought, not even for a moment, that I could be interested in anyone again." Gillian brushed a tear from her eye and Charity reached out to pat her shoulder. "He's so…rigid," Gillian wailed. "You saw what he was like. It's either his way or not at all."

They sat together, the three of them, in Charity's tiny living room, remembering Jeremy's words.

"It's true," the older woman said. "Faith is a tad forgetful. And she does tend to get so involved in the moment that everything else leaves her head. But I don't believe, I will not believe, that she is a danger to herself or anyone else."

"After they are married, Mr. Johnson would be nearby to watch out for her," Anita offered thoughtfully. "That should relieve some of Mr. Nivens's worries."

Charity shook her head. "I'm not at all convinced that worry about her safety is really what's at the bottom of this, Anita. No," she said, nibbling on her fingernail thoughtfully. "I think there's a much deeper reason why Jeremy is so opposed to this."

"He's opposed to everything," Gillian put in grumpily. "You should see the extent of this *Nutcracker* production. It's overwhelming for a little place like Mossbank. What's all the fuss for?"

"In a way, I can understand that part of it," Charity murmured. "This is his first year here, his first teaching year in America. He wants to make good; show that he's up to it."

"You mean he wants to make his mark," Anita said doubtfully. "But why?"

"I think it's to do with his future plans." Gillian's forehead was creased in a frown. "Something he said once makes me think that he's not planning on staying in Mossbank for the rest of his life. I just can't quite recall…" She fell silent, lost in thought.

"Well, you and Hope would know more about this than I," Charity said, bringing them back to the issue at hand. "But surely if he's trying to score Brownie points, as we used to call it, he's hoping that it will influence his future somewhere else. Maybe someplace with a drama school?" She glanced at Gillian for confirmation.

"No, I don't think it's that," Gillian said slowly. "His interest is in the music, not the drama. Anyway, *The Nutcracker* doesn't have any words, remember?"

"Are they really going to do a ballet?" Anita asked. Her mouth curved downward. "Roddy will kick up the biggest fuss if he has to wear a tutu."

"No, no." Gillian burst out laughing. Charity noticed the difference a smile made to that beautiful face. "There's only one little girl who actually dances; the rest just play their parts normally. Jeremy was actually quite clever when he wrote the scenes. It's quite modern."

"And the children don't mind doing it?" Charity watched carefully.

"Actually," the young teacher admitted, her eyes downcast. "They're rather enjoying it. It's just those of us who have to assemble the sets and costumes and prompt and direct who are pulling out our hair."

"The other teachers are complaining, too?" Charity tried to hold the disapproval from her voice.

"There has almost been a mutiny," Gillian admitted, bright spots of red coloring her cheeks. "We're all bogged down with the after-hours practices and workshops, etcetera. We're drowning."

"You should have asked for help," Charity chided gently. "This is a small community. We're used to pitching in. Now let's see…" She tapped her cheek thoughtfully. "I can think of several people who would help with sets. And Anita here is more than capable of directing the costume making."

"Actually, I have a trunkful of costumes that might be suitable," the woman murmured shyly. "I used to work with little theater when we lived in the East. Would you like to look?"

Charity watched as the two huddled over a list of what Gillian anticipated they would need. She was satisfied that the immediate problems would be handled, but her concern was for the young man and woman who were at loggerheads with each other.

"Thank you, Mrs. Flowerday. You're a lifesaver. Jeremy will be furious when he finds out I've enlisted all this help. He wanted it to be a surprise for the parents."

"Parents don't care about the surprise part," Charity murmured. "They just want to see their own child on stage. Don't you worry about Jeremy Nivens. I'll deal with him." She faced Gillian head-on and spoke her mind.

"Right now I'm more concerned with you and this wall you've built up between you. You've never really answered my question, but I believe you are in love with Jeremy." She waited until Gillian nodded her head. "Then it's up to you to put a stop to this mutiny, as you call it. You're going to have to try working together…find a way to make your goals mesh. That's the first step."

"Oh, but that's impossible," Gillian cried. "We're exact opposites. Whatever I say, he hates, and he's always after me for breaking some rule he's devised. He has thousands of them," she confided in a whisper.

Charity shook her head firmly. "He is your boss. And he is a coworker. He deserves your respect and your cooperation. And you love him, don't you?"

"I don't know how it came about but, yes, I do. He's so legalistic, though. And he's always…"

Charity cut the diatribe short with a smile. "My mother, God bless her, used to have a saying when we children were fighting. 'It's not what he did, it's what you do that counts.' That's the real meaning of Corinthians, don't you think?"

"You mean I should just go along with whatever he wants, meekly accepting his way?" Gillian's face was the picture of dubiousness.

"No, I'm saying that you need to find a way to get along.

The New Testament church was full of people going their own way, and the writers were continually exhorting the people to ignore the petty stuff and act in a manner pleasing to God. I think God would be pleased if you could make your workplace a happy, cohesive arena where others could see God at work."

"Keep it to myself? I have tried, you know."

"I know, dear. But the boiling point can be averted if you move away from the source of the heat or adapt to the conditions. You have to choose to understand what makes him like that...what's underneath all this need to control."

"Perhaps you're right. I've been trying to fix Jeremy for so long that I've lost my perspective about where he fits into God's plan for my life." Charity watched as the lovely face stared off into the distance. "Perhaps I need to get away and think about that."

"I know it sounds easy," Charity told her. "And I doubt that it will be, but God is teaching something here. It's up to all of us to understand what it is He wants us to learn." Charity felt the tiredness surge up in her suddenly, draining her of the strength needed to lift herself from the chair. Fervently she wished her guests would go home, but she would not ask them to leave. She let her eyes close for a moment as she whispered a prayer.

"Oh, dear. That's the boys. Thank goodness they've finally awakened." Anita grinned. "I was afraid I was going to be up all night. Roddy will be home soon from the boys' club. I'd better get going."

"I need to move, too," Gillian said. "I've gotten so comfortable here, I almost forgot I'm supposed to meet Hope for dinner downtown." She grinned at Charity's surprised look. "She's agreed to try the fried chicken place."

Charity gaped. "My dear, if you can work that miracle, you can do anything God sets before you." She accepted the soft kiss with a smile and shooed them both away, patting the smooth cheeks of Anita's sons as they toddled out the door.

"We'll start on the quilt tomorrow, Charity," Anita called from the sidewalk. "It will go quite quickly. You just wait and see."

As she walked back inside to begin her own dinner preparations, Charity decided that everything went quickly these days. Too quickly.

Slow me down, Lord, she breathed, stirring the pot of soup Anita had made earlier. *Slow me down and show me how to use what little wisdom I've accumulated to help these hurting lives.*

Jeremy's words came back then, his fear evident on the craggy lines of his white face. *And Lord,* she added in an afterthought, *please keep Faith safe and under your umbrella of care.*

And having covered every base she could think of, Charity sank down into her favorite chair, propped up her aching feet and sipped at her soup as she watched the dismal state of the world's affairs unfold on the television.

Just one other thing, Lord, she murmured as she prepared for bed a little later. *I just wanted to give a big "Thank You" that I'm not young anymore! It's far too wearing.*

Chapter Twelve

❧

"Quiet everyone!" Gillian glanced at the rosy faces spread out before her and wondered yet again at the wisdom of doing this. "Mrs. Rempel is going to help us make snow-flake Christmas cards this afternoon, so I want you all to listen very carefully, okay?"

The children nodded their heads in unison just like little robots, their eyes wide with wonder at the gray-haired woman standing at the front of the class.

Faith took her cue right on target and began her story in a hushed voice. "When I was a very tiny girl, I lived in a country called England, far across the sea."

Bethany thrust up her hand. "Is that why you talk funny?"

"Yes, dear, I expect it is." Faith smiled, losing none of her animation. "One year my father was injured at work, and for a while we had just enough money to buy our food. It was a cold dreary winter—not as cold as here, because it rained quite a lot, but still very cool." She shivered and Gillian watched the children's eyes grow wide.

"We had to spend a lot of our money on coal to heat our home, and there was nothing left over to buy Christmas presents."

"You mean there wouldn't be anything under the tree?" The boy sounded amazed at such a thing.

"We couldn't even get a tree," Faith told him sadly. "But my mother and father still wanted us to have a happy time at Christmas so they decided we should all make something to decorate our home. Then, on Christmas morning we would bring them all out and that would be our gifts to each other."

"No Nintendo?" Timothy Wentworth asked softly. Faith shook her head.

"No candy canes?" Melanie whispered.

"None."

"No Christmas oranges?"

"No," Faith smiled. "But we had lots of mother's wonderful baking. There were always gingerbread men to decorate and stars and angels. I liked to decorate the Christmas tree cookies best. I'd put one of those little silver candy balls on each branch."

"Is that what you made for your Christmas decoration?" Chad asked, as impatient as usual.

"No." Faith waited until they were all watching her and then frowned. "I didn't have anything to make. Christmas was coming closer and closer, and I couldn't think of one single thing that would be a good decoration."

"You could always string popcorn," one tiny voice volunteered. "My granny says she *always* did that."

"Or make paper chains," another offered. "You just need glue and paper."

"I suppose I could have, but my sisters were smaller and they needed to make something simple like that. Besides, I wanted to have something really spectacular to show to my family. I loved them very much and I wanted to show it, you see."

The children nodded with understanding.

"Couldn't you get a job?" Tiffany asked. "My brother shovels snow and he gets five whole dollars for it."

"Ohh!" The other kids were flabbergasted by such a huge sum.

"I don't think there was anyone in my village who could have paid five dollars for me to shovel," Faith told them softly. "So I prayed. Every night before I went to bed, I would get down on my knees and tell God that I wanted something really special for my family."

"I done that," Jonah Andrews grumbled. "I didn't do no good, though. We didn't get nothin' from God." The child who had every toy imaginable looked dismally disappointed, as if he'd expected manna to fall from the heavens, Gillian decided.

"Oh, no, dear, that's not true. We always get an answer from God. But sometimes we don't want to hear what He says and sometimes we don't like what He brings." Faith's face was shining with joy, and Gillian found herself amazed at the assurance she saw there.

How could Faith, with all the difficulties in her life, still have so much trust that God would work everything out? Gillian scorned her own untrusting attitude.

"Is that all?" Buddy Hirsch complained. "I'm hungry."

"You're always hungry," Roddy scoffed. "I bet Mrs. Rempel's gonna tell us about how they had to starve and not have any turkey dinner at all, aren't you?" he demanded, peering up at the older woman.

"I can't tell you anything if you're all talking," Faith said softly, her eyes twinkling. The children settled down immediately. "Now, I told you that I was praying every night for God to hear me, right?" A flurry of little heads nodded.

"Well, on the day before Christmas I still didn't hear God's answer. I'd waited and listened. I obeyed my mother and helped my dad. I did everything I could so that I'd be able to hear the answer, and still it didn't come. I was really disappointed because now it was too late, and I didn't have a gift for my family."

The childrens' eyes were huge as she whispered the last words. Gillian could see their mouths in round oh's of anticipation and wished suddenly that Jeremy were here to see how wonderfully his aunt related to her kids. It would be everyone's loss if Faith were locked away in some senior citizen's home, unable to share her wisdom with these little ones.

"Anyway, I was walking home, shuffling my feet through the snow. You know how you do when you're mad? Well, I was mad, really mad. I stopped in front of a store to look at the wonderful dolls in the window and I got even madder. Why couldn't my sisters and I have those dolls, I yelled at God. We deserved them, and we'd never had anything like them before."

Gillian watched twenty-eight pairs of eyes widen when Faith told them she had yelled at God. She could relate, she thought wryly. Goodness knew, she'd been yelling at God an awful lot herself lately. Especially in matters to do with Jeremy Nivens.

Why couldn't the man just admit that he was attracted to her? Just for once, why couldn't he let go of his stern facade of control and let her in past the barriers he always erected? They had something special; she knew they did. Why wouldn't he acknowledge that there was something growing between them?

"Well, as I stood there, fuming and fussing, an elderly lady spoke from behind me. She was very tiny and she had on an elegant fur coat and a wonderful hat with an ostrich feather. And on her hands she wore the finest leather gloves."

Faith pantomimed the motions, patting her head and pretending to pull on a pair of long gloves.

"'What's the matter little girl?' she asked me in a soft

voice. I glared up at her and told her I was mad." Faith's eyes surveyed her captive audience. Her voice dropped to a whisper. "'Why…why are you so angry at God? He's given you a wonderful family, a warm home and enough to eat. What's wrong with that?'"

Gillian noticed several children nodding. They were from families that were almost destitute after paying off huge loans for the land they farmed. Faith was continuing.

"Well, I just told her, 'I want Christmas presents for my family. I want to be like all the other people who give gifts under the tree. I want to give them something special.'" She shook her gray head. "That lady just stared at me. She never said a word for a very long time and then she said, 'Come with me, dear.' So I did. I followed her. All the way home."

Gillian caught Jasmine's eye before she could start on her recitation about following people you don't know. She put her finger to her lips and was gratified to see the little girl nod.

"That lady lived in a great big huge house up on the top of a hill. And when we went in and sat in front of a big warm fire, another lady brought cookies and tea. I ate as many as I could and then I sat back in my chair and listened when the lady began talking."

The children leaned forward, knowing they were getting to the good part.

"'Your name is Faith, isn't it?' she whispered in a funny soft voice. I nodded. 'And what do you want most this Christmas, Faith?' she asked me. So I told her. 'I want to be rich like you. I want to have a big house and lots of money… enough to buy presents for everyone. I want to be like other kids.'" Faith paused for a moment.

"She smiled a very funny smile and then patted me on the head. 'Do you know about God?' she asked me. I told her that I'd known about God for a long time. 'Well then,' she said. 'Can you tell me two things in the world that God created that are the same?'" Faith smiled down at them, waiting for someone to answer.

There was silence for the longest time as her charges thought through the puzzle, trying to figure it out.

"I know," Roddy bellowed, thrusting his arm up toward the ceiling. "Twins!"

Everyone agreed that God made twins the same, but Faith was shaking her head.

"Close," she told them with a smile. "Twins look an awful lot alike and they sometimes dress the same, but if you look really closely, there's always some little difference. Either they have a different look to their face or they like different things, or maybe one has a mole the other doesn't have. If you try really hard you can tell them apart."

The children appeared to be considering that.

"Well, this old lady told me that God even makes snowflakes different. Did you know there are no two snowflakes the same? Each one is just a little different from all the others. Why is that, do you suppose?" She waited a moment.

"I told the lady that I didn't know, and she said, 'God likes people and snowflakes to be themselves. He doesn't want us to try and look like or act like someone else. He wants us to be our very own special selves, just the way He made us.'" There was a light tinkling laugh.

"Well, I thought that was pretty good, so I asked her why God didn't make us all rich like her. And do you know what she said?" Every head shook as every eye fastened on Faith expectantly.

"She said, 'Oh, no, child. You don't want to be like me, all alone in this big old house with my family all dead and gone. God gave you a very special family, a unique one, all your own. Just like the snowflakes. Now you have to learn how to use all the wonderful things God gave especially to you. God doesn't want another one of me, he wants a one-of-a-kind person like you.'"

Faith's face became sad. "I felt sad for her. She had no one to share with. I had my sisters and my parents but she had no one. So I decided to give her a gift, as well as my family, by bringing everyone together. On Christmas Day we all went to her house and sang songs and sat around the fire. She asked my father if we could stay and have dinner with her, and it was the most wonderful dinner I've ever eaten."

"Was it turkey?" Roddy asked.

"No." Faith shook her head. "It was something completely different—her own special way of celebrating."

"So whenever it gets near Christmas, I like to think of that lady, and I like to look at snowflakes and see how different they are. That reminds me that God made me just the way I am."

"I didn't never see no snowflake by itself before," Roddy muttered, clearly deep in thought. "How d'ya do that?"

"That's what I'm going to show you," Faith said happily. She slipped across to the window, slid it open and carefully pulled in a huge sheet of black bristol board.

"I put this in the freezer last night, and this morning when it started to snow, I set it outside. Now the snowflakes won't melt for a minute or two and you can see how different each one is."

The children crowded around, eager to experience this hands-on information. As they oohed and aahed over the melting flakes, Gillian wondered if Faith wasn't hinting just a little at her and Jeremy's ongoing argument.

There could be no doubt that the man was different; as far removed from Michael as anyone could be. But that didn't mean she loved him any less. Perhaps God was telling her to make some adjustments.

As she and Faith worked side by side, folding and unfolding white paper that the children cut into snowflakes of every size and description, Gillian was struck again by how gently God worked. Such a great truth and yet Faith had applied it so easily. She decided to think about it again later, when she had more time.

"Jeremy?" Gillian watched as those muscular shoulders covered by a thin cotton T-shirt stretched as he set down the paintbrush he'd been wielding across the massive set several parents had constructed only that morning. "Could I speak to you for a moment? Please?"

"Yes?" His voice was not in the least welcoming, and Gillian tried to recall the verse she'd read only this morning: "Thou wilt keep him in perfect peace whose mind is stayed on Thee."

"I'm trying, Lord," she whispered. "I'm trying." She straightened her backbone and concentrated on her next words.

"I wondered if you would consider handling the youth group alone this weekend." The words came out in a rush as she waited for his explosion.

"Why? Is something wrong?" He resumed his even strokes, back and forth across the plywood.

"Not exactly. I just need to go back to Boston. Just for a day or two. To get my bearings. It's personal." She finished at last, embarrassed at having said so much.

Jeremy slowly put down his brush, dusted his hands on his paint-spattered overalls and straightened. His face was a mask of tightly controlled tension as he glared down at her.

"You're choosing *now,* when we're this close—" he held his thumb and forefinger millimeters apart "—to putting on this play?"

"I think things are pretty well in hand, thanks to the parents," she murmured reasonably. "Aren't they?"

"Perhaps at school. But what about the youth group? What are they doing tomorrow night, anyway?" He looked grim and forbidding, and Gillian's heart ached with pain.

If only he could relax a little; let someone take on a bit of the responsibility for a while. She knew it wasn't likely. He'd insisted on painting the backdrops himself, even though several very qualified drama students from the high school had offered.

"Gillian?" He was frowning down at her.

"Oh, sorry," she muttered, embarrassed at having been caught daydreaming.

"Why do you always do that?" he demanded angrily. His eyes were cold and hard.

"Do what?" Gillian asked blankly, staring at him.

"Apologize in that little-girl voice as if I'm some type of ogre." He thrust his hands into his pockets angrily.

"Oh, sorry," she said automatically and then slapped her hand over her mouth in dismay as he rolled his eyes. "I wasn't really apologizing," she tried to explain. "More like coming back down to earth."

"*Sorry* is the accepted English word for an apology," he advised her through clenched teeth. "It does not mean daydreaming."

The tide rose in her, red and hot, in answer to his nasty tone and griping words. *Don't play this game,* a little voice whispered inside her mind, and Gillian swallowed down the angry response.

"I was asking if you thought you could handle the youth group," she reminded him carefully. "They're supposed to go skating, if you recall. And then one of the parents offered to build a fire in the park and bring hot dogs for everyone to roast."

"Hah! As if anyone could feed enough to that bunch of devouring animals." He shook his head with stern disapproval.

"I just read an article that says there's far too much fat in the diets of North Americans. Especially teenagers."

Gillian smiled. She had to. The gauntlet had been thrown down so often in the past few moments, she should have been red-hot. If not for the Lord's help. And her vow to try to understand this man.

"Yes, I suppose it must seem that way to you," she nodded, considering his words. "What was your favorite food in England?"

His eyes opened wide as he stared at her, but finally a glint of humor broke through to tug at the corner of his mouth.

"Roast beef, mashed potatoes, gravy and apple pie," he admitted at last.

Gillian's eyebrows rose. "And you have the nerve to talk about our diet." She chuckled. "It's rather like the pot calling the kettle black."

"I suppose," he admitted at last. His eyes narrowed. "I don't understand the need to slather everything with ketchup, though. How do they even taste the flavor of the food?"

Gillian slipped the brush out of his hand and added a few strokes to the curve of draperies painted around the window.

"I think that's the whole purpose," she said with a chuckle. "They don't taste anything *but* the ketchup!"

He removed the brush before studying her work critically.

"I prefer to do this myself," he murmured, wiping away her work and carefully painting in a new drapery.

Gillian watched as he worked, sadness welling up inside her at his refusal to allow anyone past the shell he had created.

"You can't do it all, Jeremy," she whispered, wishing she understood this complex man. "Sooner or later you're going to have to take what other people offer. We all need each other."

She stepped back, her heel grazing the unsteady platform

behind. His hand grasped her arm, holding her steady as she regained her balance. Gillian was amazed to find herself mere inches from his quizzical gaze.

"You're very much like my aunt in some ways," he murmured, holding her gaze with his own. She felt his eyes graze across her face and felt her cheeks color at the intricate inspection he was giving her. "You always want everything to move along smoothly and happily, everyone getting along famously."

"What's wrong with that?" she demanded softly, refusing to step away from his challenge.

"It's unrealistic. Life isn't always like that, Gillian. Take you and me. You always want to look on the bright side and ignore the problems."

"And you only ever see the problems," she quipped back. "The pessimist and the optimist."

"You live in a fairy-tale world where you made Michael into Prince Charming and you were the fairy princess." He shook his head, a grim smile curving his lips as his fingers slid up her arm to twiddle absently with the bouncing curls on her shoulder. "Life is hard. There are a lot of bad things that happen. It's much easier to deal with them if you've done some preparation."

"Michael used to say 'Seize the day,'" she retorted. "He taught me not to spend my life in worry and fear for what might happen tomorrow. I want to live today to the full. Can't you let go of your inhibitions and enjoy what God has given?"

"You can't make me into Michael," he muttered, as his arms moved across her back to pull her against him. His lips grazed her forehead and moved down purposefully toward her mouth. "I am me—a different person with a different life experience."

"You don't always have to run him down," Gillian whispered, breathless with waiting as his lips moved nearer hers. "He was a wonderful man."

"I'm sure he was. And I'm equally sure I'm not nearly as wonderful. But one thing I will admit…your Michael certainly knew how to find a beautiful woman." His eyes blazed into hers. "I hope you won't be sorry, but I am going to seize the moment and kiss you."

And with that, his mouth touched hers softly, gently, drawing a response Gillian could not have stopped. In fact, she amazed herself with her own fervor as her hands just naturally moved up to his shoulders and she let her fingers rove through his crisp dark hair.

His lips were strong and sure as they kissed her, not unlike Jeremy himself. But even as he kissed her so masterfully, there was an uncertainty, a question behind his touch, a mistrust. It was as if he were afraid she would reject him now.

With the tiniest movement, Gillian answered that, holding him closer and answering with her own soft lips, drawing in a tiny gasp when his mouth moved to her neck and touched the pulse that hammered there.

It didn't last long enough.

"We shouldn't be doing this," he murmured huskily, pressing her gently away. "This is a public building. Anyone might walk in."

Gillian slowly lifted her hands away from his wide shoulders, her mind whirling with the information that was traveling to her brain. He'd kissed her. And what a kiss!

"Why not?" she managed at last. "We are supposed to be engaged." Her eyes took in the splotches of red on his cheekbones as he stepped backward and turned to focus once more on his painting.

Long and empty, the silence dragged out between them until Jeremy finally laid down his brush and turned and faced her. His voice, when it came, was soft but strong and she could hear the bitter tones underneath.

"But we both know that's a facade, don't we, Gillian?" he asked her. "I think you've made it quite clear that you're looking for someone to take your former fiancé's place. We both know that's not me." His eyes were clear and focused as they stared back at her and Gillian felt the air sizzle with electricity.

"I am who I am, Gillian. I'm not a knight in shining armor and I can't pretend to be. I hold strong opinions and I'm not afraid to say what I think. I've never been the romantic type, never even considered freezing rings in ice cubes. And I don't believe in making grand, airy gestures like all the best heroes."

He reached up and pressed back a curl that was bouncing tantalizingly near her mouth. His eyes were icy steel now and they penetrated through the foggy haze of her mind, bringing her to startled awareness. He was serious, she realized. Deadly serious.

"But when I love someone, Gillian, it will be with all of me. I won't renege on my promise, but neither will I do silly things to prove myself. I will always protect those people that I love. That's part of who I am."

"I know," she whispered sadly. "I've seen how much you care for Faith. But, Jeremy, sometimes your protection hurts the very people you say you love. Can't you just let them be?"

She stared at him for several moments before turning away, the light of hope dying inside her. His cool, implacable face never changed its look. He would insist on pushing the business with Faith, she knew. He felt it was his duty.

Help me through this, she prayed silently as she made her way out to Hope's smoothly purring car. *Let me find the answers to unlock his heart, because I love him, Lord. And I think he could love me. If he'd let himself.*

Chapter Thirteen

Jeremy breathed a sigh of relief and slowly eased his shaky legs forward. "I'll kill her for this," he told himself, easing one skate in front of the other. "If I don't die first."

It was an emotional outburst, he realized. Something he hadn't been prone to until Gillian's advent into his life. He struggled to keep his balance as a group of his ruffians swooped past, almost toppling him in their haste to move on.

"Hey, Jeremy, you gotta slide. Like this," David Crest moved slowly beside him, gliding his feet in a smooth, firm motion that did send the boy sailing over the glistening ice with athletic prowess. "No, don't walk," he ordered. "Slide."

Jeremy tried it and to his surprise found that the smooth motions propelled him forward at a rate he could almost control.

"Way to go, teach," David cheered.

That was right before he forgot to concentrate and landed on his keister. Hard.

"Whoof, that was some landing. You okay?" David's curious face peered down at him.

"Bruised," Jeremy returned acidly. "And probably damaged for life, but fine." He hoisted himself to his feet with all the elegance of a lumbering elephant and dusted off his new jeans. "It's very hard," he told the boy grimly.

"Yeah," David laughed. "Ice usually is."

"I didn't mean that. I meant learning how to skate. I don't think I'm coordinated enough for this." Jeremy glanced bitterly at the frolicking youth around him and gingerly set one foot in front of the other as he headed for the gate. "I've had enough."

"No way," David yelled and swooped up behind him, pressing gently from behind. "Now just relax and let yourself glide," he ordered, laughing. "I'll do all the work until you figure out your balance."

Before he killed her, he'd kiss her senseless, Jeremy decided, unable to do anything but let the wind whistle past his ears as his young instructor propelled him across the ice at the speed of light. It was Gillian Langford's fault that he was out here, endangering life and limb with a bunch of ungrateful kids. Bad enough that he had agreed to help with this youth group, but now she'd left him alone with them.

That was what usually happened, he reflected grimly. People generally left him and expected that he would manage. And he usually did. But it sure wasn't easy. But sometimes he found himself wishing he had a little help. Fortunately he'd had a lot of practice at going it alone in life, he told himself sternly, tamping down thoughts of his would-be fiancée and how much he missed her.

A picture of Gillian's happy, laughing face thrust itself into his mind, and he wondered how she would manage to make this cold, hard ice a positive experience. Or shed humor on the fact that he was being shoved around the ice like a sack of potatoes. She'd have a field day with that!

Somehow, thank God, he and David managed to avoid the other skaters as they moved around the edge of the oval rink. But all the same, Jeremy found himself clutching the boards with relief whenever he got near enough. Which wasn't half as often as he wanted.

"She's really going to pay for this," he griped as David whizzed him over a little nearer to the opening in the boards.

"Who?"

"Gillian," Jeremy spat out grimly. With extreme attention to detail, he stepped carefully toward the edge, lifting one foot in front of the other and promptly landed on his rear with one skate bent uncomfortably under his other leg.

"I told you, slide don't walk. Why is Gillian gonna get it?" David demanded, hauling him to his feet and nodding as Jeremy began to slip and slide across the ice like an acrobat. "She already knows how to skate. I saw her teaching the girls a double toe loop the other day."

"She's good at everything, isn't she?" Jeremy sighed. He brushed a hand across his snow-covered pants. "And I feel like an idiot. I'm going in," he said defeatedly.

David followed behind like a little puppy intent on trailing its master. "Just relax for a minute or two and then try again," he suggested. "It's not really that difficult, and it doesn't take a whole lot of skill, you know. Just practice."

"I hate skating," Jeremy told him childishly and then wished he'd kept his mouth shut. Why was it that everything the woman did managed to make him look like an incompetent, old-fashioned idiot?

"Gillian would show you how, if she was here," David told him seriously. "She's really good at teaching people things. And she never makes fun of you. I like that about her." He tugged a candy bar from his pocket and shucked the paper off in one wrist motion. "Want some?"

Jeremy shook his head and the boy popped the entire bar into his mouth. Seconds later he was talking again. "Like the other day when I was telling her about this friend of mine. Well, she's not a close friend. Not yet. But she could be. Maybe. Someday."

Jeremy prayed fervently that this wasn't going to end up in a counseling session. He had no practical experience to offer the boy when it came to women. He didn't understand them himself and he certainly didn't want to try to explain them to someone else; especially not a teenager.

So he kept silent. Which didn't seem to faze David in the least.

"You see, Myra's pretty cool, for a girl. Or she could be. But she's always snapping her gum when she talks. That gets to me." He glugged down half a bottle of soda and continued. "She's smart and funny but I get tired of always hearing the same jokes over and over." He stopped, obviously waiting for him to comment, Jeremy decided, and mentally added another point to the list of items he'd bombard Gillian with when she returned.

"D'ya think I should tell her about the stuff she does that bugs me?"

David sounded dreadfully unsure and Jeremy searched his mind for an answer. There wasn't one. "Uh, well, I guess if you want to be around her and something she's doing is bothering you, you should explain that and ask her to stop." There, that sounded okay, he decided.

"She's got this laugh, you see," David muttered, staring at his feet. "I mean she's really a good friend and everything. She even helped me do a physics assignment that was totally Greek to me. But that laugh." He shook his head dismally.

Jeremy felt inspiration strike and turned toward the boy excitedly. "Maybe you should tell me what it is that you like about her," he said helpfully. *Thank you, God. I would never have thought of that.*

David's forehead drew together in perplexity. "I dunno.

Lots of stuff. What do you like about Gillian? Besides that she's a babe."

"A what?" Jeremy stared at him aghast.

"A babe, a dish. You know—" he grinned "—easy on the eyes." He made a motion with his hands that Jeremy understood to mean Gillian's well-formed figure.

"Yes, Gillian is very lovely," he conceded absently, thinking about the vivacious, beautiful woman he was supposedly engaged to. Thinking about the way he felt every time he set eyes on her.

"Yeah, but she's no ditz," David agreed thoughtfully. "You gotta admit she's smart, too. An' she hasn't always had it so easy. My sister heard her telling one of the girls that when she was little she was pretty sick. Her parents got her to take up sports to build up her strength."

"Oh." Jeremy considered the information in a new light. For some reason he'd always thought Gillian had lived life on a bed of roses. Now it seemed that she, too, had experienced her share of problems.

"So what else do you like about her?" David pressed. "Like don't you think it's cool how she always thinks up cool things for us to do? She doesn't care if I dress differently or wear my hair like this. At least I don't think so. She never mentioned it."

Jeremy remembered Gillian's generous gift to Roddy's mother. And he recalled the way she'd gotten on her hands and knees to clean the bathroom at old Mr. Gentry's house last week when the youth group had raised money for a missionary by cleaning homes for seniors. It did seem as if his fiancée was less interested in outward appearances than getting to the heart of the matter.

"And man, can she cook. If I ever get married, I'm picking a lady who can make pies like Gillian does. Those apple pies we had at her aunt's house for the progressive supper were great!"

Jeremy would have liked to point out that he hadn't been able to taste that particular pie because David had consumed half a pie all by himself, but in the end he decided not to. After all, he was supposed to be the leader here.

"Well, anyhow, what do you think? Should I tell Myra that I don't like certain things like the way she laughs an' stuff or should I just forget it?"

There was no room for prevarication here, Jeremy realized grimly. The kid was asking the worst possible person for advice about interpersonal relationships, and Jeremy had an idea that his own experiences wouldn't exactly help David.

"The thing is, if I tell her she wears too much makeup and her skirts are too short, she's gonna get mad. And I don't really want her to be mad at me. I like her. A lot. So whadya think, Jeremy?"

Fervently, ardently, Jeremy begged God to send Gillian to get him out of this situation. He pleaded with everything he owned, but three minutes later David still sat beside him, waiting for the pearl of wisdom to leave Jeremy's lips and give him direction.

"Well, as I see it," Jeremy began, feeling his way through the maze of the feminine psyche with no clue as to his destination, "people don't generally like to hear other people talk about their faults. I mean, I don't." That's for sure, he muttered silently. "So, if you really want this girl for a friend—" he glanced at the boy for confirmation and watched the dark head nod firmly "—then I think you're going to have to accept that she is the way she is and learn to get along with that."

"You mean deal with it," David considered, scratching his head.

"Well, yes. Either that or find another friend. One who

meets your specifications." That sounded pretty good. Jeremy congratulated himself.

"And you don't think I should tell her about the gum or the makeup or other stuff?" David looked doubtful, so Jeremy hastened to clarify his position.

"Well, *if,* someday, she should *ask* if you think she's wearing too much makeup, I suppose you could tell her, kindly, what you think. I guess that's what Pastor Dave meant in his sermon on Sunday about accepting the unlovely. Don't you think?" He peered at David searchingly, hoping he wasn't being sacrilegious or something.

"I guess. My mom says kinda the same thing when my sister and I have an argument and I'm trying to tell her what my sister has done. She always waits till I'm finished and then she gives me this look and says, 'It's not what *she did,* it's what *you do* that counts.' Like I'm only responsible for me."

As the rest of the group joined them and they made their way to the park for the wiener roast, Jeremy felt the impact of David's words impinging on his skull in a never-ending tune. *It's not what she did that counts. It's what you do.*

Over and over they rolled through his brain for the rest of the evening, even when he was alone at home, with the lights turned low. They reminded him of his judgmental attitude toward Gillian. He'd argued with her about everything, and yet she had still managed to put another person's need in front of their bickering.

He thought of his aunt and the fear that gripped him when he considered the future without her. What would happen when he moved on, went back to England? Who would ensure that she stayed safe and protected if he didn't look after that now, before things got out of hand? Alzheimer's, Dr. Green had said. Progressively getting worse.

"Is it so wrong, Lord?" he prayed, pouring out his fear

and worry. "Is it so terrible to want to keep her away from the dangers of life? Am I wrong to impose my will in this matter?"

The answer came seconds later in the shrill peal of the telephone. "Jeremy?" Arthur's voice sounded strained. "You'd better come over here right away. Faith has been mugged. She needs to see a doctor."

Cold, overwhelming dread flooded his mind as Jeremy hung up and reached for his jacket. His eyes fell on the brochures that lay on the hall table describing the conditions in Sunset Retirement Home just outside of Mossbank.

He thought of his aunt, lying hurt and bleeding in the cold winter air, and rage filled him. A black, primal rage that threatened to overwhelm him. "I wasn't wrong," he said angrily, snatching up the forms and stuffing them into one pocket. "She shouldn't be left alone. It's too dangerous."

And as he sped through the icy streets, Gillian's sad green eyes stared back at him from the dark night sky. "It's not what you did or said that matters," he told her angrily. "It's what I do now that counts. It's my responsibility to protect my aunt and I'm going to do it."

"Gilly, dear, are you sure you have to go back so quickly? Couldn't you spend a few more hours with us?" Her mother's worried gaze studied her daughter's pale face with a knowing perception. "It's Jeremy, isn't it? He's the one God has sent you."

"Yes, I think so Mom," Gillian whispered tearfully. "But I can't imagine how He's going to work this one out. Especially now that Faith's been hurt. I know Jeremy will feel that it's his duty to get her into a home somewhere, away from everyone." She stopped packing long enough to stare up at her mother. "He's going to stop her wedding, Mom. I can feel it."

"Then go back and straighten it out, Gilly. God will give you the words and the ways to do what He wants. Just keep praying."

Three hours later, Gillian wearily clambered into her aunt's car and demanded, "How is she?"

Hope's face was white and strained as she faced her niece. "She's not well, Gillian. The doctor found a tumor when they did the scan. Apparently Dr. Green missed it when Jeremy took her in for a checkup. They're operating tomorrow."

"So soon?" Gillian gasped at the news, gripping the door handle with fingers suddenly gone weak. "What about the wedding?"

"Faith says she's not letting Arthur get away, tumor or no. She insists that she's going through with it. And the doctors aren't saying no." Hope's lips turned upward in the vestige of a smile. "She's tough, Gilly. And she has God on her side. She's convinced He has something very special planned."

"Can I see her?" Gillian asked quietly. "Can she talk for a while?"

"We'll go straight there. She was asking about you this morning."

To look at her, Faith was no different from any other day, save for the fact that she had several stitches along the hairline.

"I finally get to have a beauty mark," she giggled, hugging Gillian close. "I've missed you, dear. And so has Jeremy. He's been mooning around like a lost lamb without you." Her bright eyes twinkled merrily. "Well, piffle! Why don't you two go and say hello properly, while I discuss something with Hope?"

As Jeremy's hand moved under her arm, Gillian felt herself being propelled from the room. She went because she could see the stark fear in his eyes and feel the tenseness in his body.

"Come on, Jeremy," she whispered, guiding him to a soft-cushioned chair in the waiting area down the hall. "Sit down. You must be exhausted."

"I shouldn't have waited," he told her baldly. "Dr. Green said he wanted to have more tests done. I should have checked her in weeks ago. None of this would have happened if I'd done that." He glared at her furiously. "You kept insisting she'd be all right. And I knew better. It's my fault she's in there."

"Jeremy, Faith trusts in God. And I believe this is all part of His plan for her life. If she hadn't been mugged by those boys, the doctors would not likely have found the tumor until it was too late."

"It may be too late now," he told her grimly.

"I don't believe that, and you don't, either," she said sternly. "Faith is healthy and happy. She's had some wonderful times since you've been here and she's enjoyed every day that God has given her. He's not going to let her down now, when she needs Him the most. He loves her."

"So do I," she heard him whisper. "And I don't want her to die."

Gillian's reaction was immediate. She wrapped her arms around him and hugged him close against her body, trying desperately to infuse this man she loved with some of her own faith.

"She was always there," he whispered brokenly. "She always knew how much it hurt not to have a regular home and a normal family. To me she was my family, and when I'm with her everything seems like it will be okay." He looked at her, his face an agony of remorse. "I love her."

"I know," she whispered back. "I know."

Gillian sat there with him for a long time, content to hold

him, offering what comfort she could. And he held her, too, his arms a strong secure brace around her. When at last she drew away, she was prepared to tell him of her love, of the longing she had to share her love with him for as long as God gave them.

"Jeremy, when I left here, I went to Boston and I thought of what you said about me trying to make you into Michael. It's true, in a way. I did think that I could replace him...sort of show God that he hadn't taken away everything." She drew in a deep breath and continued, watching his back for some sign that he was listening.

"But what I discovered was that Michael is a part of my past. I loved him, yes. But he's gone, and the love I have now is a different kind of love." He stood there, still and unmoving.

"What I'm trying to say is that in spite of all the aunts and all their manipulations, I've fallen in love with you. I know we've argued and disagreed about just about everything over the past few months. I know that we started off on the wrong foot. But somehow, through all of that, God has shown me that what I've been feeling for you is far different from what I felt for Michael." She had to get up, try to see his face. "You were right when you said I was living in a fairyland. I was. I wanted a prince to come and carry me away from the pain of losing someone. I wanted to pretend that I was forever doomed." Gillian smiled at her own foolishness. "The star-crossed lover, if you like."

"And now?" His words were low, hushed, waiting.

"Now I've come to realize that through all of our butting of heads, I've been forced to deal with reality and accept that you are not Michael. But that through God's workings, you have made your own special place in my heart. I'm trying to say I love you, Jeremy. I have for a long time."

The silence was agonizing, and Gillian could have

screamed with tension. Instead, she stood silent, waiting for his well-thought-out reply. His answer was nothing like she'd expected.

"I suppose it's natural that you would think that," he told her baldly. "You see me as some kind of flawed character who needs your taming influence to fit into this fantasy dream you've created." He smiled halfheartedly.

"You had a wonderful home, a happy family. You're beautiful, talented. You have a way with people that draws them in toward you and makes them feel wanted; needed. And that's good. But I am not your next fixer-upper project, Gillian." He shook his head sadly. "I'm not your next Roddy Green."

"I'm so sorry," she whispered, shocked at his admission. "I never meant..."

"Don't apologize. I don't think you're even aware of it. But nonetheless, it's the way you see me," he said tiredly, shrugging off the hand she laid on his shoulder. "I admit it. I'm attracted to you. You're a very beautiful woman; what man wouldn't want to possess all that beauty? To say to the world, this is my wife. But you're not in love with me, not the real me." He shook his head. "You don't even know who I am. You've imagined a fantasy man that isn't anywhere near reality."

"But I know you've changed..." she began, trying to make him see that she wasn't dreaming anymore.

"No," he told her firmly. "I haven't changed one whit. I'm the same person I always was; the same man who lives his life by the rules that you despise so thoroughly.

"I am who I am, Gillian. In spite of all your daydreams and illusions. You can't make me change into something I'll never be, even if I wanted you to." He sighed. "I'll confess, I could easily allow myself to say what you want to hear. What we both *wish* could be true. But I know that someday you'd see me for who I really am and maybe even despise me." He paused. "I don't want either of us to be hurt that way."

"But I don't want to change you," she sputtered, standing where she was, mouth hanging open as she listened to his impassioned words.

"Yes, you do." His smile was dull and self-deprecating. "You don't love me, Gillian. Not the real me. In time I believe you'll agree that what I've said is true. In time," he added in a husky tone, "you may even thank me."

The words were quietly spoken, but underneath that cold harshness, Gillian could hear a note of…pain?

"In spite of your best attempts, I have to stick to my beliefs. You see, this is my aunt, my family we're discussing here. All right, you've encouraged this stupid idea of hers. Fine. I'm not going to oppose it any longer. If Aunt Faith wants to marry Arthur Johnson, she's free to do so. But don't expect me to be happy about it. I won't. Because it's not best for her. It's all wrong. Just like this ridiculous fiasco engagement you concocted to save your image."

Jeremy wheeled away, but felt her hand on his arm. He looked down. Perfectly shaped oval nails were buffed to a natural shine on delicate hands that could have graced a cosmetic ad.

"I'm sorry you hate me so much, Jeremy," he heard her murmur and felt a pang of remorse as he saw the diamond droplets that glimmered below her lashes. "I never realized that I was hurting you so badly. But for the record, I never considered you a challenge or a project. And I certainly don't want to change you. I just want to love you."

She sniffed delicately, and his heart softened again. But he couldn't allow himself to be moved by her tears. Not this time.

"I know you don't like my clothes. You've told me that often enough." She sniffed. "I know you think there are rules for every occasion and that I break all of them. I'm sorry about that. Really sorry. I can't help how I look, and even that seems to annoy you."

Her voice lowered as her huge emerald eyes met his. They were wide and guileless, and Jeremy felt he could drown in their depths. With every shred of willpower he had left, he restrained himself from taking her into his arms.

"I think you're a wonderful caring nephew and that Faith is so lucky to have you in her life. We all are. The way you've moved in and taken over with the youth group is a real pleasure to watch. And the school, even if I do say so, is far better run than any school I've taught in."

She lowered her voice, and he leaned in to hear her better. "I think I argued with you so much because you shook me out of my rut, made my perfect life very uncomfortable. You made me see things in a new way."

He heard the true regret in her voice and wondered at the wobble of emotion that he could discern beneath that calm facade.

"But most of all, I want to apologize for embroiling you in this silly engagement. I really did have the best of motives when I went along with Faith's error, but it's gone on too long, and I can see that it's time for me to set things right."

"I didn't mean—"

"I'm sorry, Jeremy." She cut him off. "Truly sorry. I promise I won't embarrass you again." Jeremy watched as her face drew near to his and her soft lips brushed over his cheek. "Maybe someday you'll believe that I truly didn't mean to hurt you."

He stood there, transfixed, as she walked away down the hospital corridor. He saw Reverend Dave come bursting through the door and heard his hearty greeting. Gillian's was softer but the words carried to him clearly over the shining floor tiles.

"I'm not a bride-to-be, Pastor. I never was. I made the whole thing up, and it's time I owned up to it. Could I talk to you? Privately?"

Jeremy watched dumbfounded as the two walked back out the door. Instead of relief that the whole debacle was finally over he felt…what? Sadness? A sense of loss?

He shook his head in frustration. It didn't make sense. He should be feeling relieved that he and Gillian would finally be freed from this ridiculous pretense.

Shouldn't he?

Chapter Fourteen

"All right children, this is your big night. I want each of you to do your very best. Watch carefully when Mr. Nivens gives you directions. Pay attention. Is everyone ready?"

Some looked painfully ill and others looked like overwound tops that just had to spin or they would burst. Gillian smiled gently at all of them and directed them out of her room and onto the stage. Jeremy had chosen her class to be the toys in his new revised *Nutcracker* and she was beginning to see how apt his choice had been.

Each student wore a costume. There were tin soldiers and fairy princesses. Firemen with trucks and animals galore. The music for the entire play had been adapted from the original score, and she could hear Jeremy's fine fingers in the light, bright recorded notes.

"All right, children," she whispered. "Let's begin. Everyone at attention."

They plodded onto the stage and waited stiffly for the curtain to lift, but once it had they fell into their parts naturally, keeping still as mice when Fritz and Clara and all the birthday guests celebrated.

As she watched from behind the curtain, Gillian felt a sense of pride fill her. The scenery was spectacular; Jeremy had arranged to catch all the essence of an old resplendent country house. A huge Christmas tree sparkled and glittered in the corner, lending a truly festive air to the proceedings.

At last the Sugar Plum Fairy danced across the stage, pirouetting and prancing as if born to it. When it was time for Gillian's toys to move, they twisted and turned and marched as briskly as they'd been taught without one faltering step. Their faces shone with enthusiasm, and if anyone heard the ping of the sword hitting the metal table leg, they didn't let on.

"It's going okay, isn't it?" Jeremy's voice was hushed and faintly questioning in her ear, and Gillian smiled.

"It's going perfectly," she acknowledged, smiling up at him. "You've done a wonderful job with all of it. The parents are just beaming."

He stood there, staring down at her for the longest time. And then his arms reached out and he tugged her into his embrace, his mouth hard and urgent on hers as he kissed with all the pent-up fury of a storm just unleashed.

And Gillian kissed him back, uncaring that several of the lighting students stood nearby snickering at them from the sidelines. When he finally let go, his eyes were warm and caressing.

"Thank you," he whispered.

"You're welcome." She smiled back.

He studied her quizzically for several moments before stepping away. "I have to go," he murmured and turned around, striding back into the curtains without a backward glance.

"I know," she murmured, more to herself than anyone. "But I can wait."

It was an exhausting evening for the teachers. And everyone breathed a sigh of relief as the children in the last item on the program filed onto the stage. It was time for the carols with a different groups of singers. First the glee club, which included the entire school body, filed out to fill up the stage and overflowed onto the risers in front. They gave a rousing rendition of "Frosty" and then "I Saw Mommy Kissing Santa Claus." Next were the choral singers clad in their festive red cummerbunds and bow ties.

As she seated her students in the back of the gymnasium, Gillian noted their proud stance and careful scrutiny of their leader. They kept their eyes focused on Jeremy, who stood before them in his black suit, hand upheld, ready to give the signal to begin.

Their voices rose in two of the older English carols so often heard in the vaulted cathedrals of Britain. Her own students were silent as every eye focused on the two soloists, whose clear, pure voices rose over the crowd.

And then, the pièce de résistance. The select chorus. These were Jeremy's hand-picked singers. Children who had displayed a natural ability with music. Their voices blended, falling and rising in a harmony of praise and thanksgiving for the miracle of the Christmas birth.

After the thundering applause had died away, Jeremy stepped forward to the microphone.

"Ladies and gentlemen, JFK Elementary would like to present their final number. 'O Holy Night.'"

Gillian stared. She thought they'd scrapped the idea weeks ago. Why was he now attempting this? It was complicated, not only for the singers who had a huge range of notes to cover, but also for the pantomimers who would play Mary, Joseph, shepherds and wise men.

Lord, please give us a hand here, she prayed silently. *And be with Jeremy no matter what happens.*

"It was fantastic! I've never seen such a masterpiece. Those kids deserve a medal."

Gillian grinned at the praise flowing from ecstatic parents around her. *Thank you, Lord,* she breathed, as one after another parent shook the principal's hand.

"Don't know how you did it, Mr. Nivens," one father exclaimed. "Never thought Josiah could sit still for that long."

Jeremy's face shone with the praise. "Truthfully, neither did I. I guess practice makes perfect, right Josiah?" The little boy grinned, displaying a huge gap between his teeth.

"It was a wonderful start to the Christmas holidays," Hope congratulated her later. "You must be very pleased."

"Yes, I am," Gillian agreed, stretching her toes against the fur-lined warmth of her boots. "It feels wonderful to know that he pulled it off."

A light tapping on her car window grabbed Gillian's attention, and she rolled down the glass to see Jeremy standing outside.

"I need to talk to you about this," he said clearly, holding out the envelope with her resignation inside. "I'm going to be here for a while longer, but maybe I could pick you up in a hour and we could go for coffee."

Gillian smiled. "I'm sorry but I think I've just about had it for tonight," she told him softly. "With the cookie bake planned for tomorrow and Faith's wedding the next day, I think I need to go home and relax."

He frowned. "I'd forgotten about that. Cookies, eh? How long will it take?"

"I suspect all day," Gillian grinned. "You know that bunch. They eat as much as they can. But I'm sure we'll have a few minutes to talk then, if you still want to."

He leaned his head down directly in front of hers and smiled grimly. "Oh, I'll still want to," he told her. "But I suppose it can wait."

"Why don't you relax, too," she encouraged. "Rest on your laurels. That was a fantastic closing number."

"It was good, wasn't it," he agreed. "The kids really got into it. I'll bet you were surprised that we pulled it off."

"No," she shook her head, the words coming easily. "I think you can do whatever you set your mind to. I was wrong to question that. And tonight was just the beginning for you."

"Well, we'll see." He leaned in toward her, and then glancing up at Hope, obviously thought better. He pulled his head away and straightened, staring at them both with a strange look on his face. "Good night."

"Good night."

As they drove away, Hope glanced at her niece curiously. "Why didn't you go with him? I know you still love him. You don't have to leave right away. Why not hear him out?"

Gillian leaned her head back on the headrest and closed her eyes. No one, not even Hope knew how badly she wanted to be with Jeremy tonight. But she wanted more than he could give her. She wanted it to be his shoulder she leaned on, his arms holding her closely.

"I can't, Hope. He needs time to deal with Faith's marriage, and I need to distance myself from him. He sees me as a manipulating, domineering foe. I don't want to horn in on his limelight. Besides—" she curved her gloved hand into a fist at her side "—what's the point? I'm leaving Mossbank."

The normally immaculate home of Hope Langford was bursting at the seams with laughter, cookie dough and teenagers, who were all busily engaged in preparing little care boxes for the seniors in Mossbank and the surrounding area.

Gillian had found little time to stop for even a sip of coffee let alone a discussion with Jeremy. It wasn't that he hadn't tried to speak to her. He had. Numerous times. And each time he approached she busied herself with yet another project which had resulted in more varieties of cookies than anyone had seen outside the local bakery.

"Don't you think we have about enough?" Myra asked doubtfully, casting a worried glance at the cookie sheets cooling over every available surface.

"Yes," Gillian agreed, puffing her bangs off her heated face. "This is the last batch. I purposely left the ginger snaps till last so I could bake them slowly."

It was a lie. She hadn't even intended on baking so many cookies until *he* had shown up with several boys in tow. His eyes had a strange somber look to them that she couldn't understand, but Gillian had no desire to get into it now. Not with more than twenty teens hanging around, listening in.

"I really would like to speak to you," Jeremy murmured from behind her shoulder. "Privately."

Gillian jumped, burning her hand against the hot pan as she jerked her head around to stare at him. "Ohh," she groaned between clenched teeth.

Without saying a word, Jeremy grasped her arm in his and led her to the sink. Seconds later her hand was beneath the tap and the cool relief of water removed some of the sting.

He held it there until she was sure it would freeze and only allowed her to pull away when the red area lightened to a pinkish glow.

"Sit down and relax for a moment," he ordered. "I can handle the rest of this."

"But I…"

"You've done enough. Relax."

So although she would have preferred to get away in private and have a good bawl, she sat there and sipped the hot sweet black coffee he had poured for her.

And dreamed of what could have been. As she watched Jeremy move between the groups, she fantasized that this was their home and these some of their children. The tall, skinny boy who was laughing up at Jeremy looked a lot like him;

he'd probably resemble any son Jeremy had. But it wouldn't be her son.

It was a long time before Gillian realized that the kitchen, indeed the entire house had quietened down to its usual relative silence. She gazed around at the messy kitchen, watching Jeremy scrubbing the cookie sheets. He looked perfectly at home, she decided, stifling the laugh that rose as she caught sight of the frilly white embroidered apron he wore.

"Where did everyone go?" she asked at last in a voice no one would have recognized as hers. "Why is it suddenly so quiet?"

He glanced at her over his shoulder.

"They've gone home for lunch, although I've no idea how they can eat another bite. At two o'clock those who can are coming back and we're going to deliver the cookies." His sharp gray eyes took note of her pale face and then moved to study the red patch of skin covering her hand. "How do you feel?"

"I'm fine," she told him, ignoring the whirl of her stomach as she stood to her feet. "I can do that."

He lifted the cloth beyond her reach and grinned. "Don't be silly. You've been baking for hours. The least I can do is clean up a little. We're supposed to be partners in this, remember?"

The words rang hollowly in her ears, and Gillian had to swallow down the pain. They would never be partners. She'd spoiled all that.

With a few economic moves, she had loaded the dishwasher with mixing bowls, spatulas and spoons that had littered her aunt's pristine counters. As she started the pot wash cycle, she felt his hand on her arm.

"Gillian?" His voice was low and husky and she couldn't help the shiver of awareness that moved through her.

"Yes?" She swiped the counter one last time in a business-like fashion, drained the sink and hung up the cloth.

"Will you please stop dashing about and sit down for a moment. I want to ask you something."

Dread filled her. He was going to tell her how sorry he was. That he didn't love her. Never would.

She jutted her chin out defiantly as she sat in the nearest chair. Jeremy sat down beside her, studying his hands where they lay on the tabletop. His jeans...*jeans?* She did a double take and then mocked herself.

They were perfectly pressed jeans with a knife edge crease down the front. She wondered idly if they had a brand name tag on the back pocket.

"What is it?" she whispered at last when the tension threatened to overwhelm her.

"Why did you resign?" His face was a mass of confusion as he stared at her. "I know you like living here, and I've seen you with your class. You're a natural at teaching. Why would you suddenly want to leave, when you said you intended to stay?" His eyes were a soft gray-blue, probing and searching her face for answers.

"I think it's better if I go now. Before things get any worse," she told him quietly. "I don't want to cause any more problems for you. You did a wonderful presentation at Christmas. That should help you when you decide to apply for a better position."

"But why now?" he demanded.

"It's a good time. People will assume I'm leaving because our engagement broke off. No one will blame you. You can go ahead, do your job as you planned without my interference." She refused to look at him. "It's for the best."

"Gillian?" His finger tipped her chin upward and she had to meet his gaze. He was frowning at her, as if he couldn't figure it all out. "I know I've led you to believe differently, but I really don't care what people think about this supposed engagement," he assured her quietly. "If I've learned one thing while I've been in Mossbank, it's that people will talk regardless of what you do, so you might as well try to please yourself."

There was silence in the tiny kitchen as Gillian digested this piece of information.

"Besides, I don't want you to go. I'll have to hire a substitute until the board can find another teacher. The children will be upset at losing you. It causes an awful lot of problems," he complained loudly.

"There's not really any problem," Gillian told him steadily. "Flossie Gerbrandt has agreed to cover for me until they can find someone else. She's a very good teacher and she'll be thrilled to be working with you."

"I don't want Flossie Gerbrandt," he thundered, his eyes dark with fury. "The woman follows me around constantly as it is, asking all manner of ridiculous questions."

"She's got a crush on you," Gillian told him gently. When his eyes opened wide, she nodded. "Flossie is very shy and has trouble getting a conversation started. But if you give her a chance, I'm sure you'll find you both have a lot in common."

"Hah," he grunted. "Like what?"

"Classical music, for one thing. Flossie plays the cello and she's very good." Gillian made herself say the words even though she detested it. "And she's been to England, too. You could talk about that."

"I don't want to talk about classical music or England," he barked. His eyes narrowed. "What will happen to the youth group? I can't manage it alone."

"Jeremy, you have a wonderful way with these kids once you let yourself loosen up. Why, only this morning David was telling me about the excellent advice you gave him. They respect and admire you. You'll do fine."

"What advice?" he demanded, frowning. "I don't have any advice to give teenagers. I don't know anything about them."

"Something about not pointing out his girlfriend's bubble gum," she murmured, trying to remember exactly what David had said. "I don't remember exactly."

Jeremy did. All of a sudden the conversation sounded in his mind, crystal clear. He heard himself telling David to either accept the flaws or find someone else.

What a farce it was! Here he was driving away the one person who made him feel things he'd never felt, because he couldn't accept who she was.

"Gillian, I wanted to tell you that…"

"I'm sorry," she interrupted. "I've just got to get going. I promised Faith that I'd finish her headpiece. The wedding is tomorrow, you know." She studied him for a moment. "Are you sure you won't walk her down the aisle? You are her only family."

Jeremy wished fervently that he'd never withheld himself from his aunt's wedding plans. He dearly wanted to make her happy, and since she seemed intent on going through with this wedding, he knew it was pointless to keep arguing. He owed her that much. And a lot more.

"Well, I'm sorry that you can't give in on this one issue," Gillian told him sadly. She glanced away from his searching eyes. "But I do have to go. Faith needs all the support she can get right now, and I can't let her down." She smiled in a way that made Jeremy's heart race and the blood pound in his ears. "But don't worry, I'll see you again before I leave."

"When will that be?" he asked, thoroughly out of sorts with the whole conversation. Was he never to be allowed to finish a sentence with this woman?

Gillian swept through the kitchen to the front hall, snatching up her coat and shrugging into it before he could help her. It irked him. He'd wanted to touch those bright, curling strands once more.

He'd wanted to touch *her*.

"I'm going to spend Christmas with Hope. I don't want her to be alone. But the next day I'm heading back to Boston. It's time I got on with my life. See you!" And with a wave and a halfhearted smile that tugged at his heart strings, she walked out the door.

"Wonderful," he muttered, flopping down onto the sofa. "She doesn't want Hope to be alone. Art doesn't want my aunt to be alone. Why am I the only one who'll be alone?"

"Because you want it that way."

His head whirled around in surprise. Hope Langford stood in the doorway, a frown marring the clear beauty of her face.

"I beg your pardon?" He couldn't believe she'd interrupted his private conversation. Even if it was with himself.

"You should—from a lot of people. But I'm not sure I'm one of them," Hope muttered as she hung up her coat and removed her snow boots. When she came into the room, her clear blue eyes chastised him roundly.

"You do realize that you're making everyone thoroughly miserable, don't you?"

"Me?" He stared. "What have I done?"

"You've hurt my niece, for one thing." There was a cold fury in the voice.

"But I've been trying to persuade her to stay. She won't listen. She's determined to go, so that our ridiculous 'engagement' will be terminated. She thinks people will blame her and feel sorry for me. As if I want that." Jeremy clenched his fist in anger. "I want her to stay."

"Gillian is in love with you. How do you think it feels for her to know you don't want anything to do with her—that you dislike so much about her?"

"I don't dislike her at all. I love her!" His mouth fell open in amazement. He hadn't realized the truth of the statement until just now.

"Is that why you let this supposed engagement go on so long? Is that why you called her selfish and inconsiderate and bullied her for weeks on end? Because you love her?" Hope's voice bit into him with disdain. "Some love."

"Yes, it is," he agreed in stupefied wonder.

"Are you going to try and order her around the way you've ordered Faith? You've made my niece's life a misery, Mr. Nivens. She can't even enjoy Faith's wedding, although she's worked like a trouper to make it happen. Gillian's so worried that you'll do something to spoil your aunt's happiness that she's not eating, not sleeping. Your 'love' is tearing her apart."

Jeremy winced at the scathing reprimand.

"I do love my aunt, Miss Langford. And I have no intention of spoiling her day. I wish her and Art every happiness."

"You do?"

"Of course. I was merely concerned for her safety. But since they found the tumor, well—" He swallowed down the fear and continued, needing to tell someone. "I've realized that she might only have a little while left. I want it to be a happy time." He barely caught the next words.

"It's benign."

"What?" He stared at her, afraid to believe.

"She got a phone call this morning while I was there. It was benign. Nothing to worry about. The doctor said she's fine."

"Oh, my God!" Jeremy breathed a silent prayer of thanks, sinking back onto the sofa. "I can't believe it."

"Neither could she. But she's afraid if you find out, you'll try to stop the wedding." Hope's words were blunt, but

Jeremy welcomed them. They cut to the heart of the matter, and he had no time to dawdle now.

"I'm not going to stop it," he told her grinning. "I'm going to be part of it."

Hope's face lit up like a Christmas tree, and she threw herself into his arms, pressing a soft kiss to his cheek. "Thank you, Jeremy. Thank you so much."

He grinned. "Don't thank me," he told her softly. "It's going to be my pleasure." He smiled slowly, setting her back on her feet. "But do you really think you should go around kissing the man who is engaged to your niece? Even if we are going to be related?"

Hope stared at him as her hands automatically straightened her tidy hair.

"But it's all a sham. A pretense. You're not really going to marry Gillian." Her eyes widened. Her voice dropped to a whisper. "Are you?"

For once, Jeremy felt as if the whole world was his. With a peculiar little smile, he hoisted himself from the sofa and walked slowly over to the door, yanking on his jacket as he went, mindless of the way he unevenly buttoned it.

"Yes," he whispered. "I think I am." He pulled open the door and stepped outside, completely unmoved by the icy wind or the whirling snowflakes. "She just doesn't know it yet."

As he swept out the door and down the walk, Hope rushed over to close the door, pausing a moment to watch him hurry away in his compact sports car with an unusual grinding of gears.

"My, oh my," she murmured, pressing the solid oak door into place. "Will wonders never cease?"

She was still standing there a few moments later when the doorbell rang. Half fearfully, afraid he'd come to his senses, she opened the door a crack and peered outside. A group of fifteen or twenty teenagers stood outside, grinning like a pack of wolves.

"Is Jeremy here?" one of them asked. "We're supposed to deliver the cookies this afternoon and he and Gillian were going to drive us."

Hope smiled, a wonderful heartfelt smile that lifted her stern lips and brought a glow to her eyes. "I think," she told them happily, "that we will have to make alternate arrangements. I'm afraid Jeremy and Gillian are going to be tied up."

"Property settlement," Janice Cheevers nodded knowingly. "Always happens when there's a breakup. Too bad. They were a neat couple."

"Yeah," a tall, lanky boy muttered as he brushed past Hope. "I dunno why they don't just kiss and make up. Isn't love supposed to forgive all?"

"With God's help," Hope murmured, closing her eyes in a soft prayer. "With God's help."

Chapter Fifteen

The small church was packed to capacity for Faith Rempel's wedding. Gillian had seen no one that she couldn't identify from the small community, and every single face beamed with good wishes for the elderly couple.

The Christmas decorations were glittering in the candlelight of hundreds of glowing tapers decorating the platform. She herself had arranged the silky flowers in graceful baskets which would be changed tomorrow to hold the fresh arrangements for the Christmas Eve service tomorrow night. Everything was ready.

Except for Jeremy.

No matter how hard she searched, Gillian couldn't find his face anywhere in the happy group of well-wishers. Well, why would he be there? she asked herself firmly. He'd rejected his great-aunt's decision adamantly. He wouldn't change just because she had begged him to.

Minnie Klemp pressed the loud key on the organ and everyone surged to their feet. Gillian watched as her aunt stepped down the aisle first. Hope looked magnificent in her emerald silk suit, gliding slowly down the aisle as she cradled her creamy white Persian roses gracefully across one arm.

She took her place beside Harry Conroy, the local judge and Art's longtime golf buddy.

Next came Charity, carefully following the carpeted path in her odd-gaited, delicate mincing steps, covered from head to toe in bright holly-berry red. Her roses were also white and she carried them proudly, her arthritic fingers grasping them tenderly. Her partner, Frank Bellows, slipped his arm through hers in support, and Charity smiled up at him gratefully. Gillian grinned. If she wasn't mistaken, the undertaker had a special glint in his eye when he looked at Charity Flowerday.

Then all heads focused on the back as Faith came through the door. Her wedding dress was an elegant ivory lace that lent a glow of radiance to her jubilant face. No one could say this radiant woman was too old for a bridal gown, Gillian thought fiercely. Jeremy's aunt looked blissfully exultant in the timeless silk gown.

Faith carried a bouquet of crimson red roses interspersed with deep green foliage. They were tied with a pale glossy ribbon and she held them with one hand. Her other was looped through Jeremy's!

Gillian gasped. He'd come. He'd actually relented and come to the wedding. Not only that, he was participating and from the look on his face, enjoying it.

She could only stare in disbelief as they walked slowly up the aisle. When they passed her, Jeremy's eyes rested on her for a moment and Gillian felt the same old thud-thud her heart always gave when he was around. The glint of blue in his soft gray eyes made her knees weak with love. How could she go on, knowing their own pretended engagement would never result in such a wonderful finale?

They stopped in front of her as Faith loosened one of her bright roses from the bouquet and reached past Jeremy to hand to it to her. Gillian took it with a lump in her throat, barely catching Faith's whispered words.

"For my soon-to-be great-niece."

Gillian forced herself to ignore the shaft of pain at the thought Faith's words engendered. She couldn't dwell on those words or she would burst into tears. Instead she forced herself to concentrate on the pair, young and old, moving regally down the aisle.

When the minister asked, "Who gives this woman to be married?" Gillian heard Jeremy's response in stunned disbelief. And then he handed his aunt over to her husband-to-be with careful elegance, pressing a kiss against her smooth, paper-thin cheek. A second later he was standing beside Gillian, holding her hand in his.

The entire ceremony passed by in a daze for Gillian as she kept glancing at her and Jeremy's entwined fingers. Opal Everet sang "Oh Perfect Love," Pastor Dave pronounced them husband and wife, and Arthur Johnson kissed his new bride with a gusto that brought appreciative laughs from the audience.

But other than that, Gillian heard nothing. The soloist launched into her second number, but the words held no meaning, no special significance for her. In fact, Gillian was so out of it, Jeremy had to tug on her hand to get her to stand when Mr. and Mrs. Arthur Johnson were presented to the congregation.

Gillian followed as the happy couple walked back out of the church and found her path through the church vestibule blocked.

"I have to talk to you, Gillian," Jeremy whispered urgently. "I've been trying to do that since yesterday. It's important." His eyes gleamed with some hidden fire, and Gillian could feel the tension emanating from his tall, lean body.

She didn't understand what he wanted. They had said everything there was to say. But something told her that whatever he wanted to say needed to be discussed away from the maddening crowd; without the interested gaze of the townspeople looking on.

"This is Faith and Arthur's day," she murmured, slipping past him and into the crowd. "Whatever we need to say to each other can wait. I don't want to spoil their day with another argument."

His fingers wrapped around her arm like tentacles, and he pulled her back into the protection of the pew, turning so that he shielded her from the rest of the wedding guests who were leaving the church.

"Okay," he agreed smiling. "If you insist, we'll wait. But, I need to do this now," he murmured, before his mouth came down on hers in a soft demanding kiss that left her breathless but wanting more. "And you'd better be warned. I'm going to need to do that a lot more in the future. Come on." He grasped her fingers, his eyes glittering with something she couldn't decipher. "Let's go help Auntie Fay celebrate."

And they did!

They tossed confetti on the couple until the colored circles covered their graying hair and grinning faces. They toasted them repeatedly at the reception and tinkled their glasses over and over, calling for the groom to kiss his bride. And before the couple left in their car, Jeremy tied a bunch of old cans to the bumper of Art's Jeep while Gillian whispered a few last words to Faith.

"I'm so happy for you and Arthur, Faith. You really belong together." Gillian tried to mask the jealousy she felt at the beaming smile of pure happiness Faith gave her.

"Yes, Gillian, we do. I'm so glad that God gave me another chance at love. And I have to tell you that I think He's doing the same thing for you." Faith patted her hand tenderly, the new band of gold sparkling on her finger. "I know

Jeremy loves you. And I know you love him. You may have convinced each other that you're only pretending to be engaged, but I think that's what you both really want."

"Oh, Faith," Gillian murmured, brushing a tear from the corner of her eye. "I know you're confused about this but Jeremy and I were never really engaged. You just imagined that."

Faith grinned. It was a smug, self-satisfied grin that tilted the edges of her mouth and left her green eyes sparkling like a cat's. "Did I?" she mused. "How strange."

There was a peculiar quality to those lovely eyes that had Gillian questioning her own sanity for a moment until Faith began speaking again.

"My dear Gillian," she said kindly. "I could never be confused about something so important. I deliberately threw the two of you together as part of my Christmas project. I knew that once you two learned to accept each other for who you are and stopped trying to change the other, you'd be happy together."

Faith wrapped her arm in Arthur's and pressed her cheek against his shoulder lovingly. She smiled at Gillian who was backing away from the car.

"Don't disappoint us, dear," the old woman whispered, just before the car drove off.

"Disappoint them?" Gillian whispered to herself in perplexity. "Now what in the world had the old girl meant by that? Christmas project, indeed!"

Gillian watched them go with confusion. What did any of it mean? Faith's cryptic remarks? Jeremy kissing her? What had that kiss meant? Why was he there? What had suddenly changed between them?

Her heart was full of excitement and anticipation and wonder but she tamped it down ruthlessly. Just because she had given up on her desire to stay single didn't mean that Jeremy had also had a change of heart recently.

But after all, God *did* work in mysterious ways. Didn't He?

As the newlyweds drove off to the jangle of cans, Jeremy grasped Gillian by the shoulders and turned her to face him.

"Can you walk in those things?" he asked, referring to her frivolous new shoes with their dangerously high heels. "Never mind," he muttered finally, glancing around. "I know the perfect place."

In one smooth motion he scooped her up into his arms and carried her across the street to the church. Gillian was too stunned to do anything but stare at his sudden impetuosity. Especially with half the town watching, knowing grins covering their faces.

The old church was deserted; everyone was still gathered at the hall celebrating. The tapers had long since gone out, but the Christmas tree was still lit and someone had turned on the light above the pulpit, sending a beam of white light down over the mass of bright red poinsettias. Their fragrance filled the burnished wooden building, reminding Gillian of the season. When Jeremy simply set her down on the pew and then sat beside her, staring at her through the gloom, she decided to start the ball rolling.

"We should be at the hall," she murmured finally. "The others will be wondering where we've gone to." Jeremy still said nothing, gazing down at her. Gillian fidgeted in her seat, straightening her skirt nervously.

"I owe you an apology," he murmured. "I was wrong."

"Wrong," she repeated, her brow furrowing as she peered up at him. "Why?"

"Because I tried to change you. Tried to make you and all the others into something they aren't. Something none of you were ever intended to be." He grimaced, wrapping his fingers around hers. "That's better," he murmured softly.

"Jeremy," Gillian pleaded, staring into the warmth of his soft gray eyes. "Will you please tell me what you're talking about? Why did you suddenly decide to come to the wedding?"

His eyes glittered with satisfaction. "Because I wanted to know what it would be like when you and I get married."

"What?" Gillian stared at him, her eyes wide with disbelief. "But we agreed. We've called off that silly engagement. It was just pretend, anyway."

"If you want to call it off, you go ahead. I'm not. I like being engaged to you, my darling Miss Langford. But I think I'd like being married better."

None of it made any sense to Gillian. What was he saying, for Pete's sake?

"I know this doesn't conform to the usual procedure for such occasions," he told her softly, tugging her closer beside him. His fingers slid smoothly over hers as he cradled her hands in his. "But for once, I'm going to make my own rules."

He brushed the tendril of silky hair off her forehead and pressed a kiss there. And another on the side of her neck where her pulse beat furiously. Then his hands cupped her chin and his eyes stared straight into hers, melting and drawing her into their rich shining depths.

"I love you, Miss Gillian Langford. I love you so much, I get nervous when I don't see you for even a few moments. And I'm miserable and unhappy when you're not there to brighten the day. I love the way you dedicate yourself to helping others whether they want it or not, and I'm sorry I tried to stop you from doing what you do best—simply being Gillian, the woman that God created."

Gillian felt her skin growing warm under his caressing

touch, steadily, incessantly hotter until she felt like a glowing ember that basked in the radiance of a brightly burning fire.

"I don't know what to say," she whispered.

He shook his head in amusement. "Don't tell me you're lost for words." He chuckled. "It's a miracle."

"No." She shook her head dazedly. "But this is."

"Yes," he agreed, nodding. "A Christmas miracle from God. He taught me that in Him there is only one rule. Love. And when we love someone, that love takes care of all the other rules."

His finger traced the outline of his face as he spoke. "I've lived so long with the idea that God was a stern judge who kept a detailed tally of every little mistake we made that I lost sight of the real meaning of His love for us." Jeremy brushed his mouth across her hand before continuing.

"He doesn't care if we sit or stand to sing the hymns. He doesn't care if we have the offertory before or after the special music. He doesn't even care if junior church gets canceled and the babies bawl all through the sermon. Most especially He doesn't care if Faith forgets a few things now and then. He loves her as she is."

His face was close to hers now, his breath a whisper against the sensitive skin of her face. Gillian bemusedly slid one hand lightly over the dear hard lines of his beloved face and waited patiently for him to finish.

"I finally realized that what we do isn't as important as what we think," he told her. "It doesn't matter because I can never be good enough or strict enough or wise enough."

His smile was wide and tender. "It isn't the rules or the keeping of them that's important," he murmured. "It's what you've got inside. Forcing people to obey rules will never change that."

She didn't really need to ask anymore, but Gillian knew

he was just bursting to tell her. "And what is it that you have inside?" she asked softly, half-afraid to believe.

"Love," he crowed proudly. "For you. Big and wide and all encompassing." His arms curved round her, pulling her to her feet and against his strong body.

"Big enough to forgive me for all the things I've done?" Her question was timidly quiet.

"My darling Gillian, there is nothing to forgive," he told her sincerely. "I love you just the way you are." His eyes moved over her, memorizing each detail. "God put this love in my heart and His love is never ending."

"But Jeremy, we're nothing alike," she protested mildly, hoping he'd brush away her protests.

He did.

"Thank goodness! I don't want to love someone like me." He grinned. "I know we'll have disagreements. Everyone does. But isn't His love enough to cover them all?"

She would never again see this man as rigid and unbending, Gillian decided. To her he would always be Jeremy: strong and independent, determined to do the right thing no matter what.

"I love you," he murmured in her ear, softly but clearly.

"That's good," she answered, brushing her lips against his chin. "Because I have a fair bit of that particular emotion myself. I thought maybe we could share?"

"No way," he muttered, glaring at her fiercely. "Not this time, Gillian."

Her heart dropped to the floor as she wondered if she'd been wrong once more. "Wh-what do you mean?" she stammered, staring up at him fearfully.

His arms tightened around her once before he let her go. "I mean that you did the proposing last time, Gillian Langford. This time it's my turn and I intend to follow, to the letter, all the correct and proper procedures."

He knelt in front of her, holding her hands in his, blue-gray eyes glowing with emotion. "I would very much like to be engaged to you, darling Miss Langford," he whispered softly. "For real. With a true commitment and all the expectations for our future that entails." His fingers tightened around hers. "Would you please marry me?"

"Yes," she cried, trying to tug him upward. "Yes, yes, yes."

But Jeremy Nivens had never been a man to be hurried and he wasn't about to start now. Slowly, thoughtfully, he got off his knees and stood before her. His words were soft but full of meaning. "Then would you mind wearing this ring as a token of how much I love and adore and appreciate you?" he murmured. "And as my promise that I'll never try to change you again." He snapped open the small black jeweler's case Gillian glimpsed in his hand.

She gasped at the beauty of it. It sparkled and glittered in the dimness of the old church like a fire that refused to be doused. Two slivers of glittering gold wound around out of the band and up around the high-set diamond, holding it between their grip protectively.

"It's so delicate," she whispered, awestruck as he slipped it onto her finger.

"It only looks that way," he teased, smoothing back a tendril with his finger. "Rather like you. Beautiful and fragile as a flower. But inside…ah, inside, my dear Gillian, you are a pure, clear diamond."

"It's so beautiful. I've never seen such a setting." She held up her hand and admired it in the fading light. "I never expected this," she said tearfully. "I never expected you."

"I chose this especially because it reminded me of something," he told her smiling. "It reminds me that there are two of us, different and individual in our own right. But because of God and the love He's given us, we will be joined as one and held in the palm of God's hand."

Gillian wrapped her arms around her fiancé's neck and hugged him as hard as she could, reveling in the touch of his tender yet strong mouth on hers.

"Thank you, God," she whispered, letting her eyes wing upward for a moment. "He's so much more than I deserve or dreamed of."

"What are you saying?" Jeremy demanded, tipping his head back to gaze into her starry eyes.

Gillian just beamed, letting the love that filled her heart and soul pour out on a free, unrestricted wave of undulation.

"I'm just thanking the original matchmaker," she whispered, pointing upward.

Jeremy grinned. "Yes, and you can thank Arthur and Aunt Faith later," he murmured, his lips tickling her earlobe. "Without their interference, the Lord would have had a much more difficult task."

As their heads tilted toward each other and they sealed their engagement with a long satisfying kiss, two elderly women watched for a moment longer from their hiding place in the vestibule and then tiptoed noiselessly out into the cold winter night. "I think we can consider our Christmas projects for this year a success," Charity murmured, clutching her friend's arm as they negotiated the slippery streets.

"Aren't they always," Hope agreed smugly. "Especially with a little divine assistance."

They giggled together like young girls, sticking out their tongues to catch the fluffy white snowflakes that drifted slowly down from heaven and dropped silently to earth, covering everything with a soft white blanket of peace.

And just down the street, Faith rested her head against her new husband's shoulder as their car sped away from town for the first night of their married life.

"You know, Arthur," she said happily, squeezing his hand fondly, "I can hardly wait for next Christmas. I have a real inspiration for my project next year!"

Epilogue

"**Y**ou're going to do what?" Jeremy demanded, staring at his wife in dismay. "But it's almost Christmas. We've got the pageant to plan for and the choir to rehearse. Our new drama club starts in January. You can't quit."

Gillian laughed, pressing a kiss on the tip of his nose.

"Overachieving as usual! Jeremy, darling, I intend to help you with all that, and I'll work through into the early spring but then I'm leaving JFK. At least for a little while."

Jeremy sank into his plush principal's chair and tugged her slight form onto his lap, slipping his fingers through the bright coppery strands of her lovely hair.

"I've done it again, haven't I?" he groaned, pressing his lips against her forehead. "I've pushed and bullied and made you fed up with me. Darling, I'm so sorry. I've tried, really tried not to be so…"

She cut him off midsentence.

"Jeremy Nivens, will you please let me speak?"

Her gorgeous emerald eyes flashed with temper and something he couldn't quite define. Some hint of excitement that teased and tantalized till he couldn't look away.

"Gillian, darling," he breathed anxiously, his arms tightening around her protectively. "Please don't tell me you're ill."

"I will be," she whispered. "Every morning apparently. For a few months anyway." Her face softened as she lifted one hand to cup his cheek. "I'm pregnant, Jeremy. We're going to have a baby!"

"A baby? But I hadn't planned on that till next year...er, that is, a baby?" He stared at her, struck dumb by the possibilities such a thing engendered.

"Well," Gillian huffed indignantly as a secret grin tugged at the sides of her mouth, "I am sorry that we're ahead of your all-important schedule, but I'm not taking all the blame!"

He kissed her then as the words sank in, holding her tightly and whispering a prayer of thanksgiving. When at last she could move, his wife wiggled around until her glowing eyes stared straight into his.

"There's just one thing I want to make perfectly clear," she told him firmly. "We are not, I repeat, not having six children. That's asking for problems."

Jeremy soothed her with heartfelt endearments as he placed his brown hand on her tummy.

"I'm going to be a father," he mumbled, his eyes a deep dark blue. "Me, a parent."

"Jeremy? Did you hear me? I said I'm not having six children. Two maybe. Even three. But not six. Jeremy?" The last word came out on a sigh of delight as her husband tugged her mouth down to his.

"We'll talk about it," he whispered tenderly. "Negotiate. Discuss both sides of the issue and come to some understanding. After all, we've gotten rather good at it, don't you think?"

"Mmm," she sighed. "I guess love is all about compromise, isn't it?" She grinned impishly. "Would I be compromising your male ego if I told you to shut up and kiss me?"

"I think you'd be perfectly justified, my darling Gillian. And I'd be perfectly happy to oblige."

And he was about to when a new idea suddenly struck.

"You know Faith is going to say she planned the whole thing, don't you?" he murmured, fingering her engagement ring and the gold band that protected it. "She's been talking about her 'project' for weeks now." His happy grin belied the dourness of his words.

"I'm happy to have her and the others share in it," Gillian answered, snuggling a little closer. "After all, everyone needs a little Faith, Hope and Charity. Right, darling?"

Jeremy agreed wholeheartedly with her astute assessment of the situation.

"Yes, dear."

And then he kissed her.

* * * * *

HEARTWARMING INSPIRATIONAL ROMANCE

Contemporary,
inspirational romances
with Christian characters
facing the challenges
of life and love
in today's world.

**AVAILABLE IN REGULAR
AND LARGER-PRINT FORMATS.**

For exciting stories that reflect traditional values,
visit:
www.ReaderService.com

Love Inspired®
SUSPENSE
RIVETING INSPIRATIONAL ROMANCE

Watch for our series of edge-of-your-seat suspense novels.
These contemporary tales of intrigue and romance feature Christian characters facing challenges to their faith... and their lives!

AVAILABLE IN REGULAR & LARGER-PRINT FORMATS